One Night in Tehran

LUANA EHRLICH

This book is a work of fiction. Names, characters, places and incidents either are products of the author's imagination or are used fictitiously. Any resemblance to actual persons, living or dead, events, or locales is entirely coincidental.

Visit the author's website at www.luanaehrlich.com

ISBN-13: 978-1500157234
ISBN-10: 1500157236

To Ray Allan Pollock,
for giving an eleven-year-old girl
permission to read adult spy novels.

PROLOGUE

In far northwest Iran, a few minutes after clearing the city limits of Tabriz, Rahim maneuvered his vehicle onto a rutted side road. When he popped opened the trunk of the car to let me out, I saw the car was hidden from the main highway by a small grove of trees. In spite of our seclusion, Rahim said he was still anxious about being seen by a military convoy from the nearby Tabriz missile base.

For the first time in several hours, I uncurled from my fetal position and climbed out of the vehicle, grateful to breathe some fresh air and feel the sunshine on my face. As my feet landed on the rocky terrain, Rahim handed me a black wooden cane. I wanted to wave it off, but, regrettably, I still needed some help getting around on my bum leg.

Rahim slammed the trunk lid down hard.

"You can stretch for a few minutes," he said, "but then we must get back on the road immediately. Our timing must be perfect at the border."

Rahim and I were headed for the Iranian/Turkish border, specifically the border crossing at Bazargan, Iran. He was absolutely confident he could get me out of Iran without any problems. However, during the last twenty years, I'd had a couple of incidents at other border crossings—Pakistan and Syria to be precise—so I wasn't as optimistic.

While Rahim was tinkering with the car's engine, I exercised my legs and worked out the stiffness in my arms. As usual, I was running through several "what ifs" in my mind. What if the border guards searched the trunk? What if the car broke down? What if we were driving right into a trap?

I might have felt better about any of these scenarios had either of us been armed. However, Rahim had refused to bring along a weapon. Carrying a gun in Iran without a special permit meant certain imprisonment. Imprisonment in Iran meant certain torture, so I *certainly* understood his reasons for leaving the weaponry back in Tehran.

Still, a gun might have helped my nerves.

I was surprised to hear Rahim say I could ride in the front passenger seat for the next hour. He explained the road ahead was usually deserted, except for a farm truck or two, so it seemed the perfect time to give me a brief respite from my cramped quarters.

I didn't argue with him.

However, I thought Rahim was being overly cautious having me ride in the trunk in the first place—at least until we got nearer the Turkish border. I'd been passing myself off as an Iranian of mixed ancestry back in Tehran, and now, having grown out my beard, I didn't believe a passing motorist would give me a second look.

When I climbed in the front seat, the cloying smell of ripe apples emanating from the back seat of Rahim's vehicle was especially pungent. Flat boxes of golden apples were piled almost as high as the back window, and the sweet-smelling fruit permeated the stuffy interior of the car. On the floorboard, there were several packages wrapped in colorful wedding paper. I was sure they reeked of ripe apples.

We had been back on the road for about twenty minutes when Rahim said, "Hand me one of those apples and take one for yourself, Hammid."

Although Rahim knew my true identity, he continued to address me by the name on my Swiss passport, Hammid Salimi, the passport I'd used to enter Iran two years ago. Unfortunately, it was now a name quite familiar to VEVAK, the Iranian secret police, who had already prepared a cell for me at Evin Prison in northwest Tehran.

After we had both devoured the apples, Rahim rolled down his window and threw the cores down a steep embankment.

"When you get back inside the trunk," he said, "you'll have to share your space with some of those." He gestured toward the apple boxes in the backseat.

I glanced over at him to see if he was joking, but, as usual, his brown, weather-beaten face remained impassive. Although I'd spent the last three months living with Rahim's nephew, Javad, and learning to discern Javad's emotional temperature simply by the set of his mouth or the squint of his eyes, I'd barely spent any time with Rahim. During the last two days together, he'd never made any attempt at humor, and it didn't appear he was about to start now.

I protested. "There's barely enough room for me back there."

"It will be snug with the boxes, but you will fit," he said. "If the guards open the trunk, I want them to see apples."

I felt a sudden flash of anger. "Before we left Tehran, you told me they wouldn't open the trunk at the border. You said they wouldn't even search the car."

My voice sounded harsh and loud in the small confines of the car.

However, Rahim calmly replied, "They will not search the car, Hammid. They have never searched inside. They have never searched the trunk. It is only a precaution."

He turned and looked directly at me, his penetrating black eyes willing me to trust him. It was a look I instantly recognized. I had used that same look on any number of assets, urging them to ferret out some significant nugget of intel and pass it on to me, even though I knew the odds of their being caught were high.

He returned his eyes to the road. "Surely you're acquainted with making minor changes as a plan evolves."

I took a deep breath. "You're right, of course." I suddenly felt foolish at my amateur reaction. "Planning for the unexpected is always smart. The more precautions you want to take, the better it will be for both of us. I'm sorry for questioning you."

For the first time, I saw a brief smile on his face. "There's no need to apologize," he said quietly. "The last three months have been difficult for you. Your paranoia is understandable."

Rahim shifted into a lower gear as we approached a steep incline. When we finally rounded a curve on the mountainous road, our attention was immediately drawn to two military vehicles parked on the opposite side of the road about one-half mile ahead of us. Several men were standing beside two trucks. They were smoking cigarettes and looking bored.

"It's not a roadblock," I said.

"No, we're fine."

Suddenly a man in uniform, leaning against the front bumper of the lead truck, noticed our approach and quickly took a couple of steps onto the highway. He signaled for us to pull over.

"Say nothing unless they speak to you first," Rahim said. "My papers are inside the glove box. Do not open it unless I say, 'Show them our papers.'"

"I have no papers, Rahim."

He eased the car onto the side of the road. "I put them inside the glove box," he said, "but don't open it unless I tell you to do so."

As the military officer crossed over the highway toward our car, I watched the reaction of the men standing outside the two vehicles. Although the insignia on the officer's uniform indicated he was a captain in the Iranian Revolutionary Guard Corps (IRGC), the men traveling with him were not in uniform. However, that didn't mean they weren't soldiers.

In fact, as I studied them, I knew they had to be affiliated with some aspect of Iran's vast military organization. They wore nearly identical Western clothing, had short military haircuts, and all their beards were regulation trim.

No longer bored, the men appeared alert now as their captain approached our car.

To my surprise, Rahim was opening the door and getting out of the car before the captain spoke one word to him. His behavior went against one of my favorite tenets of tradecraft: never draw attention to yourself.

The soft-spoken man I had been traveling with for two days suddenly disappeared. Instead, a loud, fast-talking stranger took his place.

"Captain," Rahim asked, "how may I assist you today? Did you have a breakdown? What a lonely stretch of road on which to be stranded."

Within seconds of greeting the captain, Rahim threw his arm around his shoulders and walked him away from our car and back across the road. There, Rahim engaged in conversation with some of the men, and, at one point, they all broke into laughter at something he said.

After a minute or two, I saw the captain draw Rahim away from the group and speak to him privately. Although I could hear none of their conversation, I tensed up when the captain gestured across the highway toward me. As Rahim continued an animated conversation with him, they began walking back across the road together.

Arriving at the car, Rahim opened the back door and pulled out two boxes of the apples we were transporting.

"Here you are, Captain. Take two of these. I'll bring two more for your men. You will not find finer apples in all of Iran."

As the captain leaned down to take the apples from Rahim, he glanced inside the interior of the car, quickly taking note of the apples, the wedding presents, and the black cane I'd placed between my legs. Lastly, his scrutiny fell on my face.

I smiled and deferentially lowered my head toward him, greeting him in Farsi. He didn't respond, but Rahim was speaking to him at the same time, so I wasn't sure he'd heard me.

The captain was already walking back to the transport trucks when Rahim stuck his head back inside the car and removed two other boxes.

Our eyes met.

He nodded at me. I nodded back.

Everything was fine.

While Rahim was distributing the apples among the men, I took the opportunity to look inside the glove box. I found three items: Rahim's passport, his travel documentation, and a small handgun.

Presumably, the handgun was my documentation had the captain demanded it.

There was something about having a fighting chance that did

wonders for my morale, and I found myself smiling.

I shut the glove box before Rahim returned.

I decided not to say anything to him about my discovery.

Without a word, Rahim got back inside the car and started the engine. As we drove past the captain and his men, several of them raised their apples to us in a goodbye salute.

"That was quite a performance, Rahim."

He continued to glance at his rear-view mirror until the group disappeared from sight.

Finally, he said, "The captain only wanted information on road conditions. He said he'd heard there were some rockslides in the area. One of the drivers was complaining about his brakes, and he was worried about the safety of his men as they made the descent."

"Who were those men? What unit did they belong to?"

"The captain didn't say, but their cigarettes came from Azerbaijan. That should tell you something."

Azerbaijan bordered Iran and was about six hours north of our location. Although it had once been a part of the Soviet Union, it was now an independent republic with close ties to Iran. Like most Iranians, the majority of the people were Shia Muslims. Tehran wanted to keep it that way. I'd heard rumors there was a unit of Iran's military specifically assigned to make sure the Sunni minority in Azerbaijan remained the minority. The unit in charge of such an operation was the *al Quds* force.

"Members of *al Quds*, then?"

"That's my guess. We've been hearing reports the Sunnis are growing in popularity. Tehran won't sit still while that happens. But that's good. Mossad likes it when Tehran is distracted."

"Why wasn't the captain interested in me?"

"I told him you were my father, plus you look harmless, Hammid."

It was true. I'd lost weight during my three-month ordeal, and, since I'd spent the time indoors, my skin had taken on an unhealthy pallor. However, I doubted I looked old enough to be his father.

"I also told him you'd fallen in the orchard and injured your leg. He wasn't surprised at your reluctance to get out of the car, if that's what you're thinking."

I remembered the way the captain had inspected the contents of our car and his lingering look at my cane. He may have believed Rahim, but he had checked out his story anyway.

"You said you were on your way to your cousin's wedding in Dogubayazit?"

"Yes, and if I hadn't given him the apples, he might have inquired further about the gifts." He flicked his hand toward the wedding presents on the backseat floorboard. "Then, I would have insisted he take one or two of those gifts for his sister."

As in most Middle Eastern countries, bribes and "gifts" were a way of life among the people, especially with military and government officials. Nothing got done without them. If you made inquiries or requested help from any bureaucrat, they expected something in return.

"You were very generous with the apples back there. Will you have enough for your friends at the border now?"

I tried not to sound worried, but whenever I found myself involved in someone else's operation, I got nervous.

He was dismissive. "Yes, there will be plenty. Now help me find the turnoff road. It leads over to a lake, but the sign is hard to see. We'll make the switch there."

He slowed down, and we both concentrated on the passing landscape. The trees were dense, and the late afternoon shadows made finding the lake road difficult.

"I think it's coming up," Rahim said.

I pointed off to my right. "There it is."

He made a sharp right turn onto a dirt road leading through a canopy of trees. One-half mile down the road, a secondary road branched off, and Rahim was able to make a U-turn at the fork in the road. Then, he pointed the car back toward the main highway.

Rahim killed the engine, and, after glancing down at his watch, he looked over at me. At that point, I knew I was about to be given The Speech, a last-minute review an operations officer usually gave to a subordinate before a critical phase commenced.

Technically, I wasn't a subordinate of Rahim's organization.

Still, I listened carefully.

"Remember the traffic at the border will move very slowly, and, once I'm pulled over, I expect there will be a long wait. At times, you will hear loud voices. That's not a cause for worry. If you hear angry voices, especially my angry voice, you should start to worry."

He paused for a long moment. Then, he opened the glove box and removed the handgun I'd seen earlier.

He handed it over to me with an understanding smile. "I'm assuming you found this already."

I checked the chamber.

It was loaded.

"Thanks, Rahim."

"Any questions?"

"No. I'm confident you've thought of everything."

We both got out of the car, and I helped him remove some of the apple boxes so he could stack them in the trunk after I was inside.

Before climbing in, I said, "Rahim, please hear me when I say I'm grateful for everything you and Javad have done for me. Perhaps, someday, I can repay you."

Rahim placed his hands on my shoulders and looked into my eyes. "That will never be necessary, Hammid," he said. "It has been God's will for us to help you."

As I tucked myself into the trunk again, I found myself hoping it was also God's will for me to make it out of Iran alive.

PART ONE

CHAPTER 1

Bill Lerner looked like a worried grandfather when he patted me on my knee in the backseat of the Lincoln Town Car and asked, "What's your state of mind, son?"

Our driver, Jamerson, gave me a quick glance in the rearview mirror.

I knew Jamerson had probably heard Lerner ask other intelligence officers that same question whenever he escorted them from Andrews AFB to one of the Agency safe houses in the quiet residential neighborhoods around McLean, Virginia.

I could hear the uncertainty in my voice as I responded, "I'm not sure, Bill, but it's good to be home."

Lerner ran his hand over his military-style haircut and shot back enthusiastically. "You bet. We'll get you debriefed, fix you up with some good grub, and then you'll be ready for some R & R."

Lerner's conversations never varied much.

His job consisted of making sure I felt safe—both he and the driver were armed—providing a listening ear if I needed to talk, and being the first in a long line of people who would bring me, a Level 1 covert operative, back to some sense of normalcy.

Lerner gestured toward my left leg, which I'd been massaging as we drove along. "That giving you trouble?"

"Yeah, a bit."

Once again, Jamerson stole a glance at me in the mirror. What was up with this guy? Was it just curiosity or something else?

I tried to dismiss my paranoia as nerves, pure and simple.

For the past several months, I'd been living on the edge in Tehran. However, three days ago, with Rahim's help, I'd made my escape from Iran, crossing the border into Turkey without incident.

Nevertheless, because I couldn't just turn my instincts on and off like a water spigot, I continued to mull over Jamerson's interest in me.

Lerner pointed to a large house at the top of a winding lane. "Well, in these new digs" he said, "you'll have some state-of-the-art rehab equipment for that leg. Support purchased this little *casa* for a song during the housing bust." He laughed. "It's been remodeled to our specifications, of course."

I didn't laugh.

I was too numb.

We pulled in front of the "*casa*," which was at least a 10,000 square-foot house. It was surrounded by gigantic oak trees, and, in the distance, at the back of the house, I spotted a large lake with a boat dock. As we pulled into the circle drive, I half expected to see a butler and several uniformed maids appear at the front door to welcome the master of the castle home.

The house was well situated on several acres of forested land and located within a gated neighborhood of similar residences. I imagined most of the well-to-do owners had their own security systems. We had entered the safe house property through a remote-controlled sliding gate, and I suspected security cameras had been tracking us ever since.

"This one is called The Gray," Lerner said.

The name made sense. Instead of addresses or numbers, the Agency used color-coded names for their safe houses, and, while the exterior of the house was blindingly white, the window shutters and the front door were painted a muted shade of bluish gray.

Previously, I had been debriefed in The Red. It was at least half the size of this one and had a red-tiled roof. There was no butler, just a slightly plump Italian cook named Angelina who had helped me gain back the weight I'd lost on a mission into Pakistan. The neighbors thought I was her son. The complexion I'd inherited from my father made it easy for me to pass myself off as an Italian, or even an Iranian of mixed ancestry.

Lerner got out of the car and headed for the front door. "Jamerson, get his kit from the trunk and meet us inside."

I took my time getting out of the car.

I paused to zip up the jacket of the tracksuit I'd been issued at the air base in Turkey, and then I leaned back inside the car and picked up the cane from the back seat. All the while, I was keeping an eye on Jamerson. He grabbed the duffel bag given to me on the flight over from Turkey, and, when he closed the trunk, our eyes met.

He motioned toward the front entrance with a slight nod of his head. "After you, sir."

I was almost six feet tall, and he was about my height, but, unlike me, he had a beefy body. I wondered how many hours he spent in the gym each day.

I hadn't seen the inside of a gym for years.

I hobbled toward the door, thankful Jamerson hadn't offered to help me.

In fact, if he had, I might have marshaled whatever strength I had left and slugged him.

Pride was a great energizer for me.

Lerner was already standing inside the giant foyer of the mansion, having keyed in the front door's security code beyond the range of my prying eyes. He was speaking in hushed tones to a middle-aged couple. I presumed they were the homeowners—at least to the other residents in the neighborhood.

After Jamerson had deposited my duffel bag on the floor, I asked him, "Ex-Marine?"

"Yes, sir."

"You served at the American Embassy in Iraq in 2008?"

There was no mistaking the pride in his voice. "Yes, sir. I'm surprised you even remembered me. You weren't in very good shape that day."

"How could I forget—?"

"Greg and Martha," Lerner said, interrupting our conversation, "let me introduce you to your newest houseguest."

As Lerner steered them in my direction, Jamerson gave me an understanding nod, and I turned my attention to the couple in charge of the safe house.

Greg was in his late fifties with a slight paunch around his middle and close-cropped gray hair. He smiled at me with a lop-sided grin. His wife was petite, had short black hair and piercing blue eyes.

I shook their outstretched hands.

"Titus Ray," I said.

Martha's smile was warm. "Welcome home, Titus."

♦♦♦♦

Martha immediately took me on a "tour" of the house. It lasted almost thirty minutes. On the first floor, besides the huge eat-in kitchen, dining room, living room, and den, there was also a study, a library, and a media room.

I was sure the basement level was like no other house in the area. Three rooms made up a mini-hospital with an operating table, x-ray apparatus, laboratory facilities, and a pharmacy. There were also fully equipped physical therapy rooms and a soundproof conference room, wired with state-of-the-art audio and video equipment.

Upstairs, along with the master suite occupied by Greg and Martha, there were six bedrooms. Security officers were in two of the bedrooms, but I was the only guest of The Gray at the moment.

As Martha escorted me to my room, she casually mentioned other facilities, so I suspected there had to be a safe room somewhere, plus a room for all the security and communications equipment. Those rooms were either located on the basement level, or in a part of the house I would have to discover for myself.

My bedroom was at the end of the upstairs hallway, the furthest from the master suite and next door to one of the security officers' rooms. As soon as Martha left me alone, I opened the wooden shutters and spent a few minutes appreciating the view.

The manicured landscape included a large boulder waterfall with a cobblestone path running alongside it. I assumed the path led down to the lake. I suspected there might even be a tunnel from the basement right down to the dock and boathouse. Most safe houses remodeled by Support had secret exits somewhere.

Within an hour of my arrival, Greg appeared at my bedroom door. He informed me I was scheduled to see Dr. Terry Howard in the basement "hospital" for a physical.

It would not be my first encounter with Terry Howard.

Howard and I had met when I was recruited by the CIA in 1980 in the middle of the Iran hostage crisis. My time at The Farm, the CIA's training facility at Camp Peary in Williamsburg, Virginia, had been full of surprises, one of which had been a case of appendicitis.

About two hours into a three-day training exercise, I had noticed a slight pain in my right side. Howard, who had just completed his residency at Massachusetts General Hospital in emergency medicine, was a member of our four-person squad, and when I popped a couple of aspirin, he started to suspect something was wrong with me. However, our team had come in last in our previous exercise, and, as the team leader, I was determined it wasn't going to happen again, so I kept ignoring my discomfort.

The task took place in and around Raleigh, North Carolina and involved locating a human target, eliminating the hostiles—another squad of trainees—and delivering the target across a "border." The border in this case was the Virginia state line.

By midnight of the first night, as my team and I were meeting together in a cheap motel on the outskirts of Raleigh, I started vomiting. After one such trip to the bathroom, Howard ignored my feeble objections and pushed on my belly. He ended his exam by asking me some ridiculous questions. Finally, he announced I was having an appendicitis attack and wanted me to check into a hospital.

I angrily disagreed and insisted on completing the task first, so Howard backed off for a couple of hours. However, after the four of us determined the location of our target, my pain became noticeably more intense.

At that point, Howard started hammering me with the facts of a burst appendix.

His lecture convinced me to work out a compromise with him. Without informing anyone at The Farm, Howard took me to the ER at Duke Raleigh Hospital and made arrangements with a surgeon to remove my diseased organ. From my hospital bed the next day, I continued to direct our mission, using one of the team members as my messenger. On the third day, our target was secured, so the team picked me up from the hospital, and we made our run for the border.

Unfortunately, we came in second.

However, none of our trainers ever found out about my emergency appendectomy. The only time they questioned me was before my initial overseas assignment. Then, the examining physician noticed my scar and remarked that someone had failed to enter my appendectomy on my medical records. At that point, I backdated the operation's date, and that was the end of it.

After our training, Dr. Terry Howard had been assigned to the Middle Eastern desk. I'd seen him a few times since then, twice for debrief exams and once in Kuwait when he was called in to examine some high-value targets before we started interrogating them. Now, since he was the attending physician at The Gray, I assumed he was assigned to Support Services permanently.

After Greg escorted me to the elevator, I told him I could make it the rest of the way on my own. Even though Greg's assignment included keeping an eye on me, he didn't voice any real objection to my small gesture of rebellion. However, as the elevator doors began to close, I noticed he hadn't moved. To reassure him, I gave him a small wave goodbye before the doors completely shut.

When I entered the exam room, Terry Howard was fussing over a set of empty vials used to draw blood; his head was bent low, trying to read the labels with a pair of bifocals perched precariously over his nose.

"Hey, Doc, how are—"

He juggled two of the vials, almost dropping one of them. "*Aaagh*! Titus, you startled me."

"Sorry. I thought you heard me." I waved my cane in his direction.

"This thing makes a lot of noise."

"No, it doesn't," he grumbled. "And don't bother apologizing. I remember how you used to like sneaking up on people."

Terry Howard had reached his late fifties with a full head of hair, no wrinkles—except for a few lines across his forehead—and he still had the slim physique he'd had when I first met him.

His grumpy demeanor remained unchanged also.

"You don't look good at all," he groused, wrapping the blood pressure cuff around my arm.

"Well, I need a haircut."

He grunted and continued taking my vitals, making meticulous notes as he probed and prodded. Lastly, he examined what had been my busted left leg.

"It was bad, huh?"

"They said I shattered my femur and tore all the knee ligaments. It wasn't pretty."

He shook his head. "With that much damage, you were either in a car accident or playing in the NFL."

"I jumped off a very high roof. Forgot to tuck and roll."

"That would do it."

Even though he had the security clearance to do so, Howard didn't question me about the particulars of my injury—that would be the job of my debriefers. He inquired relentlessly, however, about the functioning of every part of my body.

Finally, he put his hand on my knee and gave it a twist. "Did that hurt?"

The pain was excruciating.

"Ouch. Yeah!"

"Good. Maybe the surgery didn't damage your nerves too badly."

I tried massaging the pain away. "What kind of test was that?"

He ignored me and pointed to my cane. "You'll need a few weeks of rehab to get rid of your little crutch there," he said. "After that, I can't guarantee you won't continue to have some pain, but, as I recall, pain was never a big deal to you anyway."

He reached over and touched my appendix scar.

"I'll never forget how infuriated you were with me during that training run in Raleigh when I told you your appendix was about to burst. I've never seen anyone so enraged before."

Before I could protest his recollection of events, he asked me, "Have you learned to control that temper of yours yet?"

I wanted to give him a flippant answer, but in light of the decision I'd made one night in a tiny living room in Tehran, I decided to reply with the truth.

"I'm really trying, Doc, really trying."

CHAPTER 2

They left me alone for three days. At first, I figured it was because I'd arrived on Friday, and all my debriefers wanted to have a long weekend.

Later, I found out it was because Gordan Bolton—the Agency's chief of station in Turkey and the first person to greet me when Rahim released me from the trunk of his car in Dogubayazit—had suggested my bosses give me a few days off to decompress before starting my debrief.

I did nothing on Saturday except eat, sleep, and become familiar with the house. Every time I showed up in the kitchen, Martha fixed me a huge meal. For his part, Greg stayed as close to me as possible, moseying with me through the kitchen, the media room, the library, just keeping an eye on me, but willing to engage in conversation if I felt like talking.

I didn't.

I met Jim and Alex, the security officers.

Jim was an outgoing type of guy, and, like me, he was in his late forties, although his thick brown hair was already turning gray. The left side of Jim's face was disfigured by a two-inch scar running from his eye socket to his ear. However, he exuded self-confidence.

His attitude reassured me because I felt shrouded in a blanket of uncertainty.

Alex, who appeared to be in his early thirties, had curly blond hair, an acne-scarred face, and deep-set blue eyes. He barely spoke to me when we were introduced, and I had the distinct impression my presence made him nervous.

His reaction was understandable.

Covert operatives coming in from a failed mission tended to make Agency people skittish.

♦♦♦♦

After waking up on Sunday morning, I took my mug of thick black coffee outside, stared at the pool and gardens, and finally started asking myself some serious questions about my future.

Did I want to stay covert? Would I even be allowed to do so? After what happened in Tehran, were they going to offer me a desk job—analyst or such?

I thought about that for several minutes.

I decided I'd go crazy if I wasn't allowed out in the field.

The night before I'd left Tehran, Javad had asked me a question. I had answered him truthfully. However, what did that mean for my career now?

I was surprised by my feelings of helplessness and insecurity.

My emotional tenor reminded me of a time, ages ago, when Laura had left me for another man. I'd felt just as vulnerable then. Our divorce was one of the driving forces behind my accepting an offer to come to work for the CIA in the first place.

Did my life need to take a different turn now? Was it time to leave the Agency?

Praying about these questions felt like something I ought to do.

I bowed my head.

Nothing came.

Prayer wasn't a familiar practice in my life.

♦♦♦♦

By mid-morning, I was getting antsy, and, even though I was officially quarantined at The Gray until my debrief was over, I briefly considered leaving the house for a couple of hours.

I knew that the Agency's quarantine restrictions—no outside communication, television, or internet—were in place to preserve the integrity of the debrief. However, as much as I agreed with this concept in principle, trying to obey such rules always proved to be an entirely different matter altogether.

Despite my restlessness, though, I discarded my escape plans.

Instead, I wandered into the library, where I found a variety of reading choices on the shelves. There were the classics, lots of "how to" books—so I could learn about installing a toilet or making a PowerPoint presentation—and some contemporary fiction. I also found a whole shelf of religious books and different versions of the Bible.

I finally selected *A Tale of Two Cities, The Cambridge Guide to Astronomical Discovery,* and a Bible.

Then, I slipped off to my room.

Greg knocked on my door around one o'clock and asked me if I wanted some lunch. I followed him downstairs and into the kitchen where Martha was slicing up some roast beef.

When she saw me, she immediately picked up a remote control and turned off the flat-screen TV mounted on the wall in the breakfast nook.

Fox News Sunday was playing.

After putting down the remote, she looked over at Greg and silently mouthed an apology, "Sorry."

He waved her off.

He must have thought I hadn't heard anything.

Chris Wallace had been asking someone about Iran's nuclear program.

Alex was perched on a stool at the kitchen island wolfing down a sandwich. He gave me the once over, nodded his head, and left the room.

Greg grabbed the vacant stool, and I sat down next to him.

Martha placed a big roast beef sandwich in front of me, along with a small bowl of potato salad. "Thanks. This looks great."

She acknowledged my compliment with a smile. "You want

lemonade again?"

My mouth was full, so I just nodded. A few minutes later, she placed a large icy glass in front of me.

"Greg, can I get you something?" she asked her husband.

"I'll take a cup of coffee."

After she handed him a mug, a knowing look passed between them, and, seconds later, she made an excuse and left the room.

A few minutes after she left, Greg removed a sheet of paper from his shirt pocket. "Here's the schedule for your debrief tomorrow," he said. "It looks pretty straightforward. I know you've been through this drill several times."

I took the schedule and stuffed it inside my jeans pocket without looking at it.

"You like working for the Agency, Greg?"

I wasn't sure whether it was my question or the fact I was beginning to talk, but Greg smiled when he gave me his answer. "Yes, yes, I do."

He took a sip of his coffee then gestured at his surroundings. "Obviously, this is a pretty cushy job."

"Did you ever go operational, work in the field?"

His eyes shifted slightly to the left, and he hesitated a moment before answering. I had no doubt he was weighing whether it was more important to keep me talking or follow Agency rules. He decided on the former.

However, he sounded apologetic when he answered me. "Only Level 4 action, but Martha was Level 2. We met at an Agency in-house party and got married six months later."

"So you had to transfer to Support services after you were married?"

"Yeah. There were some options, but . . ." he looked over at me, then up at a camera mounted in the ceiling, "you know how difficult it would have been to live any kind of normal life, much less see each other, if either of us had stayed in Operations."

I agreed. "It wouldn't have worked."

He nodded his head, drained the last of his coffee, and walked over to the sink, carefully rinsing out his cup.

"Did Martha have a hard time adjusting?"

Looking perplexed, he asked, "Adjusting?"

"You know. Did she miss . . ." I struggled to find the right words, "her sense of purpose about what she was doing?"

He thought about my question for a moment. "I don't think she missed the ops at first. We couldn't really talk about it, of course, but I suspected her last assignment had gotten a bit ugly. I'm sure that made the change easier." He shifted uncomfortably. "Look, Titus, you know we aren't supposed to—"

"Did she stop believing?"

There was no mistaking the anger in his voice. "Believing? You mean did she stop believing her actions were helping her country?"

"No, of course not. I'm talking about that inner calling that—"

An alarm went off—a steady *beep, beep, beep.*

Suddenly, at that moment, Jim burst through a door off the kitchen.

I had just assumed the door led to the pantry.

Assumptions can get you killed.

Beep. Beep. Beep.

Jim motioned toward me. "Follow me."

Beep. Beep. Beep.

As I headed in his direction, Martha and Alex rushed into the room.

Beep. Beep. Beep

Alex quickly walked over to a wall console and entered some numbers on a key pad.

The beeping stopped.

Seconds later, the intercom from the security gate squawked. Greg started to answer it, but Jim motioned for Martha to take it.

She took a deep breath and pressed the button.

Calmly she said, "Yes."

The female voice on the other end was high-pitched and had a Boston accent. "Oh, Martha, it's me, Teresa. I just need to drive up and have you sign this petition. It won't take a minute. I hope I'm not bothering you and Greg."

Before hearing Martha's reply, Jim ushered me past the pantry door, through a false wall at the back of the pantry and into a large room. It contained a wall of security monitors, computers, and several different kinds of communications equipment.

On one of the monitors, I saw a very thin woman dressed in a pair of black slacks and a yellow blouse. She was standing outside the security gate speaking into the intercom. As I watched, she got back inside her Mercedes and waited for the gate to slide open.

Jim was watching the other video feeds from around the grounds, while also keeping an eye on a nearby computer screen as it rapidly scanned through thousands of images using the Agency's facial recognition software. As soon as a match for Teresa came up on the computer screen, he hit the button for the gate to open.

Speaking into his wrist mike, he said, "We have benign contact. Repeat. Benign contact."

Alex keyed back, "Copy. Benign contact."

Jim looked over at me. "She's just a neighbor. She called Martha earlier in the week to see if she would sign a petition to keep the city from cutting down a tree on the right-of-way. It's creating a traffic hazard." He shook his head. "Teresa's a champion of lost causes."

I took the chance to look around.

I felt sure the door on the opposite wall led to a safe room. Once a person was inside, the room could not be breached—at least not easily.

Jim glanced up at me. "Yeah, that's the safe room, but we're good right here. Martha knows how to deal with this situation."

We watched as Martha opened the front door and invited Teresa inside the foyer. They were smiling and chatting like actors in a silent movie.

Everything seemed fine, but I found myself wishing I were armed.

Along with Jim, I scanned the monitors showing the video from the grounds.

"Where's the feed from the pool house?" I asked, nervously.

He pointed to a split screen. "It's this one. It's shared with the feed from the garage."

We went back to watching the action on the screen, and I asked him to turn the audio on.

Martha and Teresa moved into the living room where Greg joined them. He was carrying a book, trying to look as if Teresa's arrival had interrupted his reading. He and Martha sat down on the sofa, and, using Greg's book for a hard surface, they signed Teresa's petition.

As they played out their deceptive scenario, I could see the differences in their operational styles firsthand.

Greg's face was stiff, devoid of any expression; his hand movements were jerky and nervous, and his voice was just a bit too loud. However, Martha appeared relaxed, even comfortable, as if she were enjoying herself. Her body posture mirrored Teresa's movements, and she stayed in sync with Teresa's conversational pattern.

After a few minutes, Jim and I watched as the three of them walked toward the front door together.

"She's consistently good," Jim said. "Greg's always twitchy, though."

My nerves eased up, and I turned away from the security console and walked around the room, poking my nose into a wall cabinet, running my hand over some books on a bookshelf.

"The gun safe is downstairs."

I turned and smiled at him. "I'm that obvious, huh?"

"I've been in your shoes, that's all."

He opened the door to a cabinet and took out a pistol.

"I keep an extra firearm in here. It would have been yours if our security had been breached."

"Good to know."

He quickly put the gun back in its hiding place.

"You didn't hear it from me though." He made a sweeping motion with his hand. "Of course, no one hears anything in here."

I made a mental note of that information. Since everything was being monitored throughout the safe house, at least the communications room was one place I could have a frank conversation without fear of blowback.

I turned my attention back to the monitors and watched Teresa pull her car into the street. When the gates closed behind her, Jim gave Alex the all clear.

I looked around the room one last time.

I said, "Well, I guess I'd better get back out there."

Jim flipped a switch to unlock the door leading through the pantry to the kitchen.

As I walked past him, he put his hand out to stop me.

"Look, Titus, I know I'm not supposed to know as much about you as I do, but there's always talk, you know that. Well . . . I want you to know, I'm here if you need anything or if you'd just like to talk to someone."

"Thanks, Jim."

I started toward the door, but then I turned back and said, "Could I ask you a question?"

"Of course."

"What's the most important thing in the world to you?"

At first, he seemed taken aback by my question.

Then, he quickly recovered and said, "I'd have to say it's my family. My wife and two kids mean everything to me."

I nodded.

"Why would you ask me that?"

"An asset asked me that question just before he was murdered."

He gave me a look of understanding.

"So, how did you answer him?"

"I never got the chance."

CHAPTER 3

On Monday morning, I awoke with a sense of relief mingled with trepidation—similar to the way I usually felt when I was about to embark on a new mission. However, unlike most of my operations, my Agency debriefing should only take a couple of days—depending on who was on the debriefing team and how they were interpreting my narrative.

When I thought about who might be assigned to my debriefing team, I decided it was time to shave off my beard. I also decided, after studying my face in the bathroom mirror, that Terry Howard was wrong; I didn't look that bad. Granted, I wasn't George Clooney handsome, but who was?

Years ago, someone had told me I was a pretty good-looking guy. Since then, no one had told me otherwise.

My trainers at The Farm had described my face as one that "blended." They considered that a good thing. Put me in a restaurant, a bus station, a mosque, and I blended right in. I didn't draw attention.

Only, as it turned out in Tehran, one time I did.

After taking a quick shower, I put on the clothing supplied for me by Support Services—a pair of dark slacks and a blue oxford shirt. My debriefers would be in very formal business attire, but I knew if I looked halfway decent and appeared to be in my right mind, that's all they expected of me. Unlike Bud Thorsen—who had a nervous breakdown after a two-year stint in Yemen and had arrived at his debriefing sessions in his pajamas—I did not want a transfer to a desk job.

At least, I didn't think so.

After I got dressed, I tried praying again. Javad and his wife, Darya, had told me it was easy, just like talking to someone. They had often prayed for me while I was living with them in Tehran, and I suspected they continued to pray for me even now.

I bowed my head and told God I wasn't looking forward to spilling my guts at the debrief. I admitted I was uncertain about my future, and it was eating away at me, and I also asked him to help me control my temper. When I finished, I decided Javad was right—praying wasn't really that hard.

Because I had no desire to stand around and make small talk with any Agency personnel, I skipped Martha's breakfast and remained in my room until Greg knocked on my door.

Then, I headed down to the festivities.

♦♦♦♦

I arrived at the lower level conference room just as Martha was coming out the door.

She gave me a fleeting smile and whispered, "I left you some cinnamon rolls. Make sure you get some." As I held the door open for her, she added, "There's also a carafe of lemonade for you."

I whispered back. "Thanks."

Although the conference table in the room could easily seat ten people, only four chairs were occupied. Douglas Carlton, my official handler and the operations officer for my mission, was seated on the right side of the table all alone.

He would be in charge of the debrief.

He was reading from a stack of papers, and I knew he was probably studying the overnight cables. Carlton was someone who prided himself on being a "detail person," and he would inform everyone of this organizational attribute at least twice in every meeting.

Carlton was bald-headed with enormous brown eyes that grew larger whenever he disagreed with something being said. He was a meticulous dresser. Today he wore a gray, pinstriped suit, long-sleeved white shirt—with the hint of a cuff showing—and a pastel-colored tie adorned with tiny, silver geometric designs.

He looked like a Wall Street banker.

Ours was a love/hate relationship.

He caught a glimpse of me out of the corner of his eye and quickly got up from his chair and started toward me. I met him halfway. He grabbed my outstretched hand and put his other hand on my shoulder, squeezing hard.

Speaking each word as if it were a sentence all by itself, he said, "So. Good. To. See. You." He pumped my hand for several seconds. "You look . . ." he paused and looked me over from head to toe, "amazingly well after all you've been through."

"I've gotten some rest," I said, "and I've been eating like a horse since I got here."

"Good." He pointed toward a credenza where an assortment of snacks and drinks were laid out. "Why don't you get yourself something to eat, and we'll get started."

As I turned to go, he patted me on the back. "I understand you didn't have any breakfast this morning."

Carlton always wanted you to know he knew more about you than you thought he did.

This personality trait accounted for the hate part of our relationship.

I grabbed a cinnamon roll and a cup of coffee and took my assigned seat at the head of the table. Carlton was seated to my left. He was distributing stacks of documents to the other three debriefers who were seated across the table from him and to my right. They had not been speaking to each other when I entered the room, and they remained focused on other tasks as I sat down.

The farthest person from me was Katherine Broward, the Agency's chief strategic analyst. She was intent on texting or entering some information on her iPhone, and she had not turned her head or met my gaze since I'd entered the room.

Katherine was also dressed in a gray business suit, but, unlike Carlton, she wore a frilly red blouse underneath her jacket. Since she had been with the Agency for less than 10 years, I put her age at around thirty-five, but discerning a woman's age was difficult for me. Discerning beauty, however, was an entirely different matter, and I knew Katherine was a very beautiful woman. She had long, honey-blond hair, green eyes, and a rather prominent chin.

At one time, Katherine and I had tried to have a relationship.

However, I'd only managed one lunch, followed by dinner a week later. Then, I was off to Afghanistan. I don't remember the excuse Katherine gave me when I asked her out upon my return, but I do remember thinking it was a very believable lie.

"Sorry, I'm late."

Every head turned as Robert Ira entered the conference room.

As I observed the look on Carlton's face, I realized he, like everyone else, seemed surprised to see the Deputy Director of Operations show up in person for the debriefing of a covert intelligence officer.

Carlton quickly got up from his chair. "Deputy Ira, this is a pleasant surprise. I didn't realize the Director was sending someone over for the debrief."

Ira placed a large black briefcase on the conference table. "I hope this isn't an inconvenience."

"No. No. Not at all," Carlton said. "Here take this seat. I'll move over."

Ira eased his large bulky body into the chair just vacated by Carlton. Then, he opened his briefcase and rummaged around inside it a moment, finally removing a laptop computer.

The Deputy's pudgy face, combined with his stringy gray hair and bulbous red nose, made him appear more like a cartoon character than a high-ranking intelligence administrator. However, I'd always suspected his looks were a bit of cunning camouflage for his devious but brilliant mind. In his position, an unappealing appearance went hand-in-hand with an unappealing job.

Robert Ira was the point man for the CIA's Director of Operations. He was sent out to look for operational and political minefields that could blow up in the Agency's face. To that end, he was tasked with assessing the successes and failures of an operation and of evaluating its financial gains and losses. His bottom-line reports to the Director were both feared and cheered. They could bring either curses or blessings on the agent involved.

I had been the recipient of both.

However, Ira seldom left Agency headquarters, preferring instead to sit in his office gathering data from operational officers, reading reports, making phone calls, and holding endless meetings. His presence at my debrief signaled someone was definitely worried about some aspect of Operation Torchlight.

Those worries were well founded.

Carlton cleared his throat and addressed the room. "First, I'd like to begin by making some introductions, then, I'll take care of the preliminaries, and, finally," Carlton paused and glanced over at me, "we'll hear from Titus."

That was partly true. They would indeed hear from me, but I, in turn, would hear from them. That's the way an operational debrief worked: I would tell my story; they would ask me questions. Some of those questions would be intended to show how much they knew, and how little I really knew.

I didn't mind that.

I've never minded finding out what others thought I didn't know.

Carlton began his introductions.

"Titus, I believe you're already acquainted with Katherine." Carlton gave her a nod. She, in turn, gave me just the briefest hint of a smile. "You're also acquainted with Mr. Haddadi, who's here to help us with any language and cultural issues we might encounter today."

Komeil Haddadi had been a high-ranking scientist in Iran's nuclear program until five years ago when he had walked into the American Embassy in London and defected—much to everyone's surprise and delight. Carlton was a member of the team who had spent several weeks interrogating him, and I'd never heard Carlton call him anything but Mr. Haddadi. However, since the two of us had spent considerable time together two years ago, while prepping for my assignment in Iran, I'd always called him Komeil.

Komeil reached across the table and clasped my hand in both of his. "So good to have you back."

As Komeil gave me a broad smile, I was reminded of pictures I'd seen of the Shah of Iran. He resembled the Shah enough to have been his brother.

Carlton finished up his introductions. "Sitting next to Mr. Haddadi is Tony Fowler. He's our outside observer for this debriefing session."

Fowler was an African-American with square, wire-rimmed glasses and a short, neat haircut. I noticed he kept fiddling with his iPad, even while Carlton was introducing everyone.

I wasn't acquainted with Tony Fowler, but we exchanged perfunctory nods.

Because Fowler was the outside observer for my debrief, it didn't surprise me we'd never met before. In fact, had we known each other, he could not have been the outside observer.

All operational debriefing sessions were assigned a person from another division, someone who had not been involved in the mission itself and who did not know the covert intelligence officer being debriefed. The reasoning behind this rule was that an outside observer brought a new perspective and provided insights not otherwise apparent to the operational team. The Director had instituted this regulation at the urging of a congressional oversight committee ten years ago, but the responsibility for choosing the outside observer had been turned over to the DDO, Robert Ira.

In my opinion, outside observers asked far too many questions during a debrief. This slowed down the whole process and interfered with the intelligence officer's flow of thought in narrating the events of an operation. Such irrelevant interrogations primarily occurred because a debrief was an invaluable opportunity for an observer to delve into operations beyond his or her intelligence scope, giving that person a treasure trove of information. Such knowledge was highly coveted and served as a powerful commodity within the walls of the Agency.

Carlton turned to his left and addressed Ira. "Once again, let me say how privileged we are to have you in the room today, Deputy Ira.

I believe you've met everyone here before?"

He smiled at Katherine and glanced briefly at the rest of us. "Yes, I have."

"I'll begin with the formalities," Carlton said, "and let me remind everyone that these sessions are being recorded."

Carlton cleared his throat yet again. When he spoke, his voice was slightly stilted.

"Session One. This is Operations Officer, Douglas Carlton, in the intelligence debrief of Titus Alan Ray, Level 1 covert operative for Operation Torchlight."

He pointed a finger in my direction. "Begin the narrative."

♦♦♦♦

"Two years ago, I entered Iran on a Swiss passport. My cover name was Hammid Salimi, the son of an Iranian watchmaker and a Swiss businesswoman. My legend was solid. I was in Tehran to open up a market for my parents' line of luxury watches and jewelry. The contacts I made among the elite in the Iranian regime were to serve as the prime recruiting ground for a cadre of assets Operations hoped would help fund the Iranian opposition and topple the government."

Not surprisingly, Fowler was the first committee member to break into my narrative. However, his eyes barely left his iPad as he threw out his questions.

"Aren't most wealthy Iranians in lock-step with the regime?" he asked. "How was such an operation even feasible?"

Carlton responded immediately. "Yes, Tony, that's an excellent question, and it's one I'll be happy to answer."

Carlton picked up a set of documents on the table, although he didn't refer to them immediately.

"All our data pointed to a great disaffection among the upper echelon of Iranian society. We heard from a variety of sources," he gestured toward Komeil, "including Mr. Haddadi, who indicated that the elite in Iran might be willing to help the opposition, despite continually receiving incentives from the government."

Mr. Haddadi shifted in his chair and opened his mouth, but before he could utter a word, Carlton began reading from the set of papers he was holding. He'd chosen several sections describing the mind-numbing psychological details about the thinking of Iran's upper class.

As his voice droned on, I knew I wasn't the only person in the room feeling sleepy.

Finally, when I couldn't stand it any longer, I interrupted him. "I recruited four assets within six months and two more the next year."

Fowler looked up from his iPad.

I added defiantly, "It was obviously a workable operation."

Fowler peered at me over the tops of his glasses, studying me for a few seconds. Then, he said, "Duly noted."

Perhaps trying to lower the testosterone in the room, Katherine spoke up.

"Our product from these recruits was extremely beneficial," she said. "Not only was Titus able to penetrate this closed community, he was also able to gain access into—"

"Well, let's not get ahead of ourselves," Carlton said, obviously trying to regain control of the meeting. "Titus, continue the narrative."

I spent almost an hour explaining how I went about identifying my targets by developing business relationships, cultivating ties in banking circles, and socializing with the affluent in Iranian society. When I got into some of the more specific details of the money I was spending to live such a lavish lifestyle, Deputy Ira started rapidly typing on his laptop.

I did not take that as a good sign.

Katherine, probably thinking the same thing, asked a question that prodded me on to a different topic. "Titus, wasn't the purchase of your apartment the reason you were able to develop a friendship with Amir Madani?"

At the mention of Amir's name, Fowler's head shot up and Ira suddenly stopped typing.

I was puzzled at their sudden interest.

"Correct," I said. "I was sitting at an outdoor café with Farid, one of my recruits, when an acquaintance of his stopped by our table. Farid introduced his friend to me as Amir."

As I described my chance encounter with Amir, I noticed a slight tic had developed below Fowler's left eye.

"I immediately recognized the man as Amir Madani," I said, "one of Iran's nuclear scientists, so I decided to use Farid to see if I could get closer to him."

"How?" Fowler asked.

"Pardon me?"

"How were you able to recognize him?"

"Well, because . . ." I hesitated for only a split second but it was just enough time for him to hit me with a barrage of other questions before I could finish answering his first one.

"Since your operational mandate was to cultivate assets to finance the opposition, what was your interest in this Amir?" he asked. "Your warrant didn't include targeting Iran's scientists, did it?"

I suddenly found myself extremely curious about Tony Fowler.

Because he was the outside observer on the committee, the position he held in the Agency was unknown to me. He could be employed in any section of Operations. Of course, everyone else in the room, except possibly Komeil, knew the name of his division.

For my part, I was beginning to suspect which door his key card might open.

However, if I were guessing correctly, it meant someone at the Agency had deliberately sabotaged my mission in Tehran.

Carlton immediately spoke up. "Of course, I authorized it."

Fowler seemed stunned. "You did?"

For several seconds, Fowler seemed to be grappling for another question. Finally, he asked, "When?"

Carlton's eyes grew wider. "When? You mean you want the actual date?" A puzzled look passed over Carlton's face. Moments later, he looked over at Ira, as if hoping the DDO might be able to clear up his confusion.

However, the deputy immediately turned his attention to his laptop, ignoring Carlton's bewildered stare.

Fowler was adamant when he answered Carlton. "No, I don't want a date. I want a timeline."

Carlton shuffled through his notes. While I had no idea what was bothering him about Fowler's question, I could tell he was simply stalling for time.

Fowler continued questioning Carlton. "Did you authorize contact before or after Titus recognized him? I want to understand how it was that Titus knew this man in the first place. There are thousands of people walking the streets of Iran. It seems odd that he would be able to—"

"I showed him pictures," Komeil said, barging into the exchange.

Fowler looked surprised. "Why would you do that?"

"Look, Tony," I said, before Komeil could answer him, "Perhaps I should have explained how I went about preparing for this mission. My oversight may have caused you some misunderstanding, and I take full responsibility for that. Let me back up and tell you about my preparation for Operation Torchlight."

I noticed a smile flicker across Katherine's face, and I wondered if she knew I was simply trying to buy Carlton time to resolve his confusion.

Fowler removed his glasses and began massaging his temples. "Sure, why don't you do that?"

I launched into a myriad of details explaining how Legends—the branch of Support Services responsible for creating false identities—had prepared my background, my credentials, and my entry into Iran. Then, I inundated Fowler with the kind of research I undertook prior to a mission. Finally, I described how Komeil and I had worked together to enable me a quick integration into Iranian society.

"I met with Komeil three times a week for two months," I said. "We only spoke Farsi when we were together. When we—"

"Why are you so fluent in Farsi?" Fowler asked. He sounded surprisingly accusatory. "Were you ever in Iran before this assignment?"

I turned to Carlton for approval. He gave me a dismissive wave of his hand. "Go ahead," he said, while continuing to look through his stack of documents.

"No, I had never been to Iran before this mission. And the language? It's just a gift. It doesn't take me long to acquire fluency in any language."

I started to elaborate about how many languages I spoke, but Fowler had no real need to know. An operational debriefing was not so much about the operative as it was about the operation. Tony Fowler was not cleared in this setting to know more about me than Carlton wanted him to know.

"Komeil briefed me on some prominent people I should get to know in Tehran," I said. "As I was studying the photographs of these people, I came across several group shots he had taken with some of his scientific colleagues while they were attending a conference together. We talked about their backgrounds, and that's how I recognized Amir Madani when I saw him that day."

I twisted open a bottle of water sitting in front of me and took a very long drink.

As I drank, Fowler appeared impatient, anxious for me to continue my narrative. I knew he wanted an explanation of why I'd decided to seek authorization to start courting Amir when my mission's objective didn't include contact with one of Iran's nuclear scientist. For some reason, such information appeared to be extremely important to him.

However, I placed the empty bottle of water back on the table and remained silent.

I waited for Fowler to ask me the question again. I needed to hear his exact words and sentence structure, to catch the nuance, and to watch his facial expression.

As the silence grew, Carlton made an elaborate show of checking his watch. "Titus," he said, "let's break for lunch and resume in two hours."

Carlton watched as Tony Fowler hurriedly left the room. Then, when the door slammed shut, he turned to Ira. "Deputy, could we have lunch together?"

I had no idea where the two of them were going for lunch, but wherever it was, I knew Carlton wasn't leaving there until Deputy Ira had served him up some satisfactory answers. When it came to getting answers, Carlton was like a kid bugging his mom for a new toy—he would never gave up until he got what he wanted.

This personality trait accounted for the love part of our relationship.

CHAPTER 4

Since I wasn't allowed to leave the grounds until clearing my debrief, I took the plate of food Martha had prepared for me and escaped onto the patio, sitting at a table beside the Olympic-size swimming pool.

It was a beautiful sunny day in April, and although the wind was chilly, I wanted the freedom of being outdoors too much to care about the temperature.

As I ate my chicken salad sandwich, I decided not to think about the dynamics occurring inside my debrief. Instead, I watched two groundskeepers cleaning out a flowerbed. They appeared to be enjoying each other's company, laughing and talking together as they worked.

However, the longer I watched them, the more I realized I wasn't just showing them passing curiosity. On a professional level, I was assessing them, scrutinizing their movements, trying to determine if they presented any real danger to me.

Since The Gray was encased in a secured environment, my obsessive exercise made me wonder if I'd been living the clandestine life too long.

Was it mentally healthy to be so suspicious? Was my wariness a sure indicator I needed to get out? Should I take the initiative and ask to be transferred to a desk job?

Yet, being a covert intelligence operative was the only thing I knew how to do, and I did it very well. I knew that.

As a kid growing up in Flint, Michigan, I thought I wanted to be a police officer or maybe an FBI agent. My parents never discouraged me, nor, for that matter, did they encourage me to pursue law enforcement. In fact, my dad, Gerald, who worked on the assembly line at GM, didn't pay much attention to me at all. In some ways, he was the typical alcoholic dad. He worked on the line all day, and then he drank himself to sleep every night. He wasn't mean, and he didn't mistreat my mom or my sister. He was simply emotionally absent from our family.

My mother, Sharon, who was a high school science teacher, relied on empirical evidence to explain her husband's behavior. "When Gerald came home from Vietnam, he was a broken man," she often told people. "He saw way too many horrible things over there, and it's haunted him ever since."

Perhaps my father experienced the most horrifying aspects of that war, but he was never willing to talk to me about any of them, and I certainly tried often enough. As a young boy, I asked him endless questions about the Army. What was like to be shot at? How did it feel to see someone die? However, his answers were always vague or monosyllabic. As a teenager, his attitude infuriated me, and we exchanged heated words on a regular basis. By the time I left for college, we were barely speaking.

As expected, my relationship with my father was a topic the Agency psychiatrists discussed with me when I applied for the CIA. At the end of those intense sessions, I finally realized my failure to bond with my father was the motivation behind my willingness to embrace Laura Hudson and her family.

Laura and I had met during my first month at the University of Michigan. Within a few weeks of being introduced, we were spending all of our time together, and, during one weekend in November, she invited me home to meet her parents.

Roman and Cynthia Hudson were welcoming, gracious people. I was immediately drawn to them, especially Roman, who owned a hardware store in a strip mall in Ann Arbor and started calling me "son" as soon as we were introduced.

Instead of returning home for Christmas during my freshman year, I spent my entire two-week break with Laura's family in Ann Arbor. It was then I learned Roman had also been in Vietnam, but there was a big difference between him and my father—he was more than willing to talk about what he'd done over there.

The first time Roman had mentioned Southeast Asia was when Laura and I had stopped by the hardware store on Christmas Eve to see if we could help with the holiday rush. Laura's mother, Cynthia, was working as a cashier, so Laura had opened up another cash register, while I went to find Roman. I located him at the back of the store in the sporting goods section where he was showing a gun to a customer.

Because I'd never been around firearms before, I watched in awe at how easily he handled the weapon, stripping it down, explaining its features, and then putting the whole thing back together in the blink of an eye. Roman noticed my fascination at his expertise, and when the customer left, he immediately began telling me stories of his time in Vietnam working for the CIA.

Laughing at himself, he said, "They called us spooks back then."

For Christmas, he gave me my first weapon, a .22 revolver, and I spent the rest of the week at the gun range. The following year, during my Spring break, two important things occurred: I asked Laura to marry me and Roman gave me a Smith & Wesson .357 magnum.

I married Laura the following June.

For a wedding present, her parents gave us the down payment on a small house near the campus. However, between both of us going to school full-time and working at our part-time jobs, I barely remembered living there. Besides that, I chose to spend most of my free time with Roman.

Roman not only continued teaching me everything he knew about weaponry, he also tutored me in the rudiments of the tradecraft he was taught during his brief time working for the Agency. I hadn't made a conscious decision to join the CIA yet, but before starting my junior year of college, I switched my major from business to international relations with a minor in languages.

By our second year of marriage, Laura was growing increasingly unhappy about my relationship with her dad. Even though I knew Laura hated all the time I was spending with Roman, I refused to change at all. When we would argue—which was often—I'd lose my temper and say incredibly cruel things to her.

Eventually, Laura found someone else. The day she asked me for a divorce, she said, "You didn't fall in love with me, Titus; you fell in love with my dad."

She was right, of course.

At first, I blamed the failure of my marriage on my disappointing family life. Later, I realized when Laura and I had met, I'd been sinking in a sea of uncertainty. Then, out of the fog, Roman had appeared to me as a lighthouse, and I'd been drawn to him as my only means of rescue.

Perhaps not surprisingly, a week after signing the final divorce papers, I was talking to a CIA recruiter.

♦♦♦♦

After finishing up my sandwich, I went back inside and put my dishes in the kitchen sink. The room was empty, so I faced the ceiling camera, raised my arm, and made a circling motion with my forefinger. Within a few seconds, Jim came through the pantry door.

"Got a problem?" he asked.

"Just a question."

He gestured for me to follow him, and we went back to his lair in the communications room. As soon as he sat down in front of the security monitors, I saw him glance up at the feed coming from the kitchen video. He noted the time on a yellow pad.

Then he pointed toward a chair. "Have a seat."

The chair he indicated faced a wall of wide-screen monitors displaying video from several different news agencies. The headlines scrolling across the screens indicated something newsworthy was happening in North Korea, and I was sorely tempted to feast my eyes on every word and satisfy my curiosity.

However, I resisted. I knew I was about to break one of the house rules, and one broken rule a day was my self-imposed quota.

Jim looked amused when I repositioned the chair so I was facing him instead of the screens. "What's your question?"

"Before I ask it, I want you to know I'm assuming several things, which will be obvious to you when I ask the question. If I'm assuming incorrectly, and you don't want to answer the question, then know for certain I won't think less of you."

He considered my statement for a couple of seconds, and then he nodded. "Okay."

"Tony Fowler."

Jim blinked his eyes several times.

I continued with my question. "Have I been playing around in his backyard?"

This time Jim's reaction was to stare at me without blinking. He did this for what seemed like a long time, but it was probably only twenty seconds or so.

I knew he'd been monitoring the feed from the video in the debriefing room during the morning session. That was his job. He could also lose his job if he revealed the identity of the outside observer to me.

However, if Jim had truly "been in my shoes," as he'd indicated to me on Sunday, then he also knew the position I was in with Tony Fowler. He understood how valuable this little bit of information was to me as I continued my narrative in the afternoon session.

He continued to hold my gaze. I waited.

"Yes," he finally said.

I suddenly realized I'd been holding my breath. "Thanks."

He pointed toward the security feed from the kitchen. "When you go back out there, I'll run this back and erase it when you move away from the kitchen sink."

"That should do it."

♦ ♦ ♦

I still had some time before my debrief was scheduled to resume, so I slipped upstairs to my bedroom. I needed a few minutes alone to get my head around what I'd discovered.

The information Jim had just confirmed for me was that Tony Fowler was head of the Nuclear Security Division (NSD). Now, it made sense why he had reacted so strongly when I'd mentioned meeting the Iranian nuclear scientist, Amir Madani.

Fowler's portfolio at NSD included running agents in any country seeking nuclear weapons, and he should have been well acquainted—at least by name—with all of Iran's nuclear personnel. Fowler's division had a number of covert operatives in Iran responsible for developing assets in their nuclear program. Perhaps one of them had even tried to recruit Amir.

Of course, from a geographic standpoint, having such a broad scope to his job description meant Fowler was required to co-ordinate his operations with other regional divisions. Otherwise, an operative from the Middle East Division and an operative from NSD might be targeting the same asset.

For example, imagine that Carlton had a covert intelligence officer in place in Tehran. Now imagine this officer had accidently met a nuclear scientist at a café and decided to develop him as an asset. In such a scenario, the correct Agency procedure called for Carlton to inform NSD of said encounter. However, Carlton could not just walk across the hall to the NSD and discuss the matter with Tony Fowler in person. No, the Agency would never allow such a direct communication between divisions. Instead, protocol called for Carlton to inform Robert Ira. Ira, in turn, was responsible for notifying Fowler and the NSD that an agent wished to pursue contact with a nuclear scientist.

If Fowler had no objection—such as he was pursuing the asset himself or had some information on him that precluded contact—Ira would then relay the message to Carlton, who would authorize his intelligence officer to develop the asset.

Now, the picture was becoming clearer.

Either Carlton had never notified Robert Ira of my request to pursue Amir—which was unlikely because Carlton had emphatically affirmed in the morning session that he'd authorized my contact—or Ira had never informed Fowler that a Middle Eastern operative was asking permission to target a nuclear scientist.

Thinking back on Fowler's behavior in the morning session, I came to the conclusion Fowler had not known about my pursuit of Amir as a CIA asset until I'd mentioned it. Was that the reason Robert Ira was at my debriefing? Had he failed to inform Fowler I was pursuing Amir Madani?

If so, why didn't the DDO follow the correct procedure and coordinate with Fowler's office on such a critical issue? For the whole field of operations to work smoothly, there had to be cooperation among the different divisions. Otherwise, operatives and assets would overlap, and it would be chaotic and dangerous for everyone, especially in a hostile environment like Iran.

Iran was one of the most difficult countries in the world in which to gather intelligence. Civilians and military personnel were taught—by the propaganda arm of Iran's elite Revolutionary Guards Corps—to be constantly on the alert for "infiltrators" and "enemies" who wanted to penetrate all aspects of society so they could exploit Iran's "secrets." In such an atmosphere, human intelligence gathering, especially in regards to Iran's nuclear program, was abysmal—so sparse as to be non-existent. Government agencies were forced to rely on satellite surveillance or the occasional defector, like Komeil Haddadi, to obtain even an inkling of what was going on inside Iran's nuclear community.

Such a shortage of intelligence had been foremost on my mind when I'd originally contacted Carlton about checking out Amir and possibly targeting him as a source. Since the NSD had done such a lousy job of finding and developing assets, now I wondered if Robert Ira had taken things a step further and simply cut the NSD division out of the loop entirely, never even informing Fowler that an intelligence officer—namely, me—had requested permission to pursue an Iranian scientist as a potential asset.

If my suspicions were correct and Ira had given Carlton the green light without informing Tony Fowler, then he'd blatantly disregarded crucial inter-division communication and had jeopardized my life. Far more importantly, his decision had contributed to—if not caused—the murder of my assets.

Now, I had a big decision to make.

CHAPTER 5

I stepped into the bathroom and splashed some cold water on my face. Then, I sat down in the overstuffed chair in front of the bedroom's fireplace and mapped out how I was going to proceed with my narrative in the afternoon session.

I could go back down to my debrief and spin my tale in such a way everyone would be placated, and no one would be blamed for the debacle of my mission.

If I took that route, I would have to minimize my contact with Amir and blame the rolling up of my network on my sloppy tradecraft. While distasteful, such a strategy would probably satisfy everyone.

Of course, using this tactic meant I would have to weave a tapestry of lies.

That would not be a problem for me.

Lying is second nature and I do it very well.

Then I considered the alternative—telling the truth.

However, I wasn't sure what the repercussions of such a decision would be. Was it even a viable option?

Whatever I decided to do, I knew my future at the Agency was about to change dramatically.

I'd been preparing myself for such a change from the moment Javad's family had come into their living room to pray for me just hours before I was to make my escape from Tehran. That night, Javad and Darya, their teenage son, Mansoor, along with Rahim, had joined hands and prayed a beautiful, fervent prayer for my well-being and safe travel through the mountains of Iran to safety in Turkey.

Javad, along with several of his relatives, owned a fruit and vegetable stand in one of Tehran's open-air markets, and Darya was a nurse who worked at a neighborhood clinic. I had been forced to live with these Iranian Christians for three months in a safe house, while hiding out from Iran's Revolutionary Guard Corps.

Each night, from my bed in a corner of their tiny living room, I had observed them at their kitchen table praying and reading their Bible together before going to bed. However, they didn't keep their beliefs private. In fact, they seemed to have an insatiable desire to share their faith—especially with me. They did this even though their pastor, Youcef, was in prison because of his proselytizing. However, they were doing something even more dangerous. Not only were they proselytizing, they were also harboring an American spy and facilitating his escape from Iran.

Before leaving them, I had thanked them profusely for their help. I had also commended them because, even though they were required to go to work every day and pretend they were just harmless Iranian citizens, they had practiced excellent tradecraft in keeping me safe.

Javad had responded to my gratitude by saying, "Oh, Hammid, it's not difficult for us to do this because we remember the words of Jesus. He said we were to be like sheep living among the wolves. He told us to be as shrewd as snakes and as innocent as doves."

Now, as I left my room to face my debriefers once again, I decided those words—to be both shrewd and innocent—might be good advice for me as well.

In reality, when it came to events in Tehran, I was both.

♦♦♦♦

Deputy Ira and Carlton were huddled together on one side of the table when I reentered the conference room. They were engaged in a whispered conversation, and from their body language, it appeared the two men had come to some sort of mutually satisfactory understanding.

I decided not to disturb them.

Instead, I walked over to the refreshment table where Katherine was pouring herself a cup of coffee.

"Enjoy your lunch?" I asked.

She tore open a packet of sweetener and dumped it into her coffee.

"I had a delicious salad, thank you. How about you?"

"I had a chicken salad sandwich with a side of contemplation."

She smiled. "I'll bet you did." Gesturing toward my leg, she asked, "Are you feeling okay? How's your leg?"

"It's getting there."

Katherine cut her eyes over to where Carlton and Ira were standing. Then, in a half whisper, she said, "I'm sorry for what happened to you, Titus."

I didn't reply because I thought she was about to add something to her statement. Instead, she abruptly turned and walked away, taking her seat at the conference table.

I poured myself a glass of lemonade and followed her over to the table, stopping to exchange greetings with Komeil. As I sat down, I realized Tony Fowler was not in the room.

I quickly ran through the possibilities of what Fowler's absence might mean.

I immediately discarded the notion he was simply playing hooky, because since the debriefing process had already begun, it would take an act of God or the intervention of the Director himself to get Fowler out of his selection as the outside observer.

However, since he must have realized the DDO had not followed the correct protocol in regards to Amir, he could have contacted Legal during lunch and stirred up a real hornet's nest. In that case, I fully expected Fowler to return to the debrief in the company of two or three other suits. If that happened, I would simply take my place in the audience, because, at that point, the ensuing confrontation between Ira and Fowler would be center stage.

As I was about to consider another possibility, Fowler walked in.

He was alone.

Rushing over to his seat, he said, "Sorry. Traffic was a mess."

Carlton placed the document he'd been holding on the pile of papers in front of him. Using both hands, he carefully aligned the edges of the stack. Finally, he looked up and addressed the group.

"We're running behind schedule," he said, "but before Titus begins his narrative again, let me explain how I like to run these debriefing sessions."

He looked down at his stack of papers again.

Nothing had moved.

"I'm a detail kind of person," he continued, "and that's why I believe in taking the time to tease out the little things. Sometimes," he looked across the table at Fowler, "it's the little things that really matter."

Fowler was giving Carlton his full attention. He hadn't even opened his iPad.

Carlton turned and addressed me directly. "Titus, go back and review for us what you knew about Amir Madani before you requested permission to approach him. Once you do that, explain what occurred after the two of you were introduced."

I nodded.

Once again, Deputy Ira opened up his laptop. Only this time, he didn't touch his keyboard. Instead, he peered across the table at Tony Fowler.

Did Fowler know he was in the deputy's crosshairs?

I would know soon enough.

♦♦♦♦

"Session Two. This is Operations Officer, Douglas Carlton, in the intelligence debrief of Titus Alan Ray, Level 1 covert operative, for Operation Torchlight."

I began the afternoon session. "When Komeil and I were discussing the backgrounds of the nuclear scientists who appeared in his conference photographs, I was intrigued by Amir Madani because he was young, he was rich, and Komeil said he was new school. I memorized his face because he seemed to be exactly the type of asset we'd profiled in the operation. Granted, since he was a scientist he wasn't really in the category of Iran's elite. However, that was the very thing that made him so interesting to me. He was both wealthy and a prominent scientist in the nuclear energy field."

"What do you mean by new school?" Katherine asked.

I smiled at her. "That's a good question."

She smiled back.

"As I understand it, the younger scientists in today's modern Iran aren't happy with their government's dependence on other nations for nuclear research and development. The regime's deference to Russia is a perfect example of this. To put it simply, they see relinquishing control of any aspect of Iran's nuclear capabilities as old school. The younger bucks are eager to show how brilliant they are in their own right."

"It's also economics," Komeil added. "Too much money goes out of Iran for such technology, and the young people of today want a strong economy so they can buy more Western music and clothes. The youth in today's Iran do not know of hardship. I can tell you many stories of how—"

Carlton cut him off. "Thank you, Mr. Haddadi."

Then, Carlton turned to me. "So, Titus, what happened after you met Amir Madani?"

"I didn't contact anyone at the Agency immediately," I said. "I wanted to make sure it was going to be worth the extra effort on my part to approach him. I had my hands full developing the six assets I was running, and I didn't want to take Amir on unless it was going to pay big dividends."

Carlton nodded. "And how did you go about doing that?"

I spent a few minutes explaining about my efforts to discover where Amir lived and worked. Then I described the way I went about putting him under surveillance for several days.

"I determined he was more involved in atomic research than Komeil had realized, and the more I observed him, the more I realized he was a very appealing prospect for recruitment. What I wasn't able to learn, however, was the origin of his wealth. He lived in Shemiran, a luxury apartment complex north of Tehran, and drove an expensive car. He certainly didn't live the lifestyle of a scientist, but I knew if he had inherited his wealth, being approached by a wealthy businessman would probably seem very natural to him."

Carlton asked, "Was this the point at which you contacted me about Amir?"

I looked directly at Fowler.

"Yes, that's the timeline," I said. "I wanted to know if the Agency had any data on him, if NSD had any knowledge of him, if an approach on my part was warranted. It bothered me about his finances and the source of his money. I wanted our analysts to do a deep data mine on that."

"And that's when my office entered the picture," Katherine said. "I found nothing in our databases indicating his money came from any outside sources, such as Iran's intelligence agency, VEVAK, or any other ministry. We scanned everything we could find. He appeared to be clean."

Fowler stood up quickly, almost tipping over his chair.

"I need to take a break," he said in a shaky voice. "I'm sorry. I'll just be a minute."

As Fowler headed for the door, Deputy Ira gave Carlton a look I'd seen several times before—usually after receiving news a terrorist we had been tracking had just been eliminated by a drone strike.

♦♦♦♦

The reek of washroom soap was still clinging to Fowler's hands when he reentered the room few minutes later. Once he sat back down, he pulled a white handkerchief out of his back pocket and started cleaning his glasses.

Carlton cleared his throat and said, "Titus, resume the narrative."

Now it was about to get ugly.

CHAPTER 6

"I knew Amir had probably been warned about the security risks of befriending strangers, so when I arranged to *accidently* run into him outside our apartment building, I immediately mentioned the friendship we both shared with Farid."

Carlton showed approval of my approaching Amir in this way by vigorously nodding his head. Fowler ignored him.

"At first, Amir seemed suspicious of me, but when I told him I'd recently purchased an apartment in the same building, he seemed to loosen up. He even gave me directions to his favorite neighborhood restaurant."

I went on to describe various ways I'd managed to meet up with Amir around the apartment complex.

"After about six weeks of casual encounters, I hosted a small party and invited him to stop by the apartment and meet some of my friends. Amir eagerly accepted, and he proved to be quite the conversationalist."

I noticed Fowler's eye tic was back.

"It was obvious he was very smart and extremely curious," I said, "so it wasn't too surprising when he began asking me some very probing questions about my background. He was particularly interested in what I was doing in Tehran, and—"

"Why did you engage him so quickly?" Fowler cut in. "Wouldn't it have been better to keep him under observation for several months?" He glanced nervously around the room, looking for affirmation. "That's correct operational procedure, isn't it?"

Before I could answer his objection, Deputy Director Ira spoke up. His tone was bone chilling. "Well, Tony, in some cases, that might be true, but, as Katherine pointed out, in all our data mining, he appeared to be clean. There was nothing," he paused dramatically after each word, ". . . zero . . . zilch . . . nada . . . indicating he could be a threat to Titus."

The room went silent.

Since the deputy wasn't on the debriefing team, he had broken procedural rules by speaking on the record. However, no one reminded him he had breached protocol.

The look on Fowler's face could only be described as panicked; I didn't really believe it was because Deputy Ira had broken the rules.

I decided to throw him a life preserver. "I admit there were some red flags which should have caught my attention," I said.

Fowler suddenly looked hopeful. "Such as?"

"One day, after having dinner with Farid, I came home and found my apartment had been searched. This was obvious to me not only by all my hidden markers being tripped, but also because whoever had searched the place had been very sloppy. Admittedly, I'm a neat freak, but I think anyone would have noticed a lamp being overturned."

"The secret police do this all the time," Komeil said. "They never need an excuse."

"Exactly what I thought, so I passed it off as just a random search. After all, I was a new face in the building, and I held a foreign passport."

"You said you weren't paying attention to several things," Fowler said. "What else did you miss?"

That wasn't exactly what I'd said, but I didn't quibble over semantics.

"I discovered I was being followed, but I knew it was probably VEVAK and not the local police, because they were very good."

Fowler sounded like a father scolding his son for running with the wrong crowd. "Those were obvious signs you should have broken off contact with Amir."

"You're right," I agreed, trying to be shrewd and innocent at the same time, "but I was relying heavily on the research Katherine's office had done on Amir. Since she had no intelligence on him, I saw no need to be overly cautious."

"How long did they follow you?" Carlton asked.

Because he already knew the answer to that question, I assumed he just trying to move the narrative along to its grisly conclusion.

"They ran surveillance on me for over two weeks, and I took extra precautions whenever I made contact with any of my assets. One day, however, Farid didn't show up for an appointment. When I tried calling him, it went to voice mail. The next day, when I was sure I'd lost my watchers, I started visiting some of the places Farid had frequented. I finally located one of his friends. He told me he was worried sick because he'd heard Farid had been arrested."

Fowler's chin fell to his chest and Komeil started shaking his head back and forth. Everyone at the Agency knew an arrest in Iran meant endless torture, no matter how minor the offense.

"I knew it was just a matter of time before Farid broke down and told them everything they wanted to know about me and the network, so I left the apartment immediately and went to ground. Once I felt safe, I started the process of alerting my other assets. Unfortunately, VEVAK had already found most of them."

Although the debriefing procedure didn't require it, I told them in excruciating detail how I'd found the bodies of three of the other six people I had recruited for Operation Torchlight. I deliberately didn't gloss over the particular aspects of each person's death, because I wanted at least two people in the room to understand how their actions had affected real flesh and blood people. This gruesome accounting took me a full thirty minutes, and before I finished, I knew everyone in the room was uncomfortable.

When my voice cracked at one point, Carlton interrupted and said, "This might be a good time for a break."

"No, I need to finish this."

When I started again, my voice was strong. "I still hadn't located my last two assets, but I knew Omid, one of the first bankers I'd recruited, had been out of town for a couple of weeks, so I went to his house. It was a tall, three-story structure located in an upscale residential area. After watching the house for a couple of hours, I determined no one was at home, so I picked the lock on the back door and went inside to wait. Omid returned home within the hour.

"After he got over the initial shock of seeing me, I explained the kind of danger he was in. However, he refused to come with me. Instead, he wanted to join his family who had gone to visit relatives on the Caspian coast. He insisted he could take his family and get out of Iran from there. I decided his plan was a good one, and we went up to his office on the third floor so he could get some cash and documents out of his safe."

I took a swig of water and continued, "As we quickly gathered the things he would need, he began chatting incessantly. It was just nerves, and he wasn't really saying anything important; it was more a stream of consciousness thing. But, as we descended the stairs to the first floor, he looked back at me and asked, 'Hammid, what is the most important thing in the world to you?' And that's when three VEVAK agents burst in the front door and shot him."

Fowler made a deep guttural sound, shot up out of his chair and shouted, "Turn off the recorder."

When no one moved, he sat back down and pleaded, his voice trembling, "Please, I need to explain."

Carlton glanced at Ira, who gave him an almost imperceptible nod. Then Carlton picked up the telephone in the center of the conference room table. "Jim," he said softly, "kill the feed."

Fowler composed himself by wiping his face with his handkerchief and gulping down some water. Then, leaning across the table toward me in a gesture of entreaty, he said, "Titus, as everyone else in this room knows, I work the Iranian desk at Nuclear Security."

The moment he divulged this, he sat back in his chair. "Now, because you know my identity, it's probably going to affect this debrief, but, frankly, I don't care. I guess they'll get someone else to be the outside observer and you can just start over. I don't know."

Deputy Ira opened his mouth as if to protest, but Fowler raised his hand and stopped him. To my surprise, the deputy remained silent. It was then I realized Ira wanted Tony Fowler to talk.

Fowler did so.

"What I do know, Titus, is our division was never," he repeated the word emphatically, "*never* informed by the DDO's office there was an agent in place in Tehran requesting permission to approach Amir Madani."

Ira clinched his teeth and asked, "What difference would it have made if we had told you?"

Fowler shouted at him, "It would have made a big difference. I would have stopped the whole thing from the outset."

Ira leaned across the table with a look of incredulity on his face. "Really? Why would you have done that?"

He sputtered. "Because . . . because . . . because Amir Madani may have been working for Iranian intelligence for years. He's a nuclear scientist, sure, but his funding comes from VEVAK. They probably recruited him to monitor the other scientists; we think he's VEVAK's eyes and ears in the nuclear community."

"Well, he's not a very good scientist," Komeil said. "In fact, he's very mediocre."

If the atmosphere in the room hadn't been about to explode, I would have laughed at Komeil's professional snobbery.

No one was laughing.

Katherine turned sideways in her chair so she could face Fowler. "If that's true, Tony, then why didn't I find anything in our databases on Amir Madani? I run the very best analysis team in the building, but we came up with nothing on him. Absolutely nothing. If you had all this intel on his activities with VEVAK, why didn't you enter it into our records?"

Even though Fowler's voice was pitched an octave higher than normal, he still managed to sound defensive. "Because we hadn't established anything with certainty."

Ira's voice was menacing. "With certainty?" Beads of sweat were popping out on the deputy's fleshy brow, but he didn't seem to notice.

"No. No. There simply wasn't clarity." Fowler shook his head in protest. "There wasn't a substantive basis yet, so I wasn't at liberty to report it. I always try to be extremely cautious in such circumstances."

Ira finally exploded. "Is that any way to run a division? No wonder the Agency doesn't have a single piece of actionable intelligence on Iran's nuclear capabilities. That's either sheer incompetence or gross stupidity."

Carlton scooted his chair away from the table. "This might be the best time to adjourn for the day. We'll make some adjustments and continue this debrief in the morning."

The committee members began gathering their belongings.

The anger inside of me had been steadily building up all afternoon, and now I wasn't able to contain it. "Remain seated," I said.

Every head turned in my direction.

I looked over at Ira, and then I deliberately turned and faced Fowler." Do you realize what your in-house political games and ineptitude have done? People have lost their lives because of you two. You owe it to them, and you owe it to me to hear the rest of this narrative."

Carlton gave me a sympathetic look, and, without consulting Ira, reached over and picked up the phone. "Jim," he said, "turn the tape back on."

After a few moments of silence, Carlton nodded at me. "Resume the narrative."

♦♦♦♦

"When the three VEVAK agents shot Omid, I returned fire. I knew I had hit at least one of them, maybe two. I raced back upstairs, scrambled out a window, and made it to the roof. One agent followed me. It was a flat roof, and I could see VEVAK didn't have the backyard covered, so when the agent started firing at me from the window, I took the only option available and jumped off the roof."

"But how did you survive?" Komeil asked. "You said it was a three-story house."

I knew he must have been hearing the account of my escape for the very first time. Unlike everyone else in the room—who didn't show much reaction to my story—Komeil had no access to classified materials or the Agency rumor mill.

"I was unconscious for several hours and didn't immediately know what had happened to me once I hit the ground," I said, "but when I came to, I was in a clinic being prepped for surgery."

Katherine responded as if something had just been confirmed for her. "Oh," she said, "the Israelis?"

"Yes," I said. "The only asset I hadn't been able to locate was Reza, and in the hospital, I discovered he had been working for Mossad, while pretending to work for us at the same time."

Ira muttered, "Not the first time that's happened."

"Evidently Mossad had more intel on Amir than we did," I said, staring at Fowler for a moment, "so they knew Amir was VEVAK. They also knew he was searching for me and for the members of my network. But, when the Israelis informed Reza he needed to leave Tehran, Reza convinced them to help him find me. Once they did, they followed me to Omid's place and observed the three VEVAK agents going inside. The Israelis decided to enter the house through the backdoor, so they drove their van through the alley to the back of Omid's house. When they arrived, I had just jumped from the roof. They shot the VEVAK agent who was about to finish me off, and then put me—"

Komeil interrupted, shaking his head in disbelief. "God must have been watching over you."

I smiled at his statement and nodded my agreement. "The Israelis put me in the back of their van and drove me over to a clinic on the outskirts of Tehran where they found a doctor willing to perform surgery on my leg. They said he was very reluctant at first, but after they promised him a substantial amount of money, he eagerly agreed.

"Mossad then contacted the DDO about what had gone down at Omid's house. Since VEVAK's security forces and Iran's Revolutionary Guard Corps were combing the city looking for me, Mossad offered the Agency one of their safe houses until my leg healed up enough for me to leave the country. I remained at the safe house for three months. Finally, one of their agents took me across the mountains into Turkey. We arrived in Dogubayazit without incident, and Gordan Bolton, our chief of station in Turkey, arranged transport back to the States for me through the air base at Incirlik."

No one said a word.

I looked over at Carlton. "End of narrative."

Carlton nodded at me. Then he picked up the house phone and told Jim to shut down the recording device. Fowler grabbed his iPad and stood up.

"Sit down, Tony," I demanded. He slowly resumed his seat. "Now you know how your petty squabbling and irresponsible negligence cost the lives of five people and endangered not only me but also several other innocent people, including the family who took care of me."

I pointed my finger at Ira. "When you bypassed NSD and didn't let them know I was in country, did you honestly think putting people's lives in danger was an effective way of dealing with an incompetent division? Did you ever once consider how your actions were going to affect me or my assets?"

Ira's face was quivering with anger as he stared back at me, but I wasn't finished with him yet.

"If you were so dissatisfied with how NSD was being run, why didn't you get out of your chair, walk down the hall, and tell them to clean up their act? Oh, wait. Doing so would have been an act of courage, and that's something you apparently know nothing about."

I turned to Fowler.

"Tony, stop questioning your intel and start acting. Whether you believe in its relevance or clarity, or whatever you want to call it, instruct your people to enter every single scrap of information you or your assets are able to uncover. It's not up to you to make judgment calls on such things. Leave that to the analysts in Katherine's office."

I addressed Carlton. "And now, I'm finished."

He nodded.

He probably felt I was finished for good. I know I did.

CHAPTER 7

When I awoke the next morning, I felt utterly alone. I knew my public condemnation of the Deputy Director would not go unpunished, and I didn't expect to be employed by the CIA at the end of the day.

Then what?

For over two decades, the Agency had given me a purpose for living and had provided my every need.

If the Agency cut me loose, what would I do? Where would I go? How would I live?

After joining the Agency, I had deliberately chosen not to own a residence in the United States. On those rare times when I found myself between overseas assignments, I had stayed in temporary housing around Langley. Besides that, except for a few items in a storage unit, I owned nothing of a personal nature.

As I thought back on it, I had only lived in the States on two occasions for an extended period of time in the last twenty years. During both of those times, I had been on an assignment. Oddly enough, both assignments had been in Oklahoma.

In 1995, I was part of a three-man team sent by the Agency to investigate the bombing of the Murrah Federal Building in Oklahoma City. The FBI was the main investigative body, but the Agency was required to send its own agents after receiving reports that Timothy McVeigh, the man apprehended immediately after the bombing, had been seen associating with a Middle Eastern man prior to leaving his Ryder truck full of explosives parked in front of the Murrah Building. When the bomb went off, he'd killed 168 people and wounded hundreds more.

A woman in Blackwell, Oklahoma had given my team a lead to a group of Arabs who appeared to have had ties to McVeigh. At least one of them had been seen with him at a gun show about a month before he'd rented the truck. We later located the guy, an Iraqi, and a couple of his buddies in Norman, Oklahoma where they had been attending The University of Oklahoma.

After setting up surveillance on him, we discovered he was part of a much larger Arab community in Norman, including some Saudis and Iranians. Most of them were college students, but several held down jobs and had families in the area.

Danny Jarrar, one of the other Arabic-speaking operatives on my team, became convinced the men under surveillance weren't really students but terrorists in training, maybe even members of a sleeper cell. However, he didn't have any evidence to back up his theory, and he couldn't convince anyone else in our division, so after we reported our findings to the FBI, we left Oklahoma.

Much later, out of curiosity, I had looked up the FBI findings on the Iraqi who had been seen with McVeigh. The Arab student had been labeled an "innocent encounter." It was obvious to me the FBI had never pursued this lead. Instead, they'd focused on McVeigh's friends and acquaintances.

However, Danny's suspicions about something going on with the Arabic students in Norman had been justified when the Agency discovered Abdul Murad, a former student at OU and an al-Qaeda operative, was the person responsible for a suicide attack in Yemen in 1996.

Six years later, Carlton gave me a second assignment in the States, and it was also in Oklahoma. For over a year, I'd been tracking an al-Qaeda operative, a Saudi, who had been one of the persons responsible for bombing our American embassies in Kenya and Tanzania. I'd lost his trail in Germany, only to learn, three months later, he was living in Florida.

In July of 2001, I convinced Carlton to send me to Florida and allow me to do a liaison with the FBI to see what the Saudi was doing on American soil. However, by the time the Agency had finished all the paperwork required for such an operation, the al-Qaeda operative had flown an American Airlines plane into one of the Twin Towers.

When Carlton called Danny Jarrar and me into his office one week after 9/11, I expected him to send us to Florida to ferret out some intelligence—albeit too late—on the Saudi. Instead, he sent us back to Norman, Oklahoma to check out the Arab community we'd reported on several years earlier.

Within a week of our arrival in Norman, we discovered some of the 19 hijackers had been enrolled at the Airmen Flight School, an aeronautical training school affiliated with the University of Oklahoma. In fact, by researching the activities of Zacarias Moussaoui, a Moroccan student who had been dismissed from the flight school, we determined al-Qaeda had been using universities as a conduit to bring operatives into the United States and to recruit other students to their Islamic cause.

Danny used his own Arabic heritage—his father was from Lebanon—to make friends with some of the Muslim students at OU. I stayed in the shadows and ran him as my asset. We obtained several bits of intel using this method. Carlton was especially pleased when we delivered Moussaoui's roommate, Hussein al-Atlas, over to the FBI for questioning.

During the two months Danny and I were living in Norman, I discovered how difficult it was for me to adjust to a "normal" American lifestyle. I felt as uncomfortable attending a football game or shopping at a Wal-Mart, as I'm sure some suburban factory worker would have felt had he been placed in Cairo, Egypt for two months.

On the other hand, Danny enjoyed our stay in Oklahoma. In fact, I caught him talking to Carlton about getting our time in the area extended. When I confronted him about it, he said he'd fallen in love with Michelle, a waitress he was dating, and he wanted to stick around the city because of her. I had threatened to tell the DDO's office he was violating procedures, and, although I wouldn't have ratted on him, my threat got his attention, and we were back at Langley within the week.

Now, remembering my stateside experiences in Oklahoma, I decided if the Deputy Director ended up firing me, I would need to find a place to live overseas, preferably, a large city.

As I rolled out of bed, someone knocked on my bedroom door.

"Hey, Titus. Can I come in?"

I slipped on a pair of jeans and opened the door. Greg was standing outside with a cell phone.

He handed it to me, whispering, "It's Mr. Carlton."

♦♦♦♦

I was still processing my conversation with Carlton when I took the elevator down to the bottom level of The Gray. He told me to report to his office by two o'clock in the afternoon. He'd given me no details about our upcoming meeting—details he so stringently required of others—and I was trying to decipher what it meant when he told me we were meeting in his office and not with the DDO.

Perhaps his office was simply my first stopover, and I would go upstairs to face DDO Robert Ira alone. However, since he also told me to get started with my physical therapy, I wondered if I still had a future with the Agency. Conversely, if I was going to be let go, maybe he was simply giving me one last chance to use the Agency's expensive facilities.

Despite my highly rated processing skills, when I entered the rehab room, the only thing I knew for certain was that my first session of physical therapy was about to begin. Possibly, after my upcoming meeting with Carlton, it would also be my last session.

As soon as I closed the door, a woman stuck her head around an office door and said, "Hi, Titus. I'm Janice, your physical therapist. I'll be with you in just one minute."

She ducked back inside the room and then reappeared in a few minutes, carrying some papers in her hand. She waved them at me. "Dr. Howard sent me over a set of recommendations to get your leg back in shape."

"Did he mention I only needed physical therapy after he examined my leg?"

She laughed lightly. "After a few sessions with me, you won't need this anymore." She leaned over and took the cane out of my hand, treating it as if it were a disgusting piece of trash. "If you'll just take a seat, I'll evaluate your leg. After that, we can get started with your therapy."

Janice was in her mid-fifties with short, curly, blond hair and brown eyes. She proved to be a no-nonsense kind of woman and refused to pay any attention to the grunts and grimaces I uttered when I was doing her exercises. However, she did reassure me several times that the workout was going to benefit my leg—eventually.

I decided to take her word for that.

After massaging and exercising my sore limb, she had me use a recumbent bicycle, instructing me to pedal backwards. I found the task easier when I focused on something else—like formulating some kind of plea I might make to the DDO to spare my career at the Agency.

Would a desk job really be that bad?

In the midst of my reverie, I glanced over at Janice. She was putting away a set of weights I'd been using earlier, and, as she did so, a gold necklace swung free from her workout jacket. Suspended from the chain was a big gold cross.

Although I wasn't a gregarious type of guy, seeing the cross struck a chord with me, so I stopped pedaling and asked her, "Why do you wear that?"

She ran her fingers around the edges of the cross. "Because it's a reminder."

"A reminder of your faith?"

"Not exactly." She appeared thoughtful for moment. "It's a constant reminder of the one in whom I put my faith."

I thought back to that night in the safe house. I nodded. "I think I get that."

My last night in Tehran, after Rahim and I had finalized the details of our trip across Iran, Javad had come to sit with me in the living room of their small house.

"Hammid," Javad had said, kneeling down beside my bed, "before you leave, I must ask you a very important question."

I already knew what that question would be because, during my confinement, our main topic of conversation had been the importance of his faith in Jesus Christ. Often, he would retrieve a worn Bible from a hidden panel in the wall and read aloud to me, stopping often to explain—as if I were a child—about sin, about forgiveness, and about how much God loved me.

I had politely replied. "Okay, Javad, ask me your question."

"Will you make a commitment to become a follower of Jesus Christ?"

"Yes, Javad, I will."

He didn't seem surprised.

♦♦♦♦

Following physical therapy, I went back upstairs to my bedroom and found the items I'd asked Greg to purchase for me after my phone call from Carlton.

My instructions had been simple: "Go to the nearest department store and buy me the most expensive suit and dress shirt you can find."

In addition to the suit and dress shirt, a couple of silk ties were laid out on the bed. Although I hadn't included the ties in my instructions, Greg obviously knew my head was on the chopping block at the Agency, and he wanted me to look my best when I stood on the guillotine.

With Greg as my chauffeur, I headed over to CIA headquarters at Langley shortly after one o'clock.

A few minutes after leaving the residential area, Greg looked over at me in the passenger seat and said, "Man, you look nice."

"Well, thanks. I clean up pretty good."

"An expensive suit helps, though."

"True. How much do I owe you?"

"It's an Armani. It set you back almost two thousand dollars." He glanced over at me to see my reaction to this news.

Knowing he was expecting it, I feigned surprise. "Wow, that much?"

Arriving in Tehran as Hammid Salimi, I'd been carrying a suitcase full of suits, some of them much more expensive than the Armani. Of course, on that mission—as well as many others—Support had clothed me free of charge.

Even so, I'd accumulated enough paychecks to have a hefty bank balance, so purchasing a nice suit wasn't going to break me. Perhaps, I might even need it in my next career, whatever that might be.

"When I get access to my bank account, I'll reimburse you."

"No hurry," he replied. "I put it on my credit card."

We rode along quietly for a few minutes.

Then he blurted out, "You could use a good haircut, though."

I considered his advice. I decided I might as well go out in style, if I was about to be given the "opportunity" to resign. "You're right. Let's find a place to get my hair cut."

"Are you sure?" he asked. "My instructions were to deliver you to Langley. There might be a problem if we stopped somewhere else."

I tried to reassure him. "No, it's okay. My debrief is over. I'm not in quarantine anymore." I pointed to a sign displaying a pair of gigantic scissors, "Pull in here."

For a moment, I thought he wasn't going to stop, but at the last minute, he reluctantly made the turn and parked in front of Anne's Styling Salon. After lending me some cash, he reminded me it wouldn't look good if I showed up late for my appointment with Carlton.

Jim had been right about Greg; he *was* a twitchy kind of guy. I promised him I would hurry, though.

Inside the salon, I was draped in a black cape by a young blond stylist with short, spiky hair.

She asked, "What kind of cut would you like?"

It was the hardest question I'd been asked in a long time.

During my time at the safe house in Tehran, my hair had grown very long—something unacceptable for men in Iran—so Rahim had insisted on cutting some of it off before we started our cross-country trek. Although he had planned for me to spend the journey huddled in the trunk of his car and out of sight, he said making me presentable was a necessary precaution in case something unforeseen happened, and I had to be seen in public. In that event, he didn't want my long hair to draw any extra attention to the two of us. After he presented his arguments, I allowed him to whack off as much of my hair as he wanted.

However, the scissors Rahim had used had been ill suited to the task, and, even if they had been razor sharp, I seriously doubted Rahim would have made it as a hairstylist at Anne's Styling Salon.

The spiky-haired lady continued to brandish her shears in front of me, waiting for an answer to her styling question.

I finally said, "I'll let you decide."

She spoke to my reflection in the mirror. "I hope you're not offended, but whoever cut your hair the last time did a really lousy job."

"I'm not offended."

She ran her fingers through my hair several times. "It won't be hard to get this in shape again. You've got really good hair."

When she finished cutting and styling my *good* hair to her satisfaction, she said, "If you want to come back some day when you have more time, I'll take care of the gray that's beginning to show up here on the sides."

"Uh . . ."

She quickly added, "Not that it looks that bad for a man your age, but I just thought you might not want that salt and pepper look just yet."

"Maybe next time."

I grabbed my cane and slowly hobbled back out to Greg's car.

I left her a modest tip—for a man my age.

CHAPTER 8

Even though he had all the right credentials, it took Greg several minutes to get through the CIA's security gates at its headquarters in Langley, Virginia.

Then, he dropped me off at the OHB or Old Headquarters Building and drove over to the parking lot of the NHB or New Headquarters Building, where Support Services was located.

Back in the 1990's, a new administration building was constructed behind the CIA's original structure. The decision was made to distinguish between the old and new buildings by simply calling them the old and new buildings. While this nomenclature may have demonstrated a lack of creativity on someone's part, I liked to believe this vanilla identification indicated the Agency had more urgent matters than naming buildings.

Carlton's office was located on the fourth floor of the OHB. After passing through two more security checkpoints in the massive lobby, I got on the elevator and hit the button for the fourth floor. However, on my way up, I changed my mind and got off on the second floor. As I made my way down a long corridor with offices on each side, I found myself savoring the musty smell of the old facility. A lot had changed at the Agency since the day I'd first stepped inside the building, but the distinctive odor of aging wood and the aura of timeless secrets had not.

Even though the badge swinging from my neck indicated I was a restricted access employee, no one paid much attention to me. I felt certain their inattentiveness meant I had the look of an executive who knew where he was going.

That was true enough.

I was headed for an alcove—my definition for it—created when the building was remodeled a few years after I had joined the Agency. Back then, computers were being installed in every room, and the installers had instructed the construction workers to leave an area through which they could conveniently access the hard wiring in the wall behind a second floor workroom. This indentation was just big enough for two people to slip inside and have a conversation without fear of being seen or overhead from the corridor.

After Simon Wassermann had shown me the alcove, we'd met there to get our stories straight on the Russian agent he'd killed in Lebanon. Since that time, I'd occasionally used the tiny space if I needed to have a private conversation with an analyst or a fellow operative, or if I just wanted to have a moment to myself.

That was what I wanted now—a moment to myself before my appointment with Carlton.

I couldn't continue wrestling with whether I should embrace a new career or not. I needed to make a decision.

Did the commitment I'd made in Tehran necessitate getting out of the Agency? How could my new life fit in with my old life?

Being a covert operative meant living a life of lies and deception. I was trained to be a con artist and a thief. How was that going to work if I was trying to follow the teachings of Jesus?

However, was I really ready to leave my clandestine life behind and find a new career?

If the DDO fired me, the decision to stay or go was out of my control. However, making a decision about my future before I entered Carlton's office put me back in control. Control was a pretty big issue for me.

When I reached the alcove, I slipped inside and asked for guidance.

A few minutes later, I had my answer.

♦♦♦♦

The key card I'd been issued at the gate gave me access to the reception room outside Carlton's office. As I entered it, Sally Jo Hartford, Carlton's secretary, was on the telephone. However, she gave me a quick smile and motioned me inside.

I sat down in a leather armchair and waited.

Carlton's outer office was decorated in muted tones of burgundy and forest green, and there were paintings of blurry pastoral landscapes hanging on opposite walls. Two leather guest chairs faced Sally Jo's desk.

As usual, her desk was uncluttered and, except for the requisite telephone and computer, held little else. It was hard for me to decide if Sally Jo's longevity as Carlton's gatekeeper was because of their shared affinity for order and symmetry or because Sally Jo related to everyone as a beneficent grandmother.

She hung up the telephone and looked me over. "Wow," she said in a soft Southern accent, "you really look spiffy!"

"Thanks. I just got my hair cut."

She continued to appraise me. "Well, it looks very modern. I expected you to show up looking half-dead today, but here you are all decked out like you're ready for a board meeting. The cane certainly adds a nice touch too."

"I just wanted to impress you, Sally Jo."

She gave me a wink, but then her expression turned serious when she pointed to the door leading to Carlton's office. "You'd better be trying to score some points with him instead. He's been upstairs in Deputy Ira's office all morning, and he's the one looking half-dead now."

She picked up the telephone and told her boss I was here.

"You can go in now." She wagged her finger at me, "And remember, Titus, he doesn't like it when you call me by my first name."

The décor in Carlton's office reflected his expensive tastes. There was a seating area on the right side of the room where guests had their choice of a damask print sofa or two matching armchairs. They were arranged in a semi-circle around a dark cherry wood coffee table. On the left side of the room was a small round cherry wood conference table with four padded brown leather chairs.

If Carlton invited a guest to sit on the right side of the room, it usually meant there would be some small talk, perhaps a commendation, and the visit would be over quickly. If Carlton invited a guest to sit on the left side of the room, it usually meant there wasn't going to be any small talk, the discussion would be serious, and the guest might wish the visit were over sooner than it would be.

Bookcases lined two sides of the room with each book perfectly in line with the one next to it. The knickknacks placed on various surfaces were understated, elegant, and classy. A dark wooden pedestal globe of the world, bathed in light from the wall of windows facing the doorway, sat in one corner of the room.

In the center of the office was Carlton's desk. It appeared heavy, solidly built, and looked even more massive than usual today because sitting alone atop the desk was a single stack of documents.

As I entered the room, Carlton was taking a sheet of paper off the stack, carefully reading it, attaching his signature without hesitation, and placing it back down, forming a second stack beside the first.

He barely looked up when I shut the door.

"Take a seat over there, Titus."

Carlton pointed to the left side of the room and went back to studying the documents. Suddenly, his head jerked up, and he stared at me for a few seconds.

"Nice suit," he said. "I like your haircut too."

I murmured my thanks and sat down in a leather chair at the small conference table.

Carlton gathered up the bundle of papers from his desk and came over to the table. When he sat down, he placed the papers between us. Then, while pressing his long, slender fingers together to form a steeple, he studied my face.

"This morning I met with the DDO about your status with the Agency."

I felt surprisingly calm.

Carlton reached over and thumped the documents a couple of times with the palm of his hand. "Here's the agreement we've reached. Now is there anything you'd like to say to me before I explain what this means for you?"

He gave the papers another thump.

"Yes."

I tried to decide where to begin. "First, please accept my apology for losing my temper yesterday with Deputy Ira. I know I must have put you in the awkward position of having to defend me."

As if he'd just tasted something sour, Carlton pursed his lips together.

Maybe, though, he was just biting his tongue.

"Whatever the deputy said this morning," I continued, "I'm sure you were backing me one hundred percent." He shrugged his shoulders as if it didn't matter, but he didn't correct me. "I don't really believe I owe anyone except you an apology. I meant every word I said, and I hope you also expressed your own disgust with the deputy's behavior."

He rubbed his hand over his baldhead in a gesture of frustration, but he still didn't reply.

"Secondly, I've given it a great deal of thought, and I hope you'll give me a chance to get my leg back in shape and return to the field." I paused for a few seconds. "Admittedly, I've thought of resigning for the first time since joining the Agency. However, after what happened to me in Tehran, I really believe I can be an even better agent in the coming months."

He looked at me thoughtfully for a few seconds.

"How long have I been your handler, Titus?"

I considered his question.

"Twenty years."

"In all that time, I don't think I've ever heard you apologize to anyone, much less to me."

I smiled. "Maybe I've never been sorry before." Then, hoping his comment was a good sign there was nothing for me to worry about, I added, "I really think I just need a few—"

"You have to go on medical leave," he said flatly.

"What? Oh, well, sure, I can do that. The physical therapist thinks I need about six weeks of rehab. My leg should be as good as new after that."

"It has to be a year."

"A year?"

"You have to go on medical leave for one year," he said calmly, reaching for the first document from his stack of papers.

"Why would I need to go on medical leave for a full year?"

He looked up from the document. His face held a look of incredulity.

It took me a few seconds, but I finally nodded my head.

"Oh, I get it. This is my punishment, isn't it?"

"It's what I negotiated your punishment down to," Carlton said. "You basically called Deputy Ira a coward, Titus. If he had his way, you'd be gone from the Agency permanently."

He pushed the first document across the table for me to read. It was the standard Agency medical leave form. It was already signed.

"Who's going to believe my broken leg merits a full year of medical leave?"

Carlton's voice held a note of exasperation. "Titus, you've been living undercover in Iran for two years. Your entire network was brought down. Not only did you break your leg, you also had to undergo emergency surgery in an underground medical facility. I can safely say no one will question why you need a year's medical leave before returning to the field again."

I decided not to respond to this logic. Instead, I started reading the document in front of me.

"This says I have to undergo an Evaluation Interview before resuming my regular duties. Does that mean Dr. Howard has to give me a checkup when the year is over?"

"No. You'll have to go through an interview process with Deputy Ira and two other people of his choosing before you'll be allowed to return to fieldwork. He insisted on that requirement. It was non-negotiable."

He picked up the next set of documents and placed them in front of me. Then, his voice took on a somber tone. "As of a few hours ago, your medical leave falls under the Security Protection Protocol."

I studied the document. "What triggered this?"

Instead of answering, he got up from the table, went over to the credenza, and pushed the intercom on his telephone console.

"Mrs. Hartford," he said, "please bring me the most recent NSA printouts."

Within a few seconds, Sally Jo handed Carlton the National Security Agency's printouts concerning recent chatter intercepts from the Middle East.

"Would either of you like something to drink?" Sally Jo asked. "Coffee? Soda?"

I gave her a smile. "I'd like some water, *Mrs. Hartford*."

Carlton was scanning the printouts and didn't look up. "I'm fine, thank you."

Sally Jo went over to a small refrigerator hidden inside a section of one of the bookcases and retrieved a bottle of water. After handing it to me, she gave my arm a quick squeeze and left the room.

Carlton folded over several sheets of the printout while walking back over to the conference table. "Mossad has a pretty good handle on the chatter coming out of Iran these days, and they think there are substantial references to you in some of their most recent intercepts. It appears someone in Tehran wasn't happy about the fact you killed two of their guys. There's talk here of revenge against the shooter."

He slapped the folded printout in front of me. After skimming the contents, I said, "Well, this would worry me if I had plans to return to Tehran for my vacation this year, but, as it turns out, I won't be leaving the States for at least a year now."

The sarcasm in my voice came out sounding harsher than I'd intended, but Carlton appeared to ignore it.

"You know how these things work. Iran has plenty of proxies they can hire to get rid of you wherever you are. And the analysts think these guys may want to send the Agency a message by killing you on American soil."

Sobered by his reply, I picked up the form for the Security Protection Protocol and looked it over.

"What's the point of the protocol?" I asked. "I'm not going to have bodyguards following me around all day."

Carlton smiled at that thought. "We both know that's not going to happen. This form simply authorizes Support to relocate you somewhere outside the D. C. area during the time you're on medical leave. They'll also provide you with housing, a legend, and whatever security setup you need for the coming year."

His explanation sounded simple, but the reality of what it meant in terms of my freedom caused me to grimace.

Carlton saw my pained expression and said, "It's actually a good thing for you, Titus. The Agency will be taking care of you as if you were on an overseas assignment."

He picked up the last document from the table.

"I've pulled your personnel file," he said. "Your family lives in Michigan, don't they?"

I nodded. "My mother and sister still live in Flint."

"That's right. Your father passed away in '92. If I remember correctly, we had to pull you out of Iraq so you could attend his funeral."

"Look, Douglas, if you think I'm going to live in Michigan during my year off, you're dead wrong."

He laid aside the data sheet. "Okay, then, where would you like to go? Where do your friends live? Is there a vacation spot you especially love?"

Feeling frustrated at his inquiries about my personal life, I asked, "Can't I decide this later?"

He was unyielding. "No, you can't. That was part of my negotiation with the DDO's office. You're out of here as of today. You'll go back to The Gray, wait a few days for Support to arrange your relocation, and then, unless something unforeseen happens, I won't see you again until next year."

"Okay." I took a swig of water to give myself time to think.

"Don't you have a place that's really familiar to you?" he asked, prodding me for an answer. "Where do you go when you're on leave?"

"I stay around the D.C. area," I said. "I visit the library or the planetarium; go to the shooting range, that sort of thing."

He shook his head and picked up my personnel file again.

After a few minutes of flipping through some pages, he looked inspired. "Here, this is perfect. You spent two months in Norman, Oklahoma back in 2001 researching that Moussaoui connection to the 9/11 hijackers."

"Yes, but—"

"And, even better," he interrupted, "you were working with Danny Jarrar then."

"Why does that make it even better?"

"I thought you knew he'd left the Agency. He's now a Deputy Director with the OSBI, the Oklahoma State Bureau of Investigation. His wife's from Oklahoma, and she insisted they move back there when they started their family. He'll be able to help Support set up security for you in the area and watch your back."

I hadn't realized Danny had gotten married. If he'd married that waitress, he was probably still mad at me for the things I'd said about her.

Carlton looked at me expectantly, waiting for my answer.

I thought back to my prayers asking for guidance and wondered if this was the way God had of working things out for me.

Finally, I relented.

"Well, why not?' I said. "At least I'm familiar with the Wal-Mart there."

Reluctantly, I signed the required documents.

When I handed them back over to Carlton, he said, "For what it's worth, I agreed with what you said to the deputy yesterday. However, for both our careers' sake, it's best if we don't talk about your accusations against the deputy ever again."

I gazed up at the ceiling for a minute as if I were actually giving this some thought. Then I nodded at him. "Understood."

He rose from the table.

I remained seated.

Carlton looked over and me and asked, "Is there something else?"

"Could I ask you a question?"

He nodded his consent.

"What's the most important thing in the world to you?"

"Ah," he said, clearly recalling my narrative during the debrief. "That's an easy one for me. It's the Agency, of course."

Of course.

CHAPTER 9

When Greg picked me up outside the OHB, I told him I'd decided to take a year's medical leave from the Agency. He showed no surprise.

As we cleared the security gate, I asked him to take me by my bank where I got some cash, removed several items from my safety deposit box, and paid him back for my new clothes and haircut. Next, he drove me over to my storage unit where I retrieved some of my guns. I also picked up a few other items, which I thought I might need during my year's absence from the area.

After that, Greg dropped me off at a car dealership, where I kicked a few tires and ended up purchasing a new Range Rover. Later in the afternoon, I called Support Services. They told me to license the vehicle out of Maryland to match the cover story they were building for me.

Having my own car gave me a sense of freedom I hadn't felt since shooting my first gun with Roman Hudson on a snowy Christmas morning years ago.

Whether it was remembering that moment, or the fact I was already beginning to feel disconnected from the Agency, I decided to give him a call. I purchased a new iPhone from an Apple store and punched in my former father-in-law's number from memory.

Although his raspy voice was showing his age, he told me he still owned the hardware store and went in to work every day. He mentioned Laura before I got around to asking about her. He said she was getting ready for her oldest son's graduation from high school and seemed very happy.

His graduation comment gave me pause, and I suddenly remembered the words of the hair stylist about the gray in my hair. I suspected I wasn't looking thirty-five anymore.

I ended the conversation before Roman had a chance to ask me about my job. Although I believed he knew I was employed by the CIA, I still maintained I was an employee of a think tank in the D.C. area. However, for some reason, lying to him about it seemed wrong to me.

After saying goodbye to Roman, I gave my sister Carla a call. We spent most of our time discussing my mother, who was living in a nursing home specializing in Alzheimer's disease, a diagnosis confirmed by doctors two years after my father passed away of liver cancer. As usual, I felt guilty about Carla carrying the burden of my mother's care, so I did what I always did after such phone calls—the next day I put a huge check in the mail to her.

Before I left the Langley area, I telephoned Katherine. She was on her way out to dinner, but she promised to call me back.

She never did, but a few weeks later, we saw each other again in Oklahoma.

♦♦♦♦

Exactly one week after my ill-fated debriefing session, I found myself entering the same conference room yet again. Only this time, I chose where I wanted to sit, and there were only two other people in the room with me. Both of them were from Support Services, specifically, Legends.

Support is a multi-faceted division in the Agency with more departments than I could ever name. However, if you were to ask any covert operative which department in Support Services was the most important one, I'm sure most would pick the one responsible for forging a plausible identity.

Legends was that department.

Josh Kellerman, a soft-spoken man in his early forties with large, tortoise-shell glasses, was sitting at the head of the table. He was looking at a PowerPoint slide on his computer. April Snyder, a redheaded woman with frizzy hair and the body of a gymnast, was walking around the room with a cup of coffee in her hand. The two of them were responsible for briefing me on the legend I would be using while living in Oklahoma for a year.

I'd been through briefings before with Kellerman, but I wasn't acquainted with April. When Kellerman had introduced her, he had called her "my assistant." I suspected that meant she was in training, which probably explained why she appeared to be slightly nervous.

They were both dressed in casual clothes—no suits today—and I was dressed in jeans and a pullover knit shirt, my traveling clothes, because I intended to head out of town once my Legends briefing was over.

Although I was going to be living in the States and not overseas, I didn't expect the briefing of my domestic legend to be much different from others Kellerman had given me when I was headed overseas. He usually used presentation software and organized his briefings under what he called The Outline. Previously, he had worked for an advertising agency and had honed his PowerPoint skills to an art. His expertise didn't go to waste at the Agency.

Kellerman picked up a remote mouse, clicked once, and a blue slide entitled "The Outline" was projected onto a large screen at the far end of the conference room. "Here's The Outline we'll be using, and it includes four essentials," he said.

Bullet points appeared in white on the screen as he spoke. "Identity, Housing, Lifestyle, and Medical Care. April will start us off this morning with Housing."

April took over the remote mouse and clicked on a slide showing an aerial view of a large house located on about thirty acres of land. I was able to see a red barn on the property, plus a small lake near the residence. Most of the surrounding land looked undeveloped.

April's voice had a slight tremor as she began speaking. "We've rented you this property located on the outskirts of Norman, Oklahoma on East Tecumseh Road. It belongs to Phillip Ortega, a professor at the University of Oklahoma, who's on sabbatical in Spain. He was scheduled to return in nine months, but I negotiated the lease for a full year."

At the mention of negotiating the lease, the tenor of April's voice changed slightly. Since she'd been responsible for negotiating with the realtor, perhaps remembering her success at this task helped to settle her nerves. At any rate, after mentioning the lease, she seemed more relaxed and continued describing my new accommodations by flashing photos of the home's interior across the screen.

"It's fully furnished, of course, and Mr. Carlton's office had a former Agency employee visit the property and arrange for some additional security systems to be installed."

I assumed she was talking about Danny Jarrar, the former field operative who was now working for OSBI. Since I knew he tended to operate with a "worst case scenario" mentality, I hoped he hadn't overdone the security thing. Too much security would only draw attention to me.

"You'll pick up the keys, security codes, and owner's instructions from Eric Hawley at the Dylard Group Real Estate Agency. His information will be included in your Kit, of course."

The Kit was given to the intelligence officer at the end of a Legends briefing. It included all the items mentioned in the briefing, plus a few extras. Kellerman usually called these extra inclusions "gifts."

April gave control of the presentation back over to Kellerman.

"Now, we'll cover Identity," Kellerman said, moving on to the next slide. "You'll be living under your given name, Titus Alan Ray. You're a Senior Fellow for Middle East Programs at the Consortium for International Studies or CIS. This is a think tank located in College Park, Maryland, and, Titus, I believe you're familiar with this enterprise."

When he glanced over at me for confirmation, I nodded. "Yes, of course."

CIS served as my cover employment for my friends and family. However, I had always been listed as a Research Analyst with them and never a Senior Fellow.

I felt my promotion was long overdue and well deserved.

Probably at least one-third of the Consortium's listed employees were really Agency employees. Given the fact the firm's initials were just one letter off from CIA, I'm not sure how many people—especially those working in the Beltway—were totally fooled by this deception.

"You're now listed as a Senior Fellow in the employee directory. We gave you a promotion because as a Senior Fellow, you're required to publish a book in your field, and the book will explain your presence in Norman. You're relocating to Norman, Oklahoma because you're collaborating with Paul Franklin, a professor in International Studies at the University of Oklahoma, on a book about Middle East policy. You'll find business cards in your Kit, along with a credit card we've established for you with your most recent paycheck from CIS."

"I hope I received a substantial raise along with my promotion," I said.

April laughed at my attempt at humor, but Kellerman just rolled on with his presentation, barely missing a beat.

"Paul Franklin has worked as a consultant for the think tank before, so he's agreed to have you as a collaborator for his book. Of course, he believes your only employment is with CIS as a Middle East expert."

"Of, course," I replied. "What's his background?"

"Previously, he was in the diplomatic corps, but he's been in academia for several years now. He no longer has any security clearance, but that shouldn't be a problem for you with your present status."

While I cringed at Kellerman's observation, it was nevertheless true. Franklin's security clearance would not be a problem for me because I would not be dealing with sensitive intelligence for the next year.

"Our next topic is Medical," Kellerman said, giving the helm back over to April.

"Because you're on medical leave," April said, "you're expected to fulfill certain requirements." She flashed a list on the screen. "As soon as you arrive in Norman, you should choose one of these facilities, where you can continue your physical therapy. This list, along with a medical insurance card, is included in your Kit."

Kellerman ended the presentation by projecting the word Lifestyle on the screen. This section described what kind of activities would be appropriate for me while living in Norman.

"You're in Norman to collaborate with Paul Franklin on a book, so you'll need to meet with him several times during the year. His contact information is in your Kit, along with an Agency encrypted laptop computer. We've downloaded the first draft of his book onto your computer. Someone from our division will be writing the sections of the book for which you will be responsible, or, if you like, you can do the writing yourself."

Well, that wasn't going to happen. I hated writing.

"In addition, of course, you'll be spending some time each week in rehab. As for the rest of your time, try pursuing activities which reflect a scholarly lifestyle—visiting libraries, museums, those sorts of things."

"The shooting range?"

"Pardon?"

"Is it okay if I go to the shooting range?" I asked. "Does a scholarly Senior Fellow do that?"

My question brought a smile to his face. "Uh . . . probably not," he said, "but we've got you covered on that too. One of the reasons we chose this location was because Mr. Carlton mentioned you might want a practice range." He returned to the slide of my new residence. "Ortega's place is not in the city limits of Norman, so it's perfectly legal for you to set up a range right here on the property."

He gestured toward the screen. "Speaking of the property, part of your lifestyle will be maintaining Professor Ortega's land. This was included in the real estate agreement. There's a tractor for mowing, equipment for tree trimming, and everything else you might need to keep up this amount of acreage. The machinery is located in the barn you see here." Using a laser beam on the remote mouse, he circled a large red barn.

Well, that wasn't going to happen. I hated mowing.

"So, Titus, this concludes The Outline." He turned off the projector and closed the lid on his computer. "Any questions?"

"You've covered everything, Josh. Another excellent presentation."

His face broke into a big smile at my compliment, and then he moved over to the credenza at the far end of the room and retrieved my Kit.

After placing all the items making up my Kit in front of me, Kellerman proceeded to go over each of them again, as if I hadn't been listening to anything he'd said. Since I was anxious to get on the road, I just nodded my head and kept my mouth shut.

Finally, he got to the end.

"The last two items are gifts from Mr. Carlton," he said, handing me the latest Thuraya encrypted satellite phone. "As I'm sure you already know, the encryption technology on this phone will prevent any of your calls from being intercepted, and you should always use it when connecting with any personnel at the Agency."

Then, placing an aluminum rifle case on the table, he said, "Mr. Carlton also wanted you to have these."

He snapped opened the latches, and I looked inside. Two rifles were nestled snugly into internal dividers, one alongside the other.

I smiled.

Now, along with the guns I'd retrieved from my personal storage unit, I felt totally prepared to write a scholarly book on the Middle East.

♦♦♦♦

After packing up my few remaining items, I spent a few minutes saying goodbye to the staff, complimenting Martha on her cooking and sharing a few laughs with Greg. Finally, I went out to the garage and tossed my luggage in the back of the Range Rover. However, seconds after saying goodbye, Greg appeared at the garage door.

"This just arrived for you." he said, handing me a messenger envelope with Agency markings on it.

"Who sent it?"

"I don't know. The guy just delivered it to the door as if you were expecting it."

"I wasn't expecting anything," I said, turning the thin envelope over in my hand, "and I never open anonymous packages."

There was an anxious note in his voice. "Perhaps we should let Jim take a look at it."

"First, tell me about the messenger."

"Uh . . ." He chewed on a fingernail as he thought for a moment. "He wasn't the usual messenger from the DDO's office. I know that for sure."

"Has he ever delivered anything here before?"

Greg's reaction was immediate. "Yes, I remember him now. He's from Tony Fowler's division, Nuclear Security."

"You're sure?"

"Positive."

I threw the envelope in the front seat and said goodbye to Greg for the second time.

Then I drove away from the mansion on a hill.

♦♦♦♦

When I pulled into an Exxon station to gas up the SUV before hitting the interstate, I opened the envelope.

Nothing exploded.

However, the contents inside the envelope definitely made my heart beat faster.

Tony Fowler had put together some raw intelligence from an asset being run by one of his operatives inside of Iran. The asset was a member of Hezbollah, the militant extremist organization responsible for Iranian terrorist operations outside their country.

The asset reported a conversation he had overhead between two of Hezbollah's top leaders regarding an American spy who had managed to escape the hands of VEVAK. According to the asset, one Hezbollah militant had told the other this American spy had recently returned to the States.

In the silence of the car's interior, I translated the last line of the Arabic conversation out loud.

"But don't worry. Ahmed will discover his location in America and kill him."

My voice sounded deafening.

PART TWO

CHAPTER 10

After entering the address for the Ortega rental property in my dashboard GPS, I left the gas station and merged onto I-495.

When I had mapped out my route earlier in the day, I had decided to travel north first and then turn south toward Oklahoma. Although the northern route was slightly longer than the southern one, I told myself it might be nice to see some of America's flyover states at ground level for the first time.

Or maybe—on an unconscious level—I had decided to take the longer route because I wasn't in a hurry to arrive in Norman.

Once I was cruising along the interstate, I thought about Fowler and the intel he'd sent me. By allowing me to have access to a raw field report, it seemed obvious he was trying to make up for all the trouble he'd caused me with Amir Madani.

After being reprimanded by the DDO, I was pretty sure Fowler was going to enter the new data into the system immediately, but I had to assume he'd sent the intel over to me first because he knew by the time the asset's product was processed and analyzed by Katherine's office, the Hezbollah hit man might have already found me.

Regrettably, this had actually happened to an experienced operative who had just returned from Bulgaria. He'd been killed outside his apartment in Bethesda, Maryland, even though there had been enough information available to prevent it from happening. The Agency had streamlined its data processing since that incident, but still, the wheels on the mammoth machine tended to move slowly.

After tuning in some country and western music on my satellite radio—putting myself in the mood for where I was headed—I checked my rearview mirror.

I spotted the red van immediately. I'd noticed it earlier at the gas station and now it was two cars behind me. I slowed down and changed lanes.

The van did the same.

Perhaps I should have been worried, but I wasn't. For one thing, a veteran operative would know that using a red vehicle to follow someone was a sure way to get noticed. Secondly, the van was following me too closely, just two cars behind. So if Ahmed the Assassin was driving the red van, he had sloppy tradecraft. That meant he was probably sloppy in other areas too.

About thirty miles later, I merged onto I-70 for the trip across West Virginia, Ohio, and Indiana. My objective was to reach Indianapolis by midnight.

I wasn't exactly sure what the van's objective might be.

♦♦♦♦

Three hours went by, and I needed to take a break, get something to eat, and make a decision.

Not surprisingly, when I pulled into a truck stop, Mr. Red Van followed me. However, when I parked near the restaurant, he went to the other side of the parking lot near the fuel pumps.

Sloppy. A target should never be out of the surveillance vehicle's sightline, especially in a parking lot.

That error made my decision for me.

I got out of the SUV, went through the lobby of the restaurant, and exited out a side door. Then I quickly walked over to the red van and knocked on the window.

It took a second, but the glass was finally lowered.

I stared into the astonished faces of two young Caucasian guys.

"Who are you?" I asked.

"We're . . . ah . . ."

I was already opening the van's door when I spotted an identification lanyard inside the cup holder between the two front seats. I grabbed it, and my suspicions were fully confirmed.

"Which one of you is John?"

"That's . . . me," the driver admitted.

"Well, John, give me your keys. Then you and your buddy go inside and get a table for us at the back. I'll be right in."

They headed for the restaurant without question.

I hollered after them, "Order me a large lemonade and a burger."

I leaned against the side of the van and punched in some numbers on my new Agency satphone.

As soon as it was answered, I asked. "Did you really believe I wasn't going to spot them?

"How did you get my private cell number?" Carlton asked, but he didn't sound too surprised to hear from me.

I ignored the question.

"They're fresh off the farm, aren't they? I mean *The Farm*." I said, emphasizing the last words so he would know I meant the Agency's training facility.

He sighed. "Yeah, they're some of Ted Cornell's new recruits at Camp Peary. He agreed to loan them out for a surveillance exercise. They were bad, huh?"

"Totally incompetent."

"I wanted someone to watch your back as you left the area," he said, "but I couldn't get my request through the proper channels before you left town, so I called Ted."

"Make sure he fails these two guys on surveillance tactics. Better yet, have him send them over to Interrogation. The instructors over there had a way of making me refocus."

"He'll get them straightened out."

"What made you think I needed an escort? Did you get access to some new intel?"

"Yes. This morning NSA reported the chatter coming out of Iran indicated VEVAK has hired a jihadist assassin. It's obvious they're fully determined to eliminate you for murdering two of their own."

"Did they identify this person?"

"Only that he's affiliated with Hezbollah."

"No name?"

"Nothing of that nature."

I decided not to mention Tony Fowler's raw field report about Ahmed, mainly because I didn't want to get Fowler in more hot water with the DDO, and also because I knew Carlton would be getting Fowler's information soon enough.

"Well, Douglas, I'm almost to Ohio, and as far as I can tell, except for a couple of greenhorns tailing me, I'm squeaky clean."

"Now that you've left this area, I'm sure you'll be fine."

He didn't sound very confident.

Then, he added, "I'll plan to stay in touch and keep you informed as events warrant."

"Is that allowed?"

A full medical leave usually meant limited contact with the Agency, especially Clandestine Operations.

"Your security protocol covers these circumstances," he said. "Just because I don't plan to see you for awhile, doesn't mean we can't communicate with each other."

That was good news to me, but I didn't want him to know that.

"Tell Ted to be on the lookout for his boys. I'm sending them home now."

"Don't be too hard on them."

After I finished the call, I went back inside the restaurant and found the two trainees. They seemed thoroughly humiliated at first, but when I shared with them my own abysmal failures in training, I thought they warmed up to me. Maybe not, but at least they enthusiastically waved goodbye when I drove off.

I pulled into Indianapolis around midnight.

♦♦♦

The next morning, after enjoying the complimentary breakfast at the hotel, I took a walk around the hotel's parking lot. I did this for a couple of reasons. First, I needed to work out the kinks in my injured leg after the previous day's long drive, and, secondly, I wanted to check out the vehicles in the parking lot.

There were three obvious rental vehicles, and I memorized their make and model in case I saw them on the road later in the day; however, all the rest appeared to be business or family cars. The last thing I did was run my security check on the Range Rover.

I did it twice.

Finally, I threw my stuff in the rear and heading south on I-70 toward Oklahoma.

It was a beautiful spring day in late April, and as I drove along, I found myself starting to relax. Of course, Carlton was right; I needed this medical leave. I was looking forward to doing some reading, studying the stars through my old telescope—I had grabbed it out of my storage unit—and even honing my cooking skills.

I switched the radio on and listened to the news. There were several reports on the President's latest political upheavals, and Israel's prime minister was warning the world about Iran's nuclear ambitions—again.

The only news coming out of Iran was good news, and, for a brief moment, I wished I were in Tehran to share it with Javad and Darya. Fox News was reporting that after three years in prison, Youcef, their pastor, had finally been released from confinement.

Pastor Youcef had been imprisoned and tortured on numerous occasions because he had adamantly refused to recant his Christian beliefs. According to Javad, Pastor Youcef had told the authorities he would willingly give his life for his faith.

Would I give my life for my new faith?

I turned off the radio and thought about that question.

I knew I would give my life for my country. That was a given. In my career, I'd often found myself in perilous situations where dying was a real possibility. However, during those times, my motivation for pressing on had been the security of America and the upholding of my own patriotic ideals.

Now, I wondered if I was as committed to Christianity as I was to my country. Would I really choose to die rather than disavow my beliefs?

It was hard for me to admit it, but I just didn't know the answer to that question. For one thing, I didn't fully understand what being a believer meant.

I had no doubt Javad could have defined it for me, but it wasn't as if I could pick up the phone and have that conversation. However, I knew what Javad would do if we were able to have such a conversation. He would open up his Bible and explain his answers from the words he read there.

I thought about that as I entered the outskirts of St. Louis.

Right then, while maneuvering through heavy traffic, I decided I needed to start reading the Bible for myself. It might be the only means of knowing God and the way to know if I had the kind of faith exhibited by Youcef, a faith I would not recant, even in the face of death.

I decided to tell God about my decision. "I don't know if you're interested in vows, God," I said out loud, "but Javad said I should start reading what you said to me. So right now, I'm making a vow to you," I paused in my prayer and gazed off at the Gateway Arch on my right. "As this arch is my witness, every day I will read something from the Bible."

I never regretted making that vow. Not even once.

CHAPTER 11

I arrived in Oklahoma City around eight o'clock in the evening. However, I decided it was too late in the day to pick up the key to the Ortega property from the realtor who was in Norman, thirty minutes away, so I drove to the south side of the city and looked around for a motel. After spotting a Comfort Inn, I got off the expressway and spent the night there, saving my arrival in Norman for the following day.

Before drifting off to sleep, though, I remembered my Gateway Arch Vow and looked around the room for a Bible.

I knew most motels provided Bibles for their guests because I had slipped into a hotel in Miami once and replaced one room's Bible with a different version of the Scriptures. Although the Bible I had placed in the nightstand looked exactly like the hotel's Bible on the outside, the Agency's tech division had equipped the new one with a special camera, enabling my asset—who was to occupy the room later in the evening—to take miniaturized photographs of some highly classified documents when he returned to his own country.

However, the Bible I found in the nightstand at the Comfort Inn had no such modifications, and I picked it up and read a random chapter.

It didn't make much sense, but I was very tired.

♦♦♦♦

At nine o'clock the next morning, I was standing in the lobby of the Dylard Group Real Estate Agency waiting for Eric Hawley. The moment the receptionist assured me that Hawley was on his way, a tall man with sandy hair, wearing a crisp white shirt and blue slacks, entered the building.

He gave me a big smile. "Hi, I'm Eric Hawley."

"I'm Titus Ray. I'm leasing the Ortega property on East Tecumseh Road."

"Oh, right. Let's go up to my office."

We took the elevator up to his office on the second floor where I signed all the necessary paperwork.

After handing me a copy of the lease, he said, "Now, if you want to follow me out to the house, I'll show you around the property."

"That won't be necessary," I quickly replied. "I'll be able to find it."

"Oh, I'm sure you could locate it, but Phillip had some extra security installed on the property this week, and when the installers came by the office to drop off the security codes, they left this manual." He picked up a thick book. "The instructions are pretty detailed. I was barely able to figure them out."

"I don't want you to go to any trouble," I said. "I could call you if I have any difficulty."

"No, no, it's no trouble. Phillip Ortega is an old friend of mine, and I've been out to his house plenty of times. I'll enjoy showing you around."

It was obvious he'd made up his mind, so I got in my car and followed him out to my new home.

On the way out there, I did a little belly-button gazing and asked myself why I was so reluctant to have him take me out to the property. Maybe it was simply the nature of my business to be guarded, holding even friendly people at a distance, or perhaps it was my loner personality—I don't need much social contact to be content.

Realizing I was going to be leading a different kind of life in Norman, I decided to view my new civilian life as if I were on assignment. To survive, I needed to adapt to the culture and environment of the area. Eric Hawley was a friendly guy. I needed to be friendly too.

I suddenly realized I might be embarking on a difficult assignment.

♦♦♦♦

I had no real need to follow Eric Hawley in order to find Tecumseh Road. Since I'd lived in Norman before, I knew there were four main roads into Norman from I-35: Tecumseh Road, Robinson, Main, and Lindsey. With the expressway virtually splitting the town into two parts, each street was labeled east or west depending on its location from I-35.

Within two minutes of leaving the real estate office, we were on Tecumseh Road. After crossing over I-35 and travelling east for almost ten miles, we arrived at Phillip Ortega's residence.

The aerial photo from Kellerman's presentation made the Ortega property appear isolated, but now I saw several other homes situated nearby. Each of them, like the Ortega property, had plenty of acreage surrounding a residence. Nevertheless, despite the acreage, I realized I had some neighbors living in close proximity to me.

Hawley stopped his Cadillac Escalade outside a brick wall fence and exited the car. By referring to an index card in his hand, he entered some numbers onto a key pad. He gave me a thumbs up when the gate swung open.

A tree-lined paved access road led up to a large modern-looking farmhouse with a wrap-around front porch. A second paved road curved south to the barn. Hawley stopped his car in front of the three-car garage attached to the residence by a breezeway.

When I walked up beside him on the driveway, he gestured expansively around the grounds and asked, "Isn't this a great place?"

"It's absolutely amazing."

I meant every word.

Several massive oak trees shaded the front lawn. About fifty yards beyond the house was the lake I had seen on Kellerman's slides. The early morning sun was shimmering off its surface, making it sparkle like a brilliant diamond. Trees and bushes lined the banks, and there was a small, wooden dock extending out over the water.

Once again, Hawley consulted his index card so he could enter the necessary numbers on a keypad at the entrance to the garage. He shook his head and said, "I really don't know why Phillip thought the property needed all this extra security. I'll have to ask him about that."

I realized he thought Philip Ortega had requested the extra security—something Danny Jarrar had probably told him. So, what was going to happen when Ortega called Hawley to check on things at home, and Hawley questioned him about why he'd added all the extra protection on his property?

This potential disaster was of Danny's own making.

Whenever we'd worked together, I'd noticed Danny had a propensity to spin a more elaborate story than was really necessary. While Danny was a great storyteller, this operational flaw had gotten him into trouble more than once, and he had a bullet hole in his right upper thigh attesting to that.

I decided I'd better clean up Danny's mess—yet again.

"Actually, Eric, you must have misunderstood the installation guys. I was the person who called up the security company and requested all this extra stuff."

He gave me an astonished look. "But, why? Our little city has to be one of the safest places on earth to live, and, as far as I know, Phillip has never had a problem out here."

I laughed, trying to sound embarrassed. "Well, Eric, I've never lived anywhere but a big city. Where I'm from, there's a burglary happening every night."

As we entered the house, he assured me, "You'll find things are much different here."

Hawley took me into every room of the house, turning on the lights, pointing out the different features and having me admire the beautiful furnishings. I agreed it was perfect for me, and that's when he started asking me some personal questions.

"Your secretary said you were writing a book with someone from the University. If I remember correctly, it was about China."

I wondered if April Snyder had made a rookie mistake and told him I was writing about the Far East. "No, the Middle East," I said.

"Oh, the Middle East," he said, nodding his head up and down as if he knew it well. "You mean Israel, the Palestinians, that sort of thing?"

"Yes, that sort of thing."

"And you're with a think tank in Washington?"

"Actually, we're located in Maryland, but we do consulting work everywhere. Here," I said, reaching inside my wallet for a business card, "let me give you one of my cards."

He glanced at it and then dropped the personal questions.

He probably noticed I was a Senior Fellow.

"Let's go out to the garage. I want to show you one last thing."

I followed him through the breezeway and out to the three-bay garage.

Pointing down at his feet where a steel door was built into the garage floor, he said, "Since you've never lived in Oklahoma before, you've probably never seen one of these."

I immediately thought I was seeing some sort of underground safe room.

"No, I've never seen anything like that."

"It's a storm shelter."

"A storm shelter."

"Here, let me show you."

He unlatched the door and slid it open on its metal rollers. After he reached down and clicked on a light, I peered inside and saw a deep gray box with two padded benches positioned opposite each other. Maybe six skinny people could fit inside.

"Wow, that's a tight fit," I said.

"When tornado season hits in about two weeks, you'll be happy Phillip decided to install it."

"I'm happy already."

♦♦♦♦

After Hawley left, I took the all-terrain vehicle from one of the garage bays and drove it up to the barn. Inside, I found Ortega's tractor and riding lawnmower, along with a workshop with plenty of carpentry tools and gardening equipment.

Professor Ortega appeared to be an industrious kind of guy.

The security company had also wired the barn—which I didn't think was necessary—so I drove around the perimeter of the property to make sure the rest of the security setup wasn't a job of overkill. Pleased with my findings, I returned to the house and unloaded my belongings from the Range Rover.

I had to assume there had been a Mrs. Ortega in the house at one time because there were several feminine touches around the place. One of the guest rooms was even wallpapered in pink flowers.

After looking over the guest bedrooms, I deposited my duffel bag in the master suite. It was decorated with dark, heavy furnishings and dominated by a king-sized bed. Two well-used, black leather lounge chairs faced a large television screen on the west wall, and there was a bookcase with a good supply of paperback books—mostly westerns—located next to a mirrored dresser on the opposite wall.

Once I put away my few belongings, I went into the main living area of the house. The living room had a massive stone fireplace with a wide-screen television mounted over it. Two recliners, an armchair, and a dark brown, oversized leather sofa were positioned around a rectangular coffee table made of distressed wood. An archway from the living room led directly into the dining room, where a wide picture window afforded a picturesque view of Ortega's lake. When I explored the kitchen, I found it was well stocked with everything I needed for cooking—except the food part.

After unpacking my telescope and putting it in the sunroom, I booted up my Agency computer to see if I had any new messages from Carlton in my inbox.

It was empty.

Around noon, I drove back into Norman. While drinking a glass of lemonade and devouring a chicken sandwich at a Chick-fil-A on Main Street, I noticed a large store in the shopping center across from the restaurant. The signage advertised it as a Mardel's store and indicated it sold books, Bibles, and gifts. I decided to check out the store before running the rest of my errands.

I needed to buy a Bible.

At the Comfort Inn the night before, since I didn't have a Bible of my own, I'd considered just slipping the hotel Bible inside my duffel bag and taking it with me. Thinking about this didn't really surprise me because some of my assignments required taking things that didn't belong to me. What surprised me was the sense of guilt I experienced when I contemplated stealing the Bible.

I could sense my world changing since that decision-making night in Tehran. It was as if I'd been dropped into an alternate universe, where using any means—moral or immoral—to achieve an objective no longer seemed as natural to me as it once was. Now, instead of doing what years of living in the shadows had taught me, I found myself looking at my actions with a different set of eyes. I was confused at times, and I wondered if I could operate effectively when I had to go back inside that shadowy world again.

♦♦♦♦

It never occurred to me buying a Bible could be intimidating, but as soon as I entered the Mardel store, I almost turned around and walked out.

On one side of the store were aisles crammed with buttons, mugs, calendars, everything from clothing to kitchenware, all with a Christian message. On the other side of the store were displays of Christian videos and worship music CD's. The center aisle contained bookshelves overflowing with Christian devotional books and religious fiction.

A smiling, silver-haired lady asked if she could assist me, and, when I mumbled something about a Bible, she led me off to an area the size of a racquetball court, where Bibles were stacked almost to the ceiling.

I wasn't able to answer any of her questions about what kind of Bible I wanted. Instead, I thought of the tiny worn Bible hidden away in Javad's living room, and I suddenly found myself wishing for one exactly like it.

Another customer drew the sales clerk away, and I was left alone to make my decision.

I muttered a quick prayer and asked for guidance.

As I continued looking at the choices, I noticed a young woman standing about six feet away from me with two opened Bibles. She had placed both on a shelf in front of her, and she looked as if she were reading from both of them at the same time.

I surprised myself by asking, "What are you doing?"

She looked up at me and laughed. "I guess I must look pretty strange," she said. "I was comparing the size of the print and trying to decide which one of these would be easier for me to read if I were standing at a lectern."

She pointed to the shelf where she'd placed the Bibles. "This is about the height of the lectern I teach from on Sunday morning."

"I see."

"Are you looking for a new Bible?"

"Yes, but I didn't realize there would be so many choices."

"You've never been to a Mardel's store before? Are you new to Norman?"

She had an air of innocence about her I found both refreshing and disconcerting at the same time.

"I just moved here."

"From where?"

"Maryland."

"Well, welcome to Norman. I'm Kristi Stellars."

"Titus Ray."

"Titus is a wonderful New Testament name. Are you attending church somewhere here in Norman, Titus?"

"Uh . . . no."

"We'd love to have you visit our church. It's Bethel Church on Lindsey Street, across from the Hollywood Shopping Center."

"Thanks, maybe I will."

"If you're looking for a Bible that is easy to read and understand, I'd recommend the English Standard Version."

"Sounds exactly like what I need."

She took one of the Bibles from the shelf and showed it to me.

"I've decided to get this one," she said. "It also has notes at the bottom of the page explaining the verses. The ladies I teach are always asking me things I don't know, so I just glance down and read the study notes."

"You teach the Bible?"

"I try, but I'm not so sure I do a very good job." She took her new Bible and placed it back in its box. "It was nice talking to you. Come visit our church. It's a real friendly place."

With members like Kristi, I knew she couldn't be exaggerating.

I grabbed a Bible exactly like the one Kristi was buying and followed her to the cash register.

Also, for the first time in my life, I considered attending a church.

CHAPTER 12

The next morning I woke up to the sound of a dog barking. It was more like a yap than a true bark, and when I looked out the patio doors toward the lake, I spotted a yellow-haired puppy chasing a squirrel around the trees bordering the water. When I opened the door and yelled, he scampered away toward the tree line.

Phillip Ortega's coffeemaker was a Keurig single-serve machine and used a small plastic cup of ground coffee. These "K-cups," as they were called, came in different brews. I chose Sumatra, brewed myself a cup, and went out to the sunroom.

While I was making a mental "To Do" list, my Agency satphone rang. The caller screen displayed Danny Jarrar's name.

"Hello, Danny," I said.

"I cannot believe you've come back to Norman."

"You know how much I loved it here."

"You were like a fish out of water, and you know it. Say, listen, I thought I'd run by and see you this morning before going into the office."

"Sure, come on over. I'll fix us some breakfast."

I'm not a great cook, maybe not even a good cook, but I like to cook.

As Carla and I were growing up, we used to fight over which one of us would get to help our mother in the kitchen. Our motivation for doing so was to avoid being stuck in the family room with my dad when he came home from work. Consequently, both Carla and I had learned to cook up some pretty decent meals.

Now, however, I simply fried up some bacon and eggs and threw a couple of slices of bread in the toaster.

When Danny called from outside the security fence, I keyed in the code for the gate. Then, five minutes later, we were sitting down at the dining room table together.

Danny was stocky, muscled up like a bodybuilder, but several inches shy of six foot. His once luxurious black hair had thinned and flecks of gray were showing up in what hair he had left. He had dark brown, almost black eyes, and beneath his generous nose was a pencil-thin moustache. Because of his Lebanese heritage, he looked as if he belonged on a sidewalk in Beirut playing checkers and discussing politics with the old-timers.

Unlike me, Danny liked to talk.

The moment he entered the house, he started talking about his job with the Oklahoma State Bureau of Investigation. Working for OSBI meant he was dealing with Oklahoma's security issues in much the same way the FBI handled national security issues. Ever since 9/11, though, state agencies and the FBI operated with a greater level of cooperation—at least on the surface—so, essentially, the FBI and OSBI worked together as one big happy family.

"So we prosecuted the guy for a computer crime, and he walked out of prison within six months," he said, finishing his story and finally digging into his plate of food.

"Sounds like you love this job."

"Well, I love being at home with my family. Michelle was lonely living out east, and she hated my Agency lifestyle. When she got pregnant, I felt I had to find employment back here. It's not as exciting for me, but it's a lot better for the three of us now."

"I have to admit I was surprised when I heard you were married."

He leaned over and punched me on my arm. "You thought I was kidding about falling in love with Michelle. See! You can be wrong sometimes."

"I'm consistently wrong when it comes to you. Remember how you knew those Arabic students back in '95 weren't really in Norman to learn engineering?"

For a few minutes, we reminisced about the good times we'd had working together years ago. However, I noticed both of us deliberately left out the bad parts.

He asked me about my cover story, and after I told him what Legends had cooked up for me, I gave him one of my newly minted business cards.

He didn't comment on my promotion to Senior Fellow.

Slipping the card inside his wallet, he asked, "Did you approve the security I had installed out here?"

"I checked on it yesterday, and it looked great. Thanks for not mounting a video camera on every fence post and giving me a security patrol."

He seemed genuinely surprised at my statement. "Now, why would I do that?" he asked. "Carlton said you needed to stay under the radar here."

I gave him a you've-got-to-be-kidding-me look. "I was going by past experience."

He smiled. "Oh, yeah, that."

"Yeah, that."

"So, what's up with this medical leave? Your leg looks gimpy, but otherwise you seem fine."

Danny loved to talk, but he also had a way of getting other people to talk, and I found myself telling him all about losing my network and hiding out in Tehran. Then, I described how I'd lost my temper during my debrief and told Deputy Ira how to do his job.

Danny almost choked on his coffee. "And he didn't fire you right away?"

"No, Carlton got my sentence reduced to a medical. Deputy Ira doesn't want to see my handsome face for a year."

"So why is Carlton concerned about your security?"

"Apparently, VEVAK didn't like it that I was able to kill two of their guys and escape their clutches. If the chatter coming out of Iran is to be believed, they're sending one of their Hezbollah friends over here to mete out some punishment on me."

He shook his head. "I don't like the sound of that."

"I'm not very fond of it myself."

Pushing aside his empty plate, he said, "Terrorist connections are part of my job at OSBI. Right now, I'm working with the FBI and Homeland Security on a human smuggling ring being run by one of the drug cartels out of Mexico. They're using the I-35 corridor from Texas on up to Oklahoma and beyond. We're not talking about some poor farm workers coming north to look for work either."

"So who are they?"

"The FBI has identified them as a group affiliated with Hezbollah. One of the Agency's operatives in Syria gave us solid intel indicating Iran and Syria have set up a joint operation smuggling Hezbollah extremists into the States. We believe they're setting up sleeper cells somewhere in this area."

I nodded. "Is Iran funding them?"

"That's what all the field reports suggest. Iran keeps threatening to bring down all kinds of havoc on us if we bomb their nuclear sites. I'm betting that's what this is all about."

"So what intel do you have so far?"

"Not much. Right now, I'm in the process of recruiting some assets in the Arabic community." He shook his head. "Of course, just like similar operations we've conducted overseas, it's going to take some time. I'm just hoping we have that kind of time."

"Speaking of your glory days in the Agency, did you ever hear of a Hezbollah hit man named Ahmed when you were running around the Middle East?"

He looked out the window and thought about my question for a few seconds. "If I remember correctly, Ahmed Al-Amin was a Hezbollah operative out of Syria. There were rumors he was an assassin. Is that the guy?"

I shrugged. "I just saw some raw data on a man named Ahmed. No surname. No confirmation either."

I removed our dirty plates from the table and placed them in the sink—cleaning up after cooking was the only part I hated about being in the kitchen.

As I rinsed off the plates, I noticed Danny getting up from the dining room table and walking over to the picture window. He appeared to be scanning the horizon beyond the lake.

After a few minutes, he asked, "Have you got everything you need out here?"

I assumed he meant weapons instead of anything else, so I assured him I was a well-armed man.

Continuing to let his gaze wander across the landscape, he said, "I want you to call me at anytime and for any reason."

"If I need backup, you'll be the first person I call."

He laughed and turned away from the window. "Yeah, I've heard that from you before, but let's hope the only scary thing you see coming at you across that prairie is a tornado barreling down on this place. You know we have some pretty big ones in this neck of the woods."

"So, I've heard."

I walked him out to his car.

However, just before he got inside, I asked him, "Do you and Michelle go to church anywhere around here?"

"That's a funny question coming from you. Is it part of your cover?"

"No, another story entirely. But yesterday I met someone who invited me to her church, and I just thought I'd ask you."

"No, we've never been to church anywhere around here," he said, getting into his car and starting to laugh. "But, hey, you probably ought to try it. That's what a Senior Fellow would do, I'll bet."

He was still laughing as he drove off.

♦♦♦♦

I went back inside, cleaned up the kitchen, and found the list of physical therapy places given to me by Kellerman. I chose one called Therapy in Motion. When I called, the receptionist suggested I come in for an evaluation around ten o'clock the following day.

I also called Professor Paul Franklin at his office on the OU campus. He didn't answer, so I left my name and cell phone number on his voice mail.

Next, I decided to go clothes shopping.

Dressing appropriately for my cover was one of the details Legends had left up to me to figure out. On my other assignments, the Kit had contained everything I needed to blend into the culture where I was living. However, the duffel bag prepared for me at the air base in Turkey had only been filled with two tracksuits and the barest of toiletry essentials, whereas the clothes in my closet at The Gray had consisted of jeans and knit shirts, plus a pair of dress pants and an oxford dress shirt. Of course, I had my new Armani suit, but I didn't think wearing it on campus would help me blend seamlessly into the environment.

There was a Dillard's department store in the shopping mall on the west side of town, and I drove over there. Besides picking out a few more shirts and a couple of dress pants, I also selected a leather jacket, a camel-colored sports coat, some dress shoes, a handful of OU shirts—to show my team spirit—and an OU ball cap.

Just as I finished paying the cashier, Paul Franklin called me back. I took my purchases and headed out to the parking lot, talking to him as I walked toward my car.

"Thanks for calling me back, Professor. I was wondering when we could get together?"

"Have you read the manuscript yet?"

"Ah . . . no, I haven't had a chance to do that."

"Well, why did you call me if you haven't done that yet? There's not much point in getting together until you've read it."

I was going back over the brief conversation in my head, trying to decide what I might have said to irritate Franklin, when I spotted a dark-skinned guy in jeans and a zipped-up hoodie standing next to my Range Rover in the parking lot. He was at the left rear wheel and was walking toward the driver's side door.

"You're right, of course. I'll get that done tonight. How about meeting tomorrow at one o'clock?"

"I have a student coming in at one."

I circled around behind the guy, stopping beside a Buick sedan and fumbling in my pocket as if I were looking for my keys.

"Okay, then, what about two?" I asked.

"Let's make it eleven in the morning."

"Eleven it is. Should we meet at your—"

The line went dead.

I slipped the phone in my pocket, dropped my packages beside the Buick, and walked up behind the guy. When I was about five feet away, he turned left at my car's front fender, meandered past the next set of parking spaces and headed toward the mall's entry doors.

Before retrieving my packages, I did a thorough check of the Range Rover's undercarriage, wheel wells, everything—a thorough check.

I found nothing.

In fact, as I thought about it, I realized I hadn't actually seen the guy touch my car.

After placing my purchases in the back seat, I sat down behind the wheel, took a long, deep breath, and turned the key in the ignition. The engine purred happily.

So did I.

♦♦♦♦

When I got home, I checked my Agency email. Carlton had forwarded a notification alert from Katherine's office indicating they were in the process of trying to confirm the veracity of a conversation one of Tony Fowler's NSD assets in Iran had overhead between two Hezbollah militants about an American spy. The agent reported Hezbollah was sending a man called Ahmed to locate and kill the American.

Carlton had added some personal words to me at the bottom of the notification: *"We have no confirmation of this name, much less an accurate identification. Remain vigilant."*

I appreciated what Tony Fowler had done by already disclosing this information to me before turning it over for analysis to Katherine's office. Like all Agency personnel, he knew information at Headquarters was a commodity—it was always needed to buy, pay back, or influence others. In Fowler's case, it seemed obvious he was trying to pay off the debt he owed me for putting my life in danger in Iran.

I sent Fowler a short encrypted email. It contained one word:

"Thanks."

Then, since I was on my computer, I pulled up Professor Franklin's manuscript.

The professor had already given our collaborative book a working title. It was *Israel and Islam: Revising the Middle East Narrative.*

If nothing else, the title was intriguing.

However, after reading the first twenty pages, I slammed the laptop's lid down so hard, I had to check back later to make sure I hadn't broken it.

Franklin's premise in "our" book was that all the conflicts between Israel and the rest of the Middle East could be resolved if the Jewish people were relocated anywhere outside present-day Israel. It was a ridiculous concept, but he had couched it in the scholarly language of academia.

He wrote as if Israel's history with the land—spanning thousands of years—simply didn't exist. In essence, he was denying there was a link between the Jewish people and the land of Israel. On this basis, he advocated there was no reason for giving the Jews their tiny strip of land in the first place. Instead, he proposed a new narrative in the peace process whereby Israel would be given the opportunity to either leave the land of their own accord or face annihilation.

His views sounded suspiciously familiar.

In the manuscript, he quoted passages from the Quran, but he omitted any references to the Bible, positioning himself squarely on the side of Iran and most Islamic militants, who were opposed to the Jewish people simply because they existed.

Trying to cool down, I walked out to the patio. Then, noticing how peaceful the lake was, I decided to trek down to the wooden dock. After walking the length of the pier, I impulsively removed my socks and shoes and dangled my feet over the side, splashing around in the cold water.

Calmer now, I sat there and thought about Franklin's manuscript.

Because my affinity for Israel was not a secret at the Agency, it occurred to me someone might be playing a cruel joke on me by coupling me up with Franklin. However, after giving this theory due consideration, I discarded it. Even though the DDO's office knew of my strong support for Israel, I couldn't believe they had paired me up with Franklin as a joke or even as a means of punishment.

Finally, I decided that since the book was a ruse and didn't have a chance of publication—at least not with my name on it—the manuscript's contents must not have been closely examined by anyone in Support Services and Franklin's beliefs had just fallen through the cracks.

Now, though, having read Franklin's manuscript and encountered his sharp-edged tone on the telephone, I couldn't wait to meet him.

CHAPTER 13

Early the next morning, I jumped out of bed, grabbed my gun from the nightstand, and went in search of a perplexing sound—something like scratching—coming from the kitchen area.

The noise, while faint in the master bedroom, increased in intensity the closer I got to the kitchen. Within a few seconds, though, I knew it wasn't coming from the kitchen. It was coming from the patio.

The puppy I'd seen chasing squirrels the day before was now at the patio doors scratching on the glass so vigorously I thought he might actually break it.

I rapped my knuckles on the sliding doors.

The startled animal looked up at me and then quickly ran back across the property.

Why were dogs so appealing to some people?

To me, this was one of life's great mysteries.

♦♦♦♦

After my initial evaluation at Therapy in Motion, my assigned therapist, Kevin, showed me the program of conditioning exercises to strengthen my leg and make my limp less noticeable. Then, the receptionist set up appointments for me to come in the following week on Monday, Wednesday, and Friday.

As I left Therapy in Motion on 24th Street, I drove south to Lindsey Street and turned east toward the OU campus and my meeting with Paul Franklin. When I came to a red light at the intersection of Lindsey and McGee, I realized I was across from the Hollywood Shopping Center, where Kristi Stellars said Bethel Church was located.

I looked to my left, and, about half a mile ahead, I could see a large building made of white stone. The front of the church was shaped like wedge, with a massive bell tower at its centermost point. The tower probably reached some 200 feet in the air. It was hard to miss, which made me wonder why I'd never noticed it when Danny and I had lived here before.

A marquee-type sign identified the building, and then right below the church's name there was a quotation. It said, "When in the Dark, Follow the Son."

I found myself smiling.

However, when I pulled into a parking garage on the OU campus, I put on my game face, or rather my scholarly face. I had dressed appropriately for my role of Senior Fellow—brown dress pants, camel-colored sports coat, white button-down shirt, and brown loafers. As I walked across the campus to Overton Hall, where the International Studies program was housed, I felt certain I could be mistaken for a beloved professor.

Most of the students going into Overton Hall were Caucasians. However, there was a smattering of Asians, Hispanics, and Arabs. The building was decorated with artwork from around the world and designed with lots of chrome and glass. It reminded me of an international corporation's headquarters more than an academic building. I found the main office as soon as I entered the building, and the receptionist directed me to Franklin's office on the third floor.

As I approached the office, I overheard two Middle Eastern students arguing in Arabic over a missed rental payment. My senses went on alert, but they paid no attention to me as I approached the reception area.

A heavy-set woman with beads in her hair looked up from her

computer and asked how she could help me.

"I'm Titus Ray. I have an appointment with Professor Franklin at eleven o'clock."

She focused on her computer once again. "He has a student with him. Please take a seat."

Fifteen minutes later, a young Arab man with a Quran under his arm left Franklin's office, and I was told to go in.

Professor Franklin sat at his desk in the center of the room. Behind him was a bank of windows providing a sweeping view of the campus and the well-kept grounds. However, my eyes were immediately drawn to the man at the desk rather than to the beautiful scenery behind it.

As I gazed on Franklin's expensive blue suit, which fit his thin, frame perfectly, I immediately realized I could have worn my Armani suit and not felt overdressed in the room with him. Franklin was at least in his sixties, with thick, silver-colored hair swept up and away from his high pale forehead. When he arose from the desk and moved forward to greet me, I wondered how many times someone had described him as a "distinguished-looking gentleman."

"Mr. Ray, I'm Dr. Paul Franklin."

He had a weak handshake.

"I'm happy to meet you Professor. You can call me Titus, though."

"Let's have a seat over here."

He indicated two upholstered chairs next to a wall of freestanding bookcases. The shelves were packed with numerous textbooks and journals on foreign relations, human rights, and international affairs. Interspersed among the books were distinctive souvenirs from around the world, plus several framed photographs of Paul Franklin with former Presidents and other recognizable dignitaries. There were also pictures of him with people I assumed to be family and friends. Not surprisingly, I spotted several copies of the Quran.

As I was about to take a seat, Franklin said, "I don't have much time. It's nearing the end of the semester, and I've got exams to grade. Let's make this quick."

Once again, I had the feeling Franklin was irritated with me. I decided to play the role of a gracious guest and charm him with my winsome personality.

"I'm sure it must be a busy time, Professor. Would it be more convenient for us to meet in about three or four weeks?"

He started walking back over to his desk. "Let me look at my calendar."

While I waited for him to find his calendar, I looked at some of his personal photographs. The most recent ones were candid shots of him playing with several small children—presumably, his grandkids.

Displayed in a prominent position, however, was a framed portrait of Paul Franklin as a young man. It was obviously taken on his wedding day. His wife was extraordinarily beautiful, and I told him so when he came back over to the seating area with his appointment book.

"Your wife is very beautiful."

"She's dead."

"Oh . . . I'm so sorry."

"The Israelis killed her."

I didn't bother to mask my surprise. "The Israelis?"

"I've been told you're a Middle East expert, Mr. Ray, so I'm assuming you know about the Sabra Refugee Camp Massacre?"

"Yes, of course. It happened back in the early 1980's in the middle of Lebanon's civil war. If I remember correctly, members of the Phalange party entered a Palestinian refugee camp and killed over three thousand people."

As I recited this account, his face turned to granite.

"Those were *Christian* Phalanges, Mr. Ray," he said, spitting out the correction, "and they were aided in that massacre by the Israelis."

"How so?"

"The Israelis sealed off the camp and prevented anyone from entering while the killing took place."

I couldn't dispute his well-documented facts, so I asked quietly, "How was your wife killed?"

At the mention of his wife, he turned away from me and looked up at their wedding picture. He didn't speak for almost a full minute, and I considered mumbling something about calling him later, but finally, he turned toward me and told me the story. His voice took on a monotone, as if he'd recited the tale a thousand times before.

"In 1980, I was the cultural affairs officer at our embassy in Beirut. I'd joined the diplomatic corps when Eloise and I were first married, but she hadn't been happy at our previous postings in Germany or Japan. She wanted to be in a country where she could make a difference. She was thrilled when I took the position offered to me in Lebanon, and she immediately went to work trying to aid the thousands of Palestinian refugees being displaced by the civil war."

At this point in the story, his voice broke slightly, but then he straightened his back and hurriedly finished the account of his wife's death.

"She happened to be in the camp the day the Israelis sealed it off following the assassination of the Lebanese President. The Israelis allowed the militant Christians to enter the camp and seek revenge on the Palestinians for killing their President. Eloise's body was found a day later. She'd been killed trying to protect some helpless child."

"Again, Professor, I am so sorry for your loss."

"I left the Foreign Service after that and raised my two daughters by myself." He nodded toward the other family photos. "I now have four grandchildren."

"I'm sure they bring you lots of happiness."

"Yes, they do," he agreed.

Then, he shook his head. "But I don't want them growing up in the kind of world we live in today. I want something better for them—a world without conflicts. Everything I do here," he gestured toward the campus scene outside his windows, "is an effort to influence tomorrow's leaders. Someday, I hope one of them will implement the right solution."

What exactly would that solution be? Perhaps a world free of Jews? If that's what he thought, then the cultured, distinguished Paul Franklin could be as dangerous as any Islamic terrorist plotting the next attack.

♦♦♦♦

As I drove away from the University, the sky was dark and cloudy, exactly like my mood. I was scheduled to meet with Professor Franklin again in four weeks, and I was thankful I didn't have to see him again until then.

However, I certainly had a better handle on why he was a bitter, angry old man who hated Israel and the Jews.

No doubt, both sides in the Arab/Israeli conflict had committed atrocities, yet Franklin had failed to mention that the Israeli commander, who had been responsible for closing down the Sabra Palestinian camp, had been forced to resign his position for the indirect part he'd played in the massacre. On the other hand, when Islamic extremists intentionally put their followers aboard airliners and blew up Americans on 9/11, they were considered heroes and cheered by Muslims around the world.

I wondered if Franklin's personal loss had so affected his thinking that he was unable—or perhaps unwilling—to see the stark differences in the two sides. But more than that, I wondered if his desire to get rid of the Jews was purely theoretical, or was he actively looking for a way to make it practical?

That question started to haunt me.

♦♦♦♦

When I returned home, I fixed myself a meal of ham, fried potatoes, and cornbread, but the moment I took the cornbread out of the oven, a movement at the patio door caught my eye.

I raced over to the glass door and slid it open.

"Get out of here! Get!"

The puppy bounded away from the door and scampered across the backyard. The moment he arrived at the lake, though, he sat down and stared at me.

I stared back.

Because the dog wasn't wearing a collar, I wondered if he'd been dumped along Tecumseh Road by some city dweller who didn't want him. Maybe they thought the dog could survive on its own or find a friendly homeowner to take him in.

Since I wasn't a homeowner or friendly, I decided the dog would have to survive on his own.

I slid the door closed and hurried back inside.

Just before sitting down, I glanced out the kitchen window. The dog was nowhere to be seen, but the wind I'd noticed earlier had picked up and the sky off to the west was dark, almost black in color.

About halfway through my meal, I turned on the television and watched the local news. The commentator had a certain twang to his voice that I was beginning to associate with Oklahoma. As I thought about how Danny was starting to add this twang to his own speech pattern, the weatherman suddenly got excited.

"Those of you living in the northeast part of Norman in Cleveland County need to take your tornado precautions *immediately*."

He sounded very serious.

"Radar shows a funnel on the ground moving due east. Go to the lowest level of your home and stay away from windows. If you have a storm shelter, go there now."

"Seriously?" I said to him, feeling paralyzed for several seconds.

Another weatherman, identified as a "storm spotter," was following the tornado, and he began describing it in detail.

At that point, I took my plate and my bottle of water and headed toward the garage, grabbing a portable radio off the kitchen counter on my way out.

As I passed by the patio doors, I heard the dog barking outside.

"Sorry, pooch," I yelled. "You're on your own."

Once inside the garage, I opened the door to the storm shelter and turned on the battery-powered light and fan. When I went back over to a workbench to pick up the food provisions I'd placed there, I heard the dog yapping yet again.

But, by the time I got back over to the storm shelter, all I could hear was the wind howling. I made my way down inside the gray box and placed my food and the radio on one of the narrow benches attached to each side of the shelter. Then, I figured out how to pull the door closed.

Seconds before latching the door, though, I made my way back up the stairs and into the kitchen. Pulling open the patio doors, I grabbed the rain-soaked dog and scrambled for the shelter. When I rounded the corner of the garage, the lights went out.

Inside the shelter, the dog was whimpering and shaking like a wet leaf. I quickly took off my new dress shirt and wrapped him in it. Then, I started trembling.

I was sure I could hear the winds howling outside, even though I was six feet underground. I even pictured the walls around me being sucked up inside the whirling mass. Trying to distract myself, I reached over and offered the dog a piece of cornbread. He gobbled it up.

"You like my cornbread?" I asked him. "I don't even like my cornbread. I guess that makes you a . . . Wait, I've got it. That makes you a corndog!"

I suddenly realized how stupid I sounded and started laughing.

Was I really sitting in a steel box in the middle of Oklahoma, holding a smelly mutt, and cowering from a storm? What was the matter with me? I had hunted down terrorists in Iraq, trained recruits in Pakistan, run a network of assets in Afghanistan, and collected intelligence in Libya. However, here I was, humbled and frightened by the sound of screeching winds coming across the prairie in America's heartland.

I opened the bottle of water, took a sip, and then poured some in my cupped hand for the puppy. He lapped it up.

When he was finished, he stared at me expectantly, as if I might know what to do next.

"Maybe we need to see what's happening out there," I said, switching on the radio.

The announcer said the tornado, after briefly touching down in some rural areas, had lifted back up in the rain-wrapped cloud. No one was reporting any injuries or damage, but some homes in Norman had lost power.

"I think that's us, dog."

He cocked his head to one side, jumped up on the bench, and grabbed the ham off my plate. After quickly devouring it, he looked up at me and started to pant, giving me the distinct impression he was grinning at me.

Maybe he liked my jokes.

We climbed out of the storm shelter into a pitch-black garage. After stumbling around and finally locating a flashlight, I vowed to prepare an emergency kit before the next storm hit.

As soon as we entered the kitchen, though, the power came back on.

I located a couple of plastic bowls. One I filled with water; the other I filled with ham and cornbread. Then I placed both of them on the floor.

I named him Stormy.

CHAPTER 14

On Sunday morning, I decided to attend Bethel church. My decision surprised me, because I was pretty sure I'd feel uncomfortable in an auditorium full of people.

One time, I had inadvertently seen what Carlton had written about me in the margin of a report: *"Works well with people; would prefer not to."*

I didn't disagree with his analysis of my personality; I wasn't a people person.

However, early Sunday morning, I changed my mind about going to church.

I had just finished my daily Bible reading. As I thought about how much my faith was being strengthened by reading it, I suddenly remembered standing in the Mardel's store all alone and asking God for guidance to choose the right Bible. That's when I'd noticed Kristi Stellars. If it hadn't been for her advice, I might never have chosen a Bible. As I thought about that encounter, it occurred to me she had also urged me to attend her church. Perhaps her invitation was God's guidance as well.

My parents had never gone to church, but Carla and I had been taken to Vacation Bible School by a neighbor when I was in the fourth grade. All I could remember about that experience was that I'd eaten a couple of red snow cones and made a raft out of Popsicle sticks. That was because a character in the Bible—a man named Paul or Saul; I can't remember exactly which one—had been shipwrecked.

I chose to wear my Armani suit to church because a suit was what I usually wore whenever I attended funerals or weddings. However, after parking my car and walking through the church parking lot, I noticed how many of the men going inside were dressed in casual clothes.

When I entered the church foyer, I was immediately greeted by several older men handing out programs. They were dressed in suits also. I relaxed then, knowing I hadn't violated some dress code by my formal attire. However, I was troubled by the fact that all the suit-wearing guys were all so much older than I was, whereas the jeans-wearing guys were about my age.

Right then, I made a mental note that the next time I came—if there was a next time—I would leave the Armani suit in the closet.

It wasn't hard to find the auditorium because I simply followed a crowd of people going in the same direction. Once I got inside, I couldn't help but notice the bustle of activity. It wasn't quiet and ethereal like a funeral. Instead, the place was buzzing with conversation and laughter.

I chose a pew about halfway down the center aisle, and as soon as I sat down, singers filed into the choir loft located on the speaker's platform. When they were all inside, the music director stepped to the pulpit and asked everyone to stand and sing with him.

The words to the songs were projected onto two large white screens. Because I wasn't much of a singer, I just read the words and listened. After the music ended, the pastor gave a welcoming speech with a particular emphasis on any visitors in the congregation. Then he instructed everyone to greet one another.

At that point, I definitely wanted to leave the building. However, once the minister, Pastor Dawson, began delivering his sermon, I decided to stay.

When his message ended, Pastor Dawson invited those who had further questions to see him after the service or call him for an appointment. Because I was trying to sort through all the questions I had about his sermon, I was surprised to hear him make this offer.

How would he ever have time to do anything but answer questions, if everyone had as many questions as I did about his message?

Another pastor came to the pulpit. He made an *urgent announcement* for volunteers in the church's Connections ministry. Although I was certain I didn't want to get "connected" with anyone, I followed his instructions and looked on the back of the program for the list of ministries needing volunteers. There were openings in The Clothes Closet, a service for needy children, in Golden Years, a meal-delivery outreach to seniors, and in English Learners, a program for non-English speakers.

The pastor urged his parishioners to consider helping out in one of the programs. He said doing so would be a blessing to someone.

I tucked the program inside my Bible and left the building.

♦♦♦♦

As I pulled through the security gate and started up the driveway at my house, Stormy ran out from behind the garage and raced my Range Rover to a stop. He started jumping around so excitedly, it made me wonder how he would act if I'd been gone for a whole day.

All during lunch, I kept thinking about the Connections announcement. Finally, I picked up the phone and called Susan Steward.

"Hi, my name is Titus Ray. Could I speak with Susan Steward, please?"

"This is Susan."

"Hi Susan, I was in your church this morning when the pastor made the announcement about getting involved in the Connections ministry. I noticed you and your husband are sponsors of English Learners and that you need another volunteer."

"That's right. Are you interested in volunteering, Mr. Ray?

"I really need to know more about the program before committing to anything."

"Okay, sure. Are you familiar with the national ESL program?"

"No, not really."

"ESL is an acronym for English as a Second Language. It's a

program for non-native speakers of English. Our participants come from the OU community and most of them are relatives of students studying there. The ESL material is already written by the national headquarters, so it's very easy to teach. In fact, my husband, Tucker, and I do most of the teaching. As a volunteer, you would simply serve as one of our aides."

"You do this free of charge?"

"Oh, yes. Our church provides this program as a means of serving our community and the international students at OU. We meet on Tuesdays and Thursdays at nine o'clock in the morning. Tucker and I are retired, and the other volunteer who works with us isn't employed. Are you available at those times?"

"Yes, I believe so."

"What kind of work do you do, Mr. Ray?"

"Please call me Titus. I'm with a think tank in Maryland, but I've relocated to Norman temporarily while collaborating on a book with a professor at the University."

"An author. How exciting!"

"Well, nothing's been published yet."

"I believe you would find the ESL work very rewarding, and as an added bonus, you'll get to meet people from around the world."

I tried to sound enthusiastic about this prospect. "That would be amazing."

"Can I sign you up?"

"I'll attend the class on Tuesday and let you know."

CHAPTER 15

On Monday, I went to physical therapy. After being humiliated by Kevin, my therapist, I left there and went over to Petco on 24th Avenue in the University Shopping Center to pick up some items for Stormy. When I got home, I wrestled Stormy into his new collar, loaded him up in the Range Rover, and took him to a vet on Alameda Avenue.

Dr. Barnett, who had been recommended to me by the receptionist at Therapy in Motion, administered several vaccinations and checked him out from nose to tail. He told me Stormy was a yellow Labrador retriever in perfect health and probably about six months old. When I mentioned I'd never owned a dog before and wasn't exactly sure what I was doing, he assured me Stormy was highly intelligent and if he needed anything, he'd let me know.

For some reason, the last thing Dr. Barnett said sounded like a warning.

"If I were you, I'd plan on him becoming a very large dog."

♦♦♦♦

Previously, when I'd lived in Norman, I'd become so bored, I'd ended up harassing Danny about his girlfriend and bugging Carlton for an overseas assignment.

Now, however, I was determined to have a different experience.

Agreeing to volunteer for the ESL class at Bethel seemed like a good first step. I knew it would keep me busy while making a difference in someone else's life—a philosophy not too different from working for the security of my country.

There were only about thirty-five cars in the church's parking lot when I turned up for my first ESL class on Tuesday. As I watched people arriving, I noticed it was an international group with no predominate ethnicity. I also saw there were more women than men heading into the building.

I remained inside my car and observed the scene for a few minutes, never wanting to become complacent about my own security. At the same time, I was determined not to overreact as I had in the parking lot when I'd seen the hooded young man walking by my car.

After being certain everyone was inside, I started to open my car door, but, at that moment, a brand new Honda Civic, with a man and a woman inside, pulled into a parking spot near my Range Rover. After the woman got out of the car, she leaned back inside and spoke in Farsi to the male driver. He answered her in Farsi.

It was a simple exchange of information about the time the woman wanted to be picked up, and the man assured her—adding a common Farsi word of romantic endearment—he'd be there to pick her up on time.

If I'd been in Tehran, I wouldn't have given the incident a second thought. However, I wasn't in Tehran, and hearing the Persian language again caused my synapses to fire.

As the man drove off, I watched the woman go through an unmarked door at the far end of the building. I entered the church through the lobby at the opposite end and quickly located the Connections desk, where an elderly woman gave me directions to the ESL classroom. Then I took an incredibly slow elevator up to the second floor.

When I arrived in the ESL classroom, the Farsi-speaking woman was already seated in a circle of about twenty men and women from various countries. They were practicing English vowel sounds. This was an exercise directed by a short, stocky, gray-haired man, who swung his arms up and down—much like a conductor leading an orchestra—while the students shouted out the sounds. The effect was comical, but they all seemed to be enjoying themselves.

A tall woman with straight blond hair and sharp, narrow features detached herself from the group.

"Are you Titus?" she asked.

"Yes. You must be Susan."

"I am. We're really glad you're here. Let me introduce you to everyone."

She stopped the exercise and introduced her husband, Tucker, who had been leading the vowel musical. Then, after she pulled a chair into the circle for me, she went around the room and instructed each student to give me their name, the country they were from, what language they spoke, and whether they were married or single.

It didn't take me long to figure out she was using my presence to conduct a quick English learning exercise for the group. However, by listening to their responses, I was able to determine there were two Japanese, three Koreans, five South Americans, two Mexicans, one Nigerian, and one Iraqi in the ESL class.

There were no Iranians in the group.

The woman in the Honda Civic, who had been speaking Farsi, said her name was Farah Karimi. After introducing herself, she said she was from Iraq, spoke Arabic, and was married.

I was mystified by her apparent deception, but after analyzing all the circumstances surrounding my spontaneously joining the ESL group, I quickly determined her presence in the class had to be a coincidence. I couldn't find any reason to believe she posed a danger to me.

However, I remained wary.

After about forty-five minutes, Susan announced it was time for a break, so the students scattered to the restrooms and to a room adjacent to the classroom, where there were several round tables, a coffee machine, and a couple of vending machines. Not surprisingly, some of the men and women separated into their different language groups, while others tried to carry on conversations with each other in broken English.

I grabbed a cup of coffee and positioned myself near a table where Farah Karimi was speaking to a group of women. As she spoke her slow, basic English, I thought I detected a definite Farsi accent to her English sentences. I learned nothing more about her, however.

Wanting to familiarize myself with the church's floor plan, I also took a quick tour of the rest of the building. My surveillance probably wasn't necessary, but I did it anyway. Except for the church offices, I found most of the building deserted.

When the students returned for the second session, they were split into several small groups, and I was put in charge of one of the groups. My responsibility consisted of listening to their grammar as they spoke to each other in English. If they made mistakes, I corrected them.

Before the class was dismissed, the other volunteer, Patty, asked how many in the group had smart phones. Nearly every hand was raised. She went on to suggest they download some word game applications and use them to help build their vocabulary.

My ears perked up when she concluded her announcement by saying, "I want to thank Farah Karimi for this helpful suggestion."

Using this as an excuse, I approached Farah the moment the class ended. Holding up my iPhone, I asked, "Could you show me the games you like to play?"

At first, she appeared puzzled by my question. Then, the words seemed to register with her, and she eagerly took my phone and started searching for the games.

As she concentrated on finding the games, I studied her features. She was a classic Persian beauty with high cheekbones and an oval-shaped face dominated by large, heavily made-up eyes. Her thick, black hair cascaded down her shoulders. Earlier, I'd seen her twirling a strand of curls nervously around her finger whenever she'd been required to speak to the class.

"This one," she said, turning my phone around and pointing to a Words with Friends application.

I nodded at her.

She also found another game called The Whirly Word.

"This one good too," she said.

I took back my phone.

"I'm sure you'd beat me in both of those games," I said with a smile.

"I no good but try hard."

Farah had obviously not learned all the rules of English grammar yet. However, she had just taught me something.

While reaching for my iPhone, the cuff of her long-sleeved blouse had pulled away from her arm to reveal a tattoo on the inside of her right wrist. The design was a small cross, and it was very similar to one I'd seen on Darya's wrist at the safe house in Tehran.

When I'd asked Darya about the tattoo, she said Iranian Christian women wore these cross tattoos to show their solidarity with other persecuted Christian women around the world.

♦♦♦♦

My schedule for the next two weeks didn't fluctuate much. I went to church on Sunday, did my rehab on Monday, Wednesday, and Friday, and helped with the ESL classes on Tuesday and Thursday. In between those times, Stormy and I explored Ortega's property.

Strangely enough, I felt content, and for the first time in many years, the Agency was only a very small blip on my radar—if it showed up at all.

However, all that changed on Friday night.

♦♦♦♦

After two weeks of volunteering in the ESL class, I was invited to a potluck dinner for the students and their spouses in the church's fellowship hall. When Susan told me about the event, she mentioned the dinner would be a wonderful time to meet the spouses of the students I was helping.

All I really cared about was meeting one spouse—Farah's husband.

The fact that I hadn't been able to discover why Farah was hiding her Iranian roots made me eager to make the acquaintance of her husband. If the opportunity presented itself, I would ask him a few probing questions. If not, I would make the opportunity happen.

On Friday night, I made a big pot of chili and brought it to the dinner. After placing it on a long table filled with a smorgasbord of dishes from around the world, Tucker grabbed me by the arm and began introducing me to the guests.

As we went from group to group, he mentioned several of their students were running late. It didn't surprise me when I learned Farah was one of them.

She was seldom on time for class either.

Farah's lack of punctuality was something I'd observed on the first day when I'd seen her using a different door than the one used by most ESL students. Later, I found out she wasn't using the lobby entrance so she could avoid taking the church's slow elevator. In order to save time, she was taking a short cut—going up the back stairs at the opposite end of the building from the lobby.

Twenty minutes after Tucker asked a blessing on the potluck meal, Farah and her husband finally arrived at the dinner. After Farah added her dish to the others, she and her husband sat down at a round table with some of the Asian couples.

I watched Farah, who exhibited an extrovert's personality, immediately begin engaging her seatmates in conversation. However, Farah's husband appeared detached, even withdrawn, from the chatter going on around him.

The meal was beginning to wind down before I made my way over to the table where they were seated. When Farah saw me, she tried practicing her rules of social introduction.

"Titus, this is my husband, Bashir," she said slowly. "Bashir, this is my friend, Titus."

In spite of his solemn countenance, Bashir Karimi was a strikingly handsome man with a well-groomed beard and dark, thick eyebrows. He immediately rose from his chair and shook hands with me. Then he gestured toward an empty chair and invited me to sit down with them.

After a few minutes of conversation with Farah about the ESL class, I asked Bashir, "Are you a student at OU?"

"Yes, I'm working on a degree in electrical engineering."

"Where did you learn to speak such good English?"

"In Iraq."

"I served in Iraq during the second Gulf war."

Bashir glanced over at his wife. "My wife said you were a writer."

His tone implied one of us had lied to him about my profession. I tried to assure him his wife wasn't the liar.

"She's correct. I'm out of the military now and writing a book on the Middle East. Since you're from that area, it would be interesting to have your input on the issues in that part of the world."

"Of course," he said. Then in a dismissive tone he added, "But I don't really follow the politics in my country anymore."

"Did you serve in the military in Iraq?"

"No, I was never in the military," he answered quickly.

Bashir's phone was resting on the table between us, and as I started to ask him another question, it beeped a couple of times and a message flashed across the screen.

"Excuse me," he said, snatching the phone from the table, "I must take care of this call."

He nodded at Farah and hurriedly made his way out of the room.

If Bashir hadn't just told me he was never in the military, the way he carried himself when he walked away from the table would have made me think otherwise. In fact, I would have guessed he had undergone extensive military training simply because of his authoritative tone and brusque manner.

Since the dinner was winding down by the time Bashir returned to the table, I didn't have a chance to resume my conversation with him. However, on my way home, I started thinking about his phone call, the one he had taken which cut short our brief time together.

In reality, Bashir had not received a phone call. The message flashing across his phone's screen had been a game notification from Words with Friends, the word game Farah had shown me the first day I'd attended the ESL class.

So why would Bashir pretend the game notification was a phone call? Was he simply using the game as an excuse to leave the table? Were my questions making him uncomfortable?

I also thought about the apparent inconsistencies in their background stories. Why was Bashir hiding his military service? Why were they both denying their Persian roots?

Maybe there was a simple explanation for their actions, but I still continued to feel uneasy about Bashir and Farah Karimi, and yet again, I wondered if their presence in Norman had anything to do with me.

However, once I entered my house and checked my email, I didn't give either one of them another thought—at least for the next forty-eight hours.

CHAPTER 16

As soon as I got home, I opened my email and saw a red box flashing. I immediately clicked on it.

It was from Simon Wassermann, another Middle Eastern operative. The two of us had been through a difficult patch many years ago, and we'd come out on the other side as pretty good friends. However, it was unusual for me to have an encrypted operative-to-operative email from him unless a joint operation was in progress.

The message was brief: *"In Chicago. Urgent we meet. Where are you? Grandma sends her love."*

Even though the email had been written more than an hour ago, I didn't respond to it immediately.

But, I had no doubt it was from Wassermann.

Once, during an arms deal, we had posed as brothers, and we'd used the "Grandma" phrase as one of our codes. However, I hadn't survived in this business without using extreme caution, so I took a few minutes to work out what I wanted to do.

In case he'd been compromised in some way, I decided not to tell him where I was living. Instead, I chose to tell him I was a couple of hours away.

I wrote back: *"In Dallas. Airport Hilton. Any time after midnight. Figure on it. Grandma loves me more."*

He responded within a couple of minutes: *"See you in Big D."*

For a few brief moments, I considered contacting Carlton, but I decided if Wassermann had wanted to bring our Operations Officer into the *"urgent we meet"* scene, he would have done so already.

I immediately put food and water out for Stormy, grabbed a couple of guns and some extra ammo, and headed for the garage. However, before driving away, I went back inside for my "go" bag. It contained everything I would need—clothes, passport, cash, and credit cards—in case I had to get out of the country quickly.

However, I was optimistic, and, when I left the house, I told Stormy I'd see him in a few hours. Then, I hit the interstate and headed south to Dallas and Simon Wassermann.

Wassermann and I had worked together several times during my career. The first time had been during my early years with the Agency when our assignment had been the surveillance of a suspected Russian agent in Mexico City.

During those endless hours of keeping the Russian under surveillance, Wassermann had maintained a steady stream of stories about how his grandparents had suffered under the Soviet's authoritarian regime before making their escape to America.

After watching the Russian for a week, I noticed the man was really getting under Wassermann's skin. To make matters worse, I was beginning to have a bad feeling about the entire operation. However, because I didn't have enough experience to pay attention to my instincts back then, I brushed aside my sense of foreboding and continued the surveillance.

One night, about three weeks into the operation, we observed the Russian bringing a young girl into his apartment. A few minutes later, he began punching her in the stomach with his fists, and, after she fell to the floor, kicking her in the face repeatedly with his boots.

Suddenly, before I had a chance to stop him, Simon pulled out his gun and raced out of our apartment and across the street. I immediately ran after him. However, by the time I arrived at the Russian's apartment, Wassermann had already burst through the door and shot him.

Although I expressed disapproval for his rash behavior, at the same time, I assured Wassermann I had his back with the Agency.

Thus, by the time the two of us were called back to Langley to give an account of the Russian's demise, we had come up with a credible tale for our debriefers.

Our story involved squabbling generals in the Russian embassy.

We spun it flawlessly.

Since then, Wassermann and I had worked together several other times, but neither of us had ever mentioned the Russian again.

Wassermann was about my age and build, and we resembled one another closely enough to have passed ourselves off as brothers—Raul and Ramon Figueroa—when we were sent into Syria to flush out a very rich and troublesome arms dealer about ten years ago. Everything went wrong on that mission, and to top it off, the Syrian was killed—though not by our hand.

I'd always suspected Mossad had done the deed, but I had no real proof of that.

Simon Wassermann was Jewish, and, at times, I'd heard some Agency people question whether his loyalties were with the U.S. or with Israel. I'd never done so. To me, he had always demonstrated an unshakable allegiance to America.

However, I knew he had access—through a back channel—into Mossad. I wasn't bothered by that. In fact, in Syria, his connections had gotten us out of a perilous situation.

Now, Wassermann wanted an urgent off-the-books meet with me.

Maybe it was just to pay back the money he owed me on a bet we'd made during our last assignment together, but, if so, why all the secrecy?

Since Wassermann had been running assets in Syria for the past year or so, I wondered if our meeting had anything to do with the Hezbollah hit man VEVAK had sent to kill me. But if that was the case, then why not bring Carlton into the picture?

I had reached the outskirts of Dallas, so I'd know soon enough.

♦ ♦ ♦ ♦

While monitoring the cars behind me, I got off I-35 and headed for a large mall in Grapevine, Texas near the Airport Hilton. Then, I employed one last counter surveillance tactic by using the mall's outer access roads. Finally, I decided I wasn't being followed and pulled into the hotel's parking lot.

I scanned the area carefully, because if Wassermann had been compromised, it was possible the opposition had already set up watchers at the Airport Hilton. Seeing nothing suspicious, I breathed a sigh of relief and got out of the Range Rover.

The wind was blowing at a steady clip as I crossed the parking lot, and I found myself hoping the thunderstorms—promised by the weatherman sometime after midnight—weren't going to affect Wassermann's flight.

As I approached the registration desk, I could hear a jazz tune and the sound of laughter drifting out from the bar and restaurant around the corner from the hotel lobby. However, the reception area itself appeared deserted. The attractive Hispanic desk clerk at the counter found the reservation I'd made online under the name of Raul Figueroa.

I knew Wassermann wouldn't have any trouble deciphering my "figure it out" sentence in the reply I'd sent back to him, and he would check in under our old operational name—Figueroa.

I told the young woman. "My brother will be arriving soon. Would you mind calling me when he's on his way up? We're big practical jokers, and I have something special planned for him when he walks in the door."

She smiled at me as if we were co-conspirators. "Oh, sure," she said. "Is he an OU fan too?"

I suddenly remembered I had on my OU ball cap. "He is."

"Well, both of you should be very careful while you're here."

"Why's that?"

"Because Texas fans carry grudges. When OU beat us at the Cotton Bowl last year, we vowed revenge." She spread her fingers apart to make the "hook 'em horns" sign for the University of Texas Longhorn football team.

"I can assure you, we'll be very careful while we're here."

♦♦♦♦

After entering my room on the fourth floor, I deposited my duffel bag on the floor and took out my laptop. Although I didn't plan on spending the night, I'd carried some luggage just for appearance's sake. However, the only items inside my bag were my laptop and some extra ammo.

After booting up my computer, I opened my email account.

It was empty.

I checked the flight schedules of planes coming in from Chicago and saw one had landed five minutes ago, and two more were landing within the next two hours. It was obvious I had some time to kill before Wassermann arrived. With that in mind, I decided to do a quick survey of the building and memorize the hotel's floor plan.

Before leaving the room, though, I turned on the Weather Channel. The radar indicated a big thunderstorm was bearing down on the metroplex area in less than two hours, but no tornadoes were in the forecast.

I took the stairs down to the first floor, and, as I waved to the desk clerk, she patted the top of her head playfully.

I had left my OU cap in the room.

When I entered the hotel's restaurant, I scanned the place as if I were meeting someone. There were only a few patrons. Perhaps the impending rain had scattered the crowd.

I sat down at the bar and ordered a cup of black coffee. Then, I did a second recon of the room.

Only one other person was sitting at the bar. He was a middle-aged, pot-bellied guy with barely enough hair to cover the top of his head. As I sat down, he glanced in my direction. Then, he saluted me a couple of times.

It was obvious he'd had few too many.

If at all possible, drinking alcohol was something I tried to avoid. When I was being vetted to join the Agency, a psychiatrist had analyzed my aversion to alcoholic beverages. He had done so in agonizing detail. Finally, after several hours of talking about it, he'd announced my attitude stemmed from my father's alcoholism. When he'd told me this, I hadn't shown any outward reaction to this diagnosis.

However, on the inside, I was screaming, "You think I don't know that, you idiot!" or something to that effect.

Occasionally, in order to maintain my cover, I took a drink, but neither the taste, nor the concept of pickling my brain held any appeal to me.

When I finished my coffee, I toured the rest of the hotel, making careful note of its exits. Then, I returned to my room. After removing my gun from its holster, I settled in for what I hoped would be a short wait.

At that moment, it occurred to me I should have prayed before leaving the house.

Javad had always prayed before he ventured outside the safe house. I'd observed him do this on numerous occasions, pausing at the door, bowing his head and taking a moment to ask for safety on the streets of Tehran.

I bowed my head and asked God to keep me safe.

Then, the phone rang.

♦♦♦♦

The clerk told me that my brother, Ramon Figueroa, had checked in and was in the elevator. When I hung up the phone, I left the room and walked across the hall to a small area containing a couple of vending machines. From there, I was able to see back down the hallway and observe the entrance to my room.

If Wassermann had been forced to bring unwanted companions, I would soon know about it.

The elevator dinged as it opened up on the fourth floor.

Simon Wassermann rounded the corner.

He was alone.

He looked tired and disheveled, as if he'd been traveling for several days, but he carefully scanned up and down the hallway as he approached the door. Then, he pulled his key card out of his pocket, quickly inserted it, and turned the knob.

He started yelling, as soon as he entered the room. "Raul, it's Ramon, your handsome brother."

I raced to the door and slipped in behind him.

Sensing my presence, he turned toward me, ready to fend off an attacker. However, when he recognized who I was, he grabbed me by the shoulders and started laughing.

Still playing the brother, he said, "Raul, it's so good to see you." Then he whispered, "Thanks for not shooting me."

After scanning the hallway again, I shut and bolted the door. When I turned around, Wassermann had already crashed on the bed.

"Boy, I'm bushed. Got anything to eat?"

While I ordered room service for us, he filled the in-room coffeepot with water and plugged it in. As it was brewing, he went inside the bathroom and stayed for at least twenty minutes.

His behavior didn't surprise me.

Wassermann was a chronological kind of thinker. He operated with both a timetable and an ongoing priority list at all times. Until he got to the part of his mental list where it was time to reveal why he wanted to see me, nothing I said was going to affect that timetable.

When he emerged from the bathroom, the coffee was ready, and he carried two cups over to a small round table in a corner of the room where I'd set up my laptop.

Removing his Agency satphone from his pocket, he said, "I need to check my messages."

As he fiddled with his cell phone, I couldn't help but notice his dirty jeans and wrinkled shirt. From the whiff of body odor I encountered when he hugged me, he'd evidently been wearing them for several days. There was little doubt he needed a shower.

Wassermann's curly black hair looked greasy, and there were more lines in his face than the last time I'd seen him. He was also much thinner.

Because he was such a big eater, his weight loss surprised me. However, he was also fidgety, throwing off tons of nervous energy.

He closed his phone with a snap. "Okay, nothing. That's good."

He took a big gulp of hot coffee.

I asked, "Are you coming in from an assignment?"

"Yeah. I'm supposed to be flying from London to D.C. tomorrow.

I'm schedule to be debriefed on Monday."

"Carlton thinks you're still in London?"

"Let's hope so."

"What were you doing in Chicago?"

"Waiting to hear from you. Yesterday, I flew from London to New York. I'd heard you were on medical leave, and I thought maybe you'd gone back to Michigan, but, even if you hadn't, I knew I could get a flight out of O'Hare to wherever you were staying. So, after landing in New York, I caught a flight to Chicago and emailed you."

"No wonder you look—"

There was a sharp knock at the door.

Both of us sprang up from our chairs. Since I had a gun, I signaled for him to answer the door while I covered him from the bathroom.

"Who is it?" Wassermann asked.

"Room service."

He unlocked the door, swinging it all the way open and casually stepping behind it as I covered him.

CHAPTER 17

It really was room service. However, Wassermann elected to roll the cart in the room himself.

After quickly devouring some food, he began explaining his reason for contacting me.

As I predicted, he began chronologically.

"For the past two years, I've been in Damascus running a couple of assets inside a Hezbollah group. Their leader takes his orders straight from Iran."

"What kind of assets were you running?"

He gave me an irritated look. "Slow down. I'm getting to that."

"Sorry. Lost my head."

"I recruited two people, a man and a woman, inside a group calling itself *Asaib al Haq* or League of the Righteous. I targeted a man named Talib because a reliable source told me he needed the money and was willing to get inside the group and work for the Agency. Sure enough, within six months, he was giving me some valuable stuff."

Wassermann concentrated on his eating for several minutes.

When I couldn't stand it any longer, I asked, "And the woman you recruited?"

He took a drink of water before answering. "Rasha was a peripheral person, a cousin of one of the group's leaders. In reality, she didn't have much access to their plans and knew next to nothing of actionable intelligence. However, she prepared meals for the leaders and was excellent at identifying people in the organization and giving us intel on members attending their meetings."

Wassermann paused while drowning his French fries in ketchup.

I prodded him. "I'm assuming all this background has something to do with me?"

"Hold on, I'm getting to that." He stuffed a big forkful of French fries in his mouth. "You know, when we first met, you had a lot more patience."

"I was younger then."

"And better looking."

I held up my hands in mock surrender. "I'm *patiently* listening now."

"Good. Here's where it gets interesting. The first high-quality piece of intelligence from Talib detailed how *Asaib al Haq* was bringing operatives into the U.S. He said they were working with the Mexican drug cartels to bring them across our southern border. Once Hezbollah members got here, they were supposed to organize deep cover cells and wait for further instructions."

I interjected, "I recently had an OSBI agent outline the same scenario. He's in the process of trying to locate those cells right now."

He nodded. "That piece of intelligence came from my network." He gestured at me with his fork. "Now, this is where you come into the picture."

"About time."

He ignored my comment. "Talib told me three weeks ago that Ahmed Al-Amin—someone I know Hezbollah has used in the past for assassinations—attended an *Asaib al Haq* meeting in Damascus. It was a send off celebration for a team of agents leaving for Mexico."

"Was Al-Amin giving them a pep talk before they left?"

"Not exactly. Talib said Ahmed Al-Amin was going to Mexico with this group, but he wasn't going to be setting up cells in the States or waiting for orders, because he already had his orders. Do you want to venture a guess as to why Ahmed was coming to the States?"

"To kill me?"

Wassermann seemed surprised. "You already know this?"

"I was given some raw data on someone named Ahmed, but that was all, and it hasn't been verified yet. Was I mentioned by name?"

"No, and I didn't know it was you until much later. Talib just heard VEVAK had been hunting an American spy who had escaped from Iran, and he said they had hired Ahmed to kill him."

"So how did you find out the American spy was me?"

Wassermann took a deep breath and pushed himself away from the table. He stared at me for a second.

I knew that look. He was about to step off into some deep water, and he was giving himself a moment to turn around and walk away.

He decided to take the plunge.

"Years ago, you held my career in your hands, and to this day I'm not sure why you chose to feed Carlton the lies we told him about how that Russian got killed in Mexico. However, what I'm about to tell you today will mean you have control over my career once again, because I'm going to give you the means to destroy it, if you choose to do so."

I shook my head at him. "I've never regretted saving your career, Simon."

He looked at me without saying a word.

I decided to push him. "So tell me how you knew Ahmed was coming to the States to hunt me down."

He shifted nervously in his seat. Finally, he blurted out, "Because my controller in Mossad told me."

I'm pretty adept at managing my facial expressions, so I suppressed my shock at his admission. While I'd been certain Wassermann had a back channel into the Israeli spy organization, it never occurred to me he was a full-fledged Mossad operative. If he was discovered working for Mossad while also working for the CIA, he would be arrested for treason. My knowledge of his activities could make me guilty as well.

I must not have suppressed my feelings all that well, because he took one look at my face and hurriedly assured me, "I've never passed them any classified information, Titus."

"Let's not go into what you've done or not done for Mossad, Simon," I said, while trying to keep the anger out of my voice. "Just tell me what you know about Ahmed."

"I gave my controller in Mossad the information I'd obtained from Talib about the American spy, and that's when they let me know you were the operative VEVAK had targeted. My controller told me your Iranian network had been busted, and Mossad agents had saved your life. He also said Mossad had recently given the Agency some intercepts indicating Hezbollah was coming after you in the States, but they didn't specifically know which Hezbollah agent VEVAK had sent."

"So I'm guessing Mossad told you not to tell the Agency you knew the identity of the American spy because they knew such information would have revealed your relationship to them."

"Yes, but I'd already made up my mind I was going to contact you, whether Mossad approved or not."

The pace of Wassermann's narrative picked up now that his secret was out. "I also felt I owed it to you to find out as much as I could about Ahmed, so I asked Talib to make some inquiries about him. I told him to find out where Ahmed might be staying in the States, what name he was using—in other words, all the details Talib could discover that might be useful to you."

"That was pretty dangerous for him, Simon."

He sounded defensive. "I knew that, but I warned him several times to be careful. However, after I gave him the assignment, several days went by, and I didn't hear from him. Naturally, I got worried, so I made contact with Rasha. She was frightened and refused to have anything to do with me. I realized she knew something about Talib, so I bribed her to tell me what happened to him and promised I would never contact her again. That's when she said the head of *Asaib al Haq* had executed Talib—shot him in the head—after accusing him of being an Israeli spy."

Wassermann was suddenly quiet, staring down at his plate for several seconds.

The images of my own dead assets suddenly flashed in front of me. "I'm sorry, Simon. I know how that feels."

He didn't respond.

Trying to change the subject, I asked him, "So you decided to get out?"

He looked up at me and nodded. "There was nothing else I could do. Plus, I wanted you to have this information as soon as possible. I contacted Carlton and told him my main asset had been killed. We both agreed my mission had been compromised, so I flew to London within a few hours of talking to Rasha."

Wassermann got up and paced around the room. "I'm sorry I can't give you any more details about Ahmed. I'm positive he's in the States right now."

"Chatter out of NSA confirms that."

He walked back over to the table and sat down. After a few seconds, he picked up his fork and started mindlessly pushing the remaining scraps of food around on his plate.

While I knew he must have been waiting for me to condemn him for his treasonous revelation, I was still processing how I was going to deal with it.

A strained silence lingered between us for a few moments.

Finally, I made a decision.

"Don't worry, Simon, your career choices are your own. I won't be the one to judge you."

As soon as the words were out of my mouth, a loud crash of thunder shook the hotel.

Both of us jumped.

The moment I started laughing, Wassermann joined me, and the tension between us quickly disappeared.

"There's a big thunderstorm coming," I said, pointing at my iPhone on the table between us, "but my weather app says no tornadoes are in the forecast."

"Is that why you've been looking at your phone? Are you afraid of storms now?"

"Nothing bothers me about storms," I reassured both of us.

♦♦♦♦

Wassermann said he was still hungry, so I urged him to finish what was left of my dinner, while I gave him the specifics of what had happened to me in Tehran. I also explained why the DDO had put me on a year's medical leave.

He shook his head. "I would give a year's salary to see the video of your debrief." Then, he turned serious. "I don't believe there's much chance of Ahmed finding you in Oklahoma, but don't let your guard down."

"Why do you think I had you meet me here?"

"You did the right thing."

"Yeah, but I'm not used to hiding out from the hunter; I'm used to being the hunter."

He grinned. "When I get back to Langley, I'll try and spin a story about Ahmed Al-Amin to Carlton. Maybe he'll let me go after him for you."

"You don't owe me anything, Simon."

He ignored me and grabbed the room service menu. "Let's have some dessert."

Wasserman decided he wanted some chocolate cake, and he insisted I pick out a dessert too, even though I said I was leaving soon.

After calling room service, he asked, "Hey, don't I still owe you some money on that bet we made?"

"Yeah, pay up."

He grinned. "Well, I'm a bit short of funds right now, but give me your address in Norman, and I'll send you a check."

After giving him one of my cards, he told me his plans were to spend a couple of nights in Dallas before flying to Langley for his debrief with Carlton on Monday morning. Since I knew how vulnerable he felt without a weapon, I put on my jacket and ball cap and went out to my car to grab my extra Sig for him.

As I walked out of the hotel, I checked for any changes in the scenery.

A few cars were gone from the parking lot. At this late hour, those were probably bar patrons or hotel staff. One car had arrived and was parked a few spaces beyond mine. It looked like a rental car, so I figured it belonged to Wassermann. There was also a dark-colored Dodge van parked on the far side of the parking lot away from the other vehicles. I knew I hadn't seen it before. However, no one appeared to be inside, so I dismissed it.

When I thought about it later, though, I realized the van's windows were heavily tinted, and I shouldn't have assumed it was unoccupied.

Inside the Range Rover, I inserted my extra handgun in my waistband and covered it with my jacket. The rain arrived the second I slammed the car door.

I made a mad dash for the lobby, darting inside just as it started to pour.

When I laid the gun in front of Wassermann, he was already halfway through his chocolate cake. "Are you driving the black Toyota parked in the second row?"

"Yeah. Everything look okay?"

"I think so. Did you detect surveillance on any of your flights?"

"From Damascus to London, I knew I had a watcher, but I lost him at Heathrow. From London to New York I spotted two Arabs traveling separately, but they had lots of eye contact, so I made sure I lost them before I caught the plane to Chicago."

"And from Chicago to Dallas?"

"There was one Arab couple, but they had some kids with them. Of course, about half the passengers were Hispanic looking, and, with what Hezbollah's doing in Mexico . . . well, I was concerned, but, yeah, I'm sure I came in clean. Of course, once I got to the airport and rented the car, I made several circuits around the area before coming here to the hotel."

"I think we're good then. I'm headed back to Norman now."

He lifted the aluminum warmer from the plate next to him. "At least eat the apple pie I ordered for you."

The vanilla ice cream was just beginning to melt, so I sat down and started devouring it while Simon checked out the gun I'd given him.

"Thanks for this," he said, slapping me on the shoulder as he got up from the table, "and thanks for being so understanding about . . . ah . . . the other."

"And thank *you* for coming halfway around the world to give me this information," I replied.

"Enough happy talk. I'm going out to the car to get my duffel bag, and then I'm taking a long, hot shower. I know I must smell awful."

"It's pouring rain. Wear my jacket or you'll get soaked."

"What's up with you and the weather reports all the time?" he asked, but he put on my jacket, slipped my spare gun inside his pocket and grabbed my OU ball cap, checking out the hallway before closing the door behind him.

That was the last time I saw Wassermann alive.

CHAPTER 18

I finished my apple pie, loaded my computer back in my duffel bag, and waited for Wassermann to return.

The storm had intensified with lots of lightning and earsplitting thunder. Whether it was the storm or Wassermann's absence, I began to grow increasingly anxious. However, out of sheer habit, I spent the next five minutes wiping down the room for fingerprints.

Then, as all the instinctive synapses in my brain began firing at the same time, I grabbed my duffel bag and quickly left the room.

In order to avoid the lobby, I ran down the back stairs and exited out a side door behind the hotel. At that point, I took out my gun and made my way to the parking lot in the blinding rain.

The first thing I noticed, as I remained crouched behind a trash barrel on the west side of the hotel, was the absence of the Dodge van.

Then, I focused on Wassermann's car and saw he wasn't anywhere near it. Finally, my eyes spotted a crumpled heap, about the dimensions of a fallen man, positioned twenty feet away from my Range Rover.

I cautiously made my way over to the spot and found Simon Wasserman on his back with a gunshot wound in the center of his forehead. Raindrops were pelting his lifeless eyes, and the blood pouring from his body was merging with the dirt and grime on the concrete surface and flowing rapidly down the street.

I checked for signs of life.

I found none.

He'd never even had a chance to draw the gun I'd given him.

The killing shot had probably come from a high-powered rifle some distance away, say from a Dodge van on the far side of the parking lot.

As my emotions started to get the best of me, I grabbed his shoulders, leaned into his face, and said, "Goodbye friend, your debt's been paid."

My training kicked in, and I quickly removed my jacket, ball cap, and gun from his body, throwing them into the duffel bag. At the last second, I remembered the business card I'd given him, and I also lifted it from his pants pocket.

After I got inside my Range Rover, I scanned the area one more time. However, I was sure the killer had left as soon as he'd made the shot.

The downpour continued as I drove out of the parking lot.

Once I made my way back to I-35, I pulled into a Love's Truck Stop and parked where I was completely hidden by some eighteen-wheelers. I sat there for several minutes until I could feel my heartbeat slow to a normal rhythm. Then, I laid my head back on the headrest and let my emotions roam free. Finally, I reached underneath the passenger seat for my Agency satphone and contacted Carlton.

♦♦♦♦

I woke him up.

He mumbled, "Where are you? What's that noise?"

"I'm in my car outside of Dallas, Texas and it's pouring down rain."

"Talk."

"First, you need to call the FBI in Dallas and have them secure a murder scene in the parking lot of the Airport Hilton in Grapevine, Texas. Simon Wassermann is dead."

When I spoke those words, Carlton made a hissing sound as if he were sucking extra air into his lungs.

I continued, "Next, have the local and state police be on the lookout for a late model Dodge van, dark blue, with heavily tinted windows."

"License plate number?"

"I have no idea. The passenger will be of Arabic descent, but possibly passing himself off as Hispanic."

"Anything else?"

"Whatever happens, don't let the press get wind of the murder and release a photo of Wassermann."

"Are you hot now?"

"Negative. I'm heading back up I-35 to Norman."

"I'll call you back."

He hung up.

Once again, I was grateful Carlton was my handler. I understood how desperately he wanted to know what was going on, but instead, he trusted his agent's on-site analysis and simply responded by doing his own job, keeping his questions and judgments until a more appropriate time.

I pulled out of the truck stop and onto the expressway. As I drove north, I began asking myself what just happened and why my friend was dead.

If Wassermann had been followed from the airport and was the intended target of the Dodge van killer, then why wasn't he taken out before reaching the hotel? Why would someone wait and risk a shot in front of a hotel when the hit could have been done in a less conspicuous environment?

I thought back to Wassermann's statements about being certain he had a tail on the flight from Damascus to London. If someone had wanted to kill him, why didn't they do it before Wassermann left Syria? Why would an assassin follow him halfway around the world to take him out?

Wassermann's death made no sense if he was the intended target.

On the other hand, it made perfect sense if I was the assassin's mark.

Since Hezbollah was sophisticated enough to be dropping sleeper cells into the United States, they probably had the means to draw some analysis threads between Wassermann and me. When Wassermann and I had posed as the Figueroa brothers, we had operated out of Syria, and it wouldn't have been hard for Iran or Hezbollah to draw a connection between the two of us.

Then again, maybe Hezbollah knew Wassermann was running Talib and had set the whole thing up, hoping he would lead Ahmed straight to me. Perhaps that was why Ahmed was in Damascus in the first place.

At the hotel, when Wassermann was telling me about all the great intel he was getting from Talib, a yellow caution light had been going off in my head. The whole scenario had sounded a little too convenient for my taste. Even now, Talib was probably alive and living the good life in Syria, having betrayed Wasserman, while enabling a surveillance team to follow him to my doorstep.

On Wassermann's trip back to the States and on to Dallas, Hezbollah could have set up a "leapfrog" type of surveillance with one operative tailing him on one leg of the journey, then handing him off to another agent for the next leg and continuing on like that all the way to Dallas.

If that's the way it went down, then the operative tailing Wassermann on the flight into Dallas must have transmitted his flight information to Ahmed before leaving Chicago. Ahmed would have had a two-hour window to position himself at the airport and tail Wassermann to the hotel. Although Wassermann had sworn he was clean, his fatigue could have made him careless.

I thought back to when I'd first spotted the van in the hotel's parking lot. It wasn't raining then, so the light from the hotel's security poles would have been bright enough for Ahmed to identify me, even though I'd been wearing the ball cap.

At that point, I was an easy target.

Why hadn't he made the kill shot then?

Perhaps the shooter wasn't ready yet. Maybe the rifle's scope hadn't been attached, or he hadn't done the necessary surveillance. Thirty minutes later, when Wassermann had appeared wearing my jacket and cap, the assassin had taken the shot, and Wassermann had gone down, sacrificing his own life for mine.

This scenario all made sense to me, but as so often happened, Carlton might read the tea leaves differently.

♦♦♦♦

I don't remember much of the trip back to Norman, except when I reached Denton, Texas, about an hour from the Oklahoma border, I saw the sun coming up over the horizon. At that point, I realized the rain had stopped and my windshield wipers were squeaking like crazy.

By the time I pulled into my driveway, the sun was fully up.

I paused for a few seconds before going inside the house and thanked God I was still around to enjoy the early spring morning.

The moment I entered the house, Stormy greeted me enthusiastically, but then, after sniffing at my clothes, he sulked around, refusing to let me out of his sight.

Was it possible he could sense my loss? Could he know my heavy heart?

After I got out of my wet clothes, I took a hot shower and cooked myself a huge breakfast. When I was on my second cup of coffee, my Agency satphone rang.

Carlton sounded awake and in full operational mode now. "What's your status?"

"Home in Norman safe and sound."

"The FBI is handling everything at the hotel in Dallas. They've cited national security interests and cut out the local authorities. Nothing definitive has turned up on the van yet, but the police have been alerted. Simon's body is being flown to Andrews, and the Agency will handle the arrangements with his family."

"I think Simon's been married a couple of times, but he doesn't have any kids. I believe his parents live on Long Island. He has a sister in San Diego and a brother in Detroit. You could find their phone numbers in his files. Oh, and I also think there's a sister in Chicago."

Sounding concerned, he asked, "Are you okay?"

I suddenly realized I'd been babbling.

"Simon took that hit for me. I'm trying to deal with it, that's all."

"You don't know for certain that's what happened. We'll do a complete analysis when we get there."

"You're coming here? I thought I'd have to—"

"Katherine and I are on an afternoon flight to Oklahoma City," Carlton said, cutting me off.. "It arrives at 4:07. American Airlines. Meet us curbside."

I didn't protest.

CHAPTER 19

After sleeping soundly for almost five hours, I got up, ate a sandwich and decided to check out Ortega's guest rooms.

I wanted to be prepared in case Carlton decided to accept an invitation to stay with me—Katherine too, of course.

Before receiving Carlton's phone call earlier, I had anticipated being ordered back to Langley. There, in a conference room at Headquarters, I would have been required to give Carlton and a couple of analysts an "incident" debrief.

Intelligence officers sometimes called these sessions "mini-debriefings," but to me they bore little resemblance to a debriefing, mini or otherwise.

Basically, an incident debrief was a recorded accounting of a clandestine officer's involvement in a non-operational event. If the event required the intervention of local law enforcement, then the questioning of the officer might become pretty intense.

There was only one reason Carlton had gone to the trouble of convincing the DDO he needed to come to me instead of vice versa—he continued to be worried about my security. He thought I was still a target, and he believed Norman was a safer place for me than the D. C. area.

I was hoping he was right, but now, I had my doubts.

♦♦♦♦

While driving to the airport, I got a call from Carlton saying their plane had landed early. By the time I arrived, he and Katherine were standing on the curb outside the American Airlines terminal.

I was happy to see both of them.

Despite having been awakened by me in the middle of the night, managing my crisis since dawn, and traveling for almost three hours, Carlton looked well rested. Unlike most people, travel seemed to energize him. He wore a pair of light-colored slacks with a dark navy blazer over a crisp white shirt. However, since it was Saturday, he wasn't wearing a tie.

Katherine, on the other hand, was dressed very casually in a pair of jeans, a light green silky blouse, and black boots. Her sunglasses were perched on top of her head, and the Oklahoma wind was blowing her hair in every direction.

She looked quite beautiful.

Carlton urged Katherine to ride in the front seat with me, and, except for this brief exchange, he remained silent as we drove the short distance back to Norman.

However, Carlton's reticence was not a surprise to me because I knew his preference was to hear the details of any crisis in a prescribed and orderly fashion and not in a conversational back and forth.

As we pulled up to Ortega's house, Katherine said, "This is a gorgeous place."

Carlton murmured, "Nice," from the backseat.

We all got out of the car, and, at that moment, Stormy come bounding out from behind the garage.

He headed straight for Carlton, dirty paws and all.

I shouted his name once, and, whether it was my urgent tone or Carlton's scowl, he immediately whirled around and ran toward me, obediently plopping himself down beside my feet.

I was as surprised by his behavior as anyone.

"What a cute dog," Katherine said, leaning over and rubbing Stormy's head. "Did he come with the property?"

"No, he just showed up one day."

Carlton nodded approvingly. "Well trained animal."

Katherine wanted a tour of the house, and, although I knew I must have sounded like a real estate agent showing her around, she laughed at my commentary. For a few short minutes, I forgot all about Wassermann and the real purpose of her visit.

However, I was brought back to reality when we returned to the living area and saw Carlton standing at the dining room table adjusting a video camera. It was aimed at the head of the table.

He looked up as we entered the room. "Let's get started, shall we?"

♦♦♦♦

When I sat down, Carlton said quietly, "Begin by telling us what you and Simon Wassermann were doing at the Airport Hilton last night."

Around the Agency, Carlton had a reputation for controlling his emotions and maintaining his composure, even in the most stressful of circumstances. After years of working with him, though, I had no doubt he was seething with anger and frustration, not only at me, but also at Wassermann.

Although he might not show his feelings outwardly, I knew there were numerous ways he could demonstrate his displeasure with me—from assigning me a boring, tedious mission to partnering me up with a less-than-desirable operative.

For that reason, and because I desperately wanted to capture Wassermann's killer, I decided to tell him the whole truth.

Beginning with the first email I'd received from Wassermann, to the phone call I'd made at Love's Truck Stop, I told him everything—every last detail about what had been done and said, both by me and by Wassermann, in the last twenty-four hours.

While I was relating all this, Katherine was busy at her computer, communicating with her office back at Langley and building a timeline of Wassermann's last hours.

When I finished my meticulous account, Carlton was the first to speak.

"I should have suspected something was going on when Simon asked me if you were on an assignment. I was the one who told him about your medical leave."

Strangely enough, I felt our situations were suddenly reversed, and I found myself taking on the handler's role of offering support to Carlton. "There was nothing suspicious about that question, Douglas. You knew we were friends."

"He was a double agent. There's no other way to look at it. I badly misjudged him."

"Simon was—"

"We've got the video from the hotel parking lot." Katherine announced, turning her computer around so we could all see it.

As I'd been relating my story, Katherine had been entering an approximate time when each of the events at the hotel had unfolded. Her timeline now appeared on the left side of her computer screen, while the grainy black and white videos from two CCTV cameras in the hotel's parking lot were being displayed on the right.

Supporting my hypothesis of how the murder had gone down, the dark blue van had pulled into a parking space just moments before I'd come out of the hotel to retrieve my extra gun for Wassermann. Eighteen minutes later, in the midst of a downpour, Wassermann was seen coming out of the hotel wearing the same jacket and cap that I'd been wearing just minutes before. It would have been easy for anyone to make the assumption the figure running through the rain was me.

As we watched the rest of the video, knowing we were about to see Wassermann shot, I felt the tension in the room rise. The poor video quality made it less difficult that I'd anticipated, though, and, when it actually happened, it appeared as if Wassermann had simply crumpled to the ground.

The video taken from the outside portico of the hotel showed the van leaving the parking lot within two minutes of Wassermann's being hit. The van turned east on a feeder road and quickly disappeared from view.

After the video had ended, Carlton excused himself to make a phone call, while Katherine carried on an extended conversation with one of her analysts back at Langley. I retrieved a bottle of water from the refrigerator and sat back down at the dining room table, plotting how I might go about finding Simon Wassermann's killer and—the most difficult task of all—convincing Carlton to authorize it.

When Carlton returned, Katherine said, "They found the van abandoned in Waco. It's registered to a Venezuelan student at the University of Texas in Austin."

"Stolen?" Carlton asked.

"They're not sure. It hasn't been reported stolen, but neither have they been able to locate the owner."

I shook my head. "It wasn't a Venezuelan student who shot Simon. It was Ahmed."

"They're enhancing the video from the hotel parking lot, so maybe we'll get a look inside the van," Katherine said. "I'm not very hopeful, though, not with those weather conditions and the poor lighting."

"He's probably headed back to Mexico," I said.

"My people are working with NSA to identify any overseas communication coming out of Texas," Katherine said. "If Ahmed really thinks he killed you, he'll be letting Tehran know. We're sure of that."

"Do we have any information on those Hezbollah cells already set up here in the States?" I asked Carlton. "They could be helping Ahmed escape the country right now. Danny Jarrar is working with the Feds on this. He told me they were—"

Carlton quickly cut me off. "We don't know for certain it was Ahmed who shot Simon."

"I'm positive it was."

He gave me a long look. "Okay, I'll give Danny Jarrar a call, but we have to let Homeland Security handle this, Titus."

However, he turned to Katherine and said, "Do a complete workup on Ahmed Al-Amin—biography, photos, locations, associates, anything you can find."

While Katherine talked to Langley, Carlton began to break down the video equipment he'd used to record my account of Wassermann's murder.

I asked him, "Could I fix you a cup of coffee? Something to eat?"

"Nothing for me. We're heading back to Langley," he looked at his watch, "in about two hours."

"You're not staying over?"

"We need to get back. I have a meeting scheduled with Deputy Ira, plus Katherine needs to coordinate with her team."

While Carlton was reloading his video case, making sure everything fit together perfectly, I paced around the room, trying to decide how to approach him about what I wanted.

Finally, I gave up figuring out how to be subtle and just blurted it out. "I need to be in on this."

Carlton stopped what he was doing. "You know that's not possible."

"If it's because of Simon's relationship to Mossad, I had no idea he—"

"That's not it and you know it." He took me by the arm and steered me away from Katherine. "The FBI and Homeland Security will be handling this, Titus. And besides, Deputy Ira would never allow you to become involved. You're on medical leave, remember?"

"What if Ahmed makes it out of the country? He's killed an American intelligence officer on American soil. Surely, the Agency will be authorized to go after him, bring him to justice, send him to Gitmo, put him on trial, one of the above, something."

"We'll cross that bridge when we come to it. I still need verification it was Ahmed who killed Wassermann."

"At least consider me for the mission if it gets authorized."

He looked up at the ceiling for a few seconds. "If we get the go ahead to go after him . . . I might consider thinking about it."

At least he didn't nix the idea entirely.

♦♦♦♦

After Carlton stepped into the living room to call Danny Jarrar, I asked Katherine if I could fix her a sandwich or bring her a cup of coffee. She agreed to both.

When I set the plate in front of her, I said, "I hope you like meatloaf sandwiches."

She looked surprised. "Is this homemade meatloaf? Did you make this yourself?"

I laughed at the look on her face. "You didn't know I could cook? What kind of analyst are you?"

She smiled as she carefully cut the sandwich into quarters. "Look, Titus, I wanted to explain why I never called you back a few weeks ago."

I assured her, "It wasn't a big deal."

After she took a delicate bite from one of the quarters, she wiped her mouth with her napkin and said, "I thought about calling you back, but I'm seeing someone, and I think it's pretty serious."

"I completely understand."

She nodded. "Good."

"Is he someone I know? Someone at the Agency? Another intelligence officer?"

I suddenly realized I was asking way too many questions.

"Are you kidding? No."

She seemed genuinely shocked at my implication she was dating someone from work.

"Forgive me for asking," I said, "but why is dating someone from the Agency so surprising?"

"Because it's impossible to sustain a relationship with schedules like ours. Look at me. It's Saturday afternoon, and I'm sitting here in Oklahoma analyzing data when I should be on a golf date back in Virginia right now. I can't have a relationship with someone who works a schedule like mine. We'd never see each other. It's hard enough as it is."

"No, you're right. It wouldn't work."

We sat there in silence for a few moments.

Obviously trying to change the subject, she said, "I noticed you're not using your cane anymore. Is your leg better?"

"Much better."

She pushed her plate aside and leaned across the table toward me. "I know with all that's happened to you, it may seem strange to say this, but you seem better too."

"Really? In what way?"

"I don't know exactly," she said, pausing to consider my question.

"Are you happier? More at peace maybe?"

In response to her question, I decided to take the opportunity to tell her about my experience of faith in Tehran. As I did so, she listened with an intensity I found a little disconcerting. However, the more I talked, the more I became convinced she was drawn to what I was saying.

When I finished, she replied, "I've tried to read the Bible before, but it's never made any sense to me."

"I used to feel that way too. Now, though, there are moments when the words seem to reach up and grab me."

She looked thoughtful, as if she were analyzing some critical data. "Perhaps you need to have this experience of faith before you can really understand the words."

♦♦♦♦

Carlton returned to the dining room. "Katherine, please excuse us. Titus and I need to talk." He turned to me and gestured down the hallway. "Shall we go out to your sunroom?"

Since the sunroom was located away from the main part of the house, I couldn't imagine how he knew Ortega's place had a sunroom. However, when he went down the hall ahead of me, I decided Legends must have supplied him with the floor plans to the house—one of those details he was so fond of having.

As soon as we entered the room, he asked, "Is that your old telescope?"

"Yeah. I got it out of storage."

"That's good. " He sat down in a white wicker chair and looked around. "This is all working for you, isn't it?"

"I'm adjusting."

"Are you meeting people? Danny told me you were attending church. Is that right?"

I gave him my schedule for the past three weeks, and while I was telling him about working with the ESL class at the church, I was debating with myself whether I should mention my concerns about Paul Franklin or not. I kept going back and forth because I had so few details about what Franklin was doing, and it occurred to me I might be making way too much of the bitterness and ravings of an old man.

In the end, he made the decision for me.

"And what about Paul Franklin? Have you met him yet?"

"Unfortunately, yes."

"You didn't get along?"

"It was more than that. The book we're supposed to be writing together is a piece of anti-Semitic garbage. He believes all Jews should be kicked out of Israel, and if they get annihilated when they're leaving, all the better."

"I had no idea. How could I have missed that?"

He looked genuinely perplexed, and, for some strange reason, I felt a small measure of pleasure in knowing something he didn't know.

"I'm certain Franklin's views weren't examined when Legends set me up with him at CIS, and who knows if anyone at the think tank really investigated him. I mean, why should they? He's been a member of the diplomatic corps."

"In what capacity?"

"He was the cultural affairs officer at our embassy in Beirut in 1980. He was there during the Sabra massacre, and his wife happened to be in the refugee camp that day. She was murdered along with the Palestinians."

Carlton nodded his head several times as if remembering the circumstances. "So he blames the Jews for his wife's death?"

"Yes, and I believe the Arabic students on campus aren't shy about knocking on his door. He's definitely not hiding his affinity for Islam either."

Carlton remained thoughtful for several seconds, and then he shook his head. "I don't like this. Why didn't you tell me sooner?"

"I've looked at Franklin from several different angles, and I can't see how he could be an actual threat to me. He thinks I was a researcher at CIS before I was promoted to Senior Fellow. He treats me as inconsequential. My cover is good with him."

"I'm going to have Katherine run some background on him, see who he's been emailing, what political blogs he's been reading, that sort of thing."

He got up from the chair and walked over to the windows. He appeared to be taking a closer look at the lake, but I knew his restlessness was simply an indicator he was assessing all the dots and trying to connect them.

"You need to be extremely careful, Titus. Ahmed is still out there."

"He thinks he killed me."

"If that's true, let's hope nothing happens to change his mind."

PART THREE

CHAPTER 20

As I drove to the ESL class on Tuesday morning, I continued to monitor my environment for any kind of surveillance. Earlier in the day, Carlton had informed me there was no indication Ahmed had contacted his home base in Iran and reported the assassination of the American spy. He also said the FBI could find no trace of Ahmed or the Venezuelan student who owned the van.

I figured Ahmed had gone to ground and hadn't left the States yet. That alone was enough to keep me alert.

When I pulled into the church's parking lot, I surveyed the area for any suspicious vehicles. Although there were a few I'd never seen before, most of the cars looked familiar to me. However, I did take note of a late model black Nissan sedan parked at the far end of the lot close to the church's back entrance. It drew my attention because most vehicles in the parking lot were located closer to the church's front entrance. However, the windows of the Nissan weren't tinted, and I could see there was no one inside.

When I arrived in the ESL classroom, Susan stopped me just as I was about to go into the break room to make coffee. "Would you mind leading the conversation portion during the second session?" she asked. "Patty has a dental appointment and won't be here today."

"Uh . . . I'm not sure I'm qualified to do that."

She laughed at my hesitancy. "Of course you are. I've seen you in the small groups, and you're an excellent facilitator. Just pick out some discussion topics from this booklet and moderate the group as they try to talk with each other."

I had watched Patty conduct the discussion exercise before, and I couldn't recall her doing much more than giving an occasional grammar correction, so I took the booklet Susan offered me. While Tucker led the group in repeating the alphabet, I sat down at a desk in a corner of the room and picked out the topics I wanted to use.

When Tucker turned the class over to Susan a few minutes later, I glanced up and noticed Farah Karimi was absent from the group. Although she was usually late to class, I'd never known her to miss any of the sessions.

However, I forgot all about Farah when I suddenly realized the next break was scheduled in less than fifteen minutes, and I'd been so intent on studying the discussion booklet, I hadn't made coffee for the students. I rushed over to the break room and started filling the large coffee urn with water. When I opened a drawer and saw there weren't any more coffee packets, I stopped by the classroom and told Susan I was going downstairs to get some more coffee from the church's kitchen.

Instead of taking the slow elevator, though, I tried to save time by using the back stairs at the far end of the hallway,

That's when I discovered Farah Karimi.

She was lying in a pool of blood on the tiled floor of the stairs' half landing.

Instinctively, I drew my gun and cautiously descended the steps.

The stairwell consisted of two sets of stairs joined at a landing. Farah had ascended the first set of stairs, and then, evidently, she had turned at the landing to ascend the second set of stairs.

However, she'd never made it past the first step.

As I moved toward the landing, I looked over the railing to see if the area was clear.

It was.

Her assailant was gone.

I hurried to her side and checked for a pulse.

She had none.

Her head lay on the floor at an odd angle, and when I examined it, I realized her throat had been slashed. All the blood around her was from a knife wound, not a gunshot wound as I'd initially thought when I'd first seen her from the top of the stairs.

I had to make a quick decision.

Should I leave the scene and try to find the killer? Should I call 911 and wait for the police to arrive?

What would Titus Ray, Senior Fellow at a prestigious think tank, most likely do?

I called 911.

However, I also skirted around Farah's body, descended the steps to the first floor, and carefully opened the door to the hallway.

It was empty.

A door to my left led outside. A door to my right led to the kitchen.

I went through the door to my left and surveyed the parking lot. Twenty to thirty cars were parked in the lot, and I could see no movement in any of them, nor were there any cars leaving the area. The scene looked exactly the way I'd seen it earlier that morning.

I turned to go back inside.

Then, I remembered the Nissan.

I looked again.

It was gone.

I hurried back up the stairs to the second floor, trying to maintain my focus as I passed Farah's body once again. When I entered the hallway leading to the ESL classroom, I holstered my gun. Just before opening the door, I breathed a quick prayer.

The students were still seated, and Susan was pointing to a poster depicting a produce arrangement at a grocery store and asking her pupils to name the different vegetables. Tucker was standing off to the side watching them.

I motioned to Tucker, and he walked over to me as I stood beside the door. By this time, I could hear police sirens faintly in the distance.

"Tucker," I whispered, "Farah's had a horrible accident on the back stairwell. I've called 911, so the police and an ambulance will be here any minute. You need to keep everyone inside. I'm going downstairs to show the police where she's located."

His face registered shock. "Oh, no, no, no," he said, "I can't believe it." He looked around frantically, as if he should be doing something.

I was afraid he might be getting hysterical.

"I have to go now."

"Sure, sure," he replied, still sounding anxious. "I'll take care of things here."

♦♦♦♦

The Norman Police Department sent three squad cars.

After showing them where I'd found Farah, an officer named Freeman explained that, since I had been the first person to discover Farah's body, departmental regulations required him to keep me isolated until their investigator arrived.

"Sure, I understand," I responded, wondering if regulations also required Officer Freeman to check me for a weapon.

That would be awkward.

"This may take awhile," he said. "A city councilman and his wife were murdered last night, and most of our detectives are tied up on the west side of town right now."

I assured him I didn't mind waiting.

After he put me in a church staff member's office, he asked me not to use my cell phone or leave the room. To help me remember these "requests," he stationed another officer outside the door.

However, he did not check me for a weapon.

As soon as the police officer shut the door, I paced the small office and mentally processed the murder scene.

The moment I'd seen Farah's body on the stairs, I'd experienced a flashback to Wassermann's murder on Friday night and thought Ahmed had shot her as well. Now, even though I knew her throat had been slashed, I still questioned whether Ahmed could be the person responsible for her death.

However, what possible motive could he have for killing her?

Perhaps he was on his way up to the second floor to find me, and she had interrupted him. If that was the case, why did he leave after murdering her? Why not continue on up to the second floor and finish me off?

I considered the scene on the stairwell and the state in which I'd found Farah's body. There were no signs of a struggle. The murderer had simply slashed her throat.

In fact, it looked very much like a combat kill, similar to what I'd seen many times before in Afghanistan. I had no doubt Ahmed was capable of such an act. On the other hand, if Farah's husband, Bashir, was a trained military officer, he was probably as skilled with a knife as he was with a gun.

Did Bashir have something to do with his wife's death?

I remembered the dinner on Friday night and Bashir's strange behavior. It was obvious the guy had some secrets, but I found it hard to believe Bashir had killed his own wife. However, I knew the police would consider him the most likely suspect.

However, Bashir might not be their only suspect, because it suddenly occurred to me that my situation looked precarious as well.

Not only had I called in Farah's murder, but when I'd examined her neck wound, I had also deposited my DNA on her body. This created the possibility the NPD would look at me as the prime suspect in her killing and not even consider her husband.

Although I knew I could contact Carlton if the police took their suspicions too far, I decided to see how things played out before I did that. My gut feeling was that Farah's death was not a random killing, but whether or not her murder had anything to do with me was something I needed to find out. To do so, I would have to find a way to get close to her murder investigation.

The moment I started entertaining some possibilities of how I might go about doing that, Officer Freeman opened the door and stepped inside.

"Mr. Ray, would you come with me, please?"

We took the elevator up to the second floor, and as we passed the ESL classroom, I glanced in.

Tucker was involved in an animated conversation with a police officer, while the students were sitting around in small groups. They looked disoriented. I could see Susan standing in a corner of the room all by herself. She was weeping.

"Would you mind stepping in here for just a moment, sir?"

The officer ushered me into another classroom two doors away from the ESL room, and then he keyed his shoulder mike and told someone I was in Room 223.

"Have a seat, sir. Detective Saxon will be right with you."

CHAPTER 21

A couple of minutes passed before Detective Saxon entered the room. When she did, she paused at the doorway, took out a small notebook, and made a quick notation.

The detective was wearing a long-sleeved, black and silver blouse over a pair of dark slacks. Her brownish-black hair was pulled away from her face and fastened at the nape of her neck. Her minimalist hairstyle accented her large, almond-shaped eyes and oval face. Big silver earrings dangled from her ears. Whenever she moved, they twirled around like a set of wind chimes.

"Mr. Ray, I'm Detective Nikki Saxon."

I stood up and extended my hand. "Please call me Titus."

She gave me a firm, quick handshake.

She wasn't wearing a wedding ring.

"Titus," she replied, while writing in her notebook, "I understand you were the person who called 911. Is that right?"

"Yes."

"And you discovered the body?"

"Yes."

"Please tell me exactly what happened and begin with what you were doing before you discovered . . ." she paused and looked at her notebook, "Farah Karimi. When you're finished, I'm going to take you down the hall so you can retrace your steps and show me exactly what you did after you discovered her body. Will that work?"

"I can do that."

I quickly explained my actions, beginning with when I left the classroom and ending with when I returned to the room and informed Tucker that I had called the police.

As I was relating my story, the detective leaned against the wall and took notes. Several times, I saw her bob her head up and down as if she were agreeing with my actions.

When I finished the account, she paced around the room for a few seconds, tapping her pen against her notebook. All the while, her earrings moved in a kind of hypnotic rhythm.

As I watched her circling the room, I wondered how much coffee she'd consumed that morning.

She suddenly turned toward me and asked, "Tucker Steward identified you as a volunteer in the English class. Is that correct?"

"Yes."

"How long have you been a volunteer?"

"I was starting my fourth week today."

She closed her notebook and asked, "Is there anything else you'd like to say?"

"No, I believe that's it."

She walked over to the door and spoke to one of the uniforms in the hallway.

When she returned, she said, "We need to wait here a few more minutes. The students are being released from the classroom now."

I responded, "This has been a difficult day for them." Then, I quickly added, "For me too."

"I'm sure it has."

The detective walked over to the windows and looked down on the parking lot, chewing on a fingernail as she observed the scene below. Her actions made me reconsider my original assessment about her coffee consumption.

Instead, I wondered if Detective Saxon was worried about something.

I guessed her age to be around thirty, so I suspected she hadn't worked many murder cases before. More than likely, all the seasoned detectives were involved in the big publicity-grabbing homicide Officer Freeman had mentioned.

Maybe inexperience was the reason for her apparent anxiety.

She turned away from the window, picked up her notebook and said, "I was going to do this later, but since we have to wait, why don't you go ahead and tell me something about yourself. Start with where you work."

"I'm employed by a think tank in College Park, Maryland called the Consortium for International Studies. It goes by the initials CIS."

"You're a long way from home, Titus."

"I've relocated to Norman temporarily so I can work on a book with Paul Franklin. He's employed at the University."

"Professor Franklin from International Studies?"

"Yes. You know him?"

"Only through reputation."

I was tempted to ask her to expand on that answer, but since she was doing the interrogating, I finished summarizing my bio and gave her my address.

"East Tecumseh Road," she said slowly, as if trying to remember something. "I don't recall any rental property out that way, and I'm sure there aren't any apartment buildings. Are you living with someone?"

"No, I live alone. I'm leasing the property from Phillip Ortega. He's in Spain on a sabbatical."

"Another OU professor."

"You also know him?"

She smiled for the first time. "I graduated from OU. I took some of his classes."

An officer motioned to her from the door, and she followed him out into the hallway, returning a few seconds later.

"Okay, Titus, I'm ready to go over your statement again. Let's walk down the hall to the ESL classroom now."

With the detective and another officer trailing me, I retraced my steps, beginning in the classroom and then proceeding to the stairwell. However, I stopped a few feet short of the stairwell door because officers had already strung yellow crime scene tape around the entrance

The detective lifted the tape, and we ducked underneath it. As I opened the door, I paused and explained how I'd stopped on the first step because I'd seen Farah's body on the landing.

Now, all I could see was a stark outline where Farah Karimi's body had fallen. Dried pools of blood remained behind. A crime tech was still processing the scene, and another police officer was standing on the descending steps watching him work.

The distinctive odor of death hovered over the close quarters.

"Describe what you saw."

"I saw lots of blood, and I could tell she wasn't moving."

"Did you hear any noises or unusual sounds before you opened the door?"

"No."

"Other than her body, did you notice anything after you opened the door?"

"No."

"What did you do after you saw her body?"

"I went down the stairs and checked for a pulse."

"Is that how you got that blood on your shoe?"

I looked down, and, for the first time, I saw a dark discoloration on the outside edge of my right shoe.

"Yes. I tried to be careful, but . . ."

"What did you do after you checked her pulse?"

"I called 911."

"And then?"

Should I tell her I went down the stairs and checked the parking lot to see if I could spot Farah's killer? Should I tell the detective about the Nissan? Would a scholarly fellow do that?

"I returned to the classroom and told Tucker about Farah."

"Fine. Let's go back down the hall. I have a few more questions for you."

When Detective Saxon and I got back to the classroom, she had me take a seat while she consulted her notes.

"I've just reread the statement Tucker Steward made to an officer," she said, looking down at her notebook. "Mr. Steward says when you returned to the classroom, you told him Farah Karimi had suffered an accident."

She raised her head and looked at me with an intensity that might unnerve a guilty man.

"Yes, I did say that."

"Why?"

"I was concerned about telling him she'd been murdered. Until the police arrived and told him something different, I thought it might be better just to say Farah was involved in a serious accident. I didn't want him to get hysterical."

"Is he ordinarily an emotional guy?"

"Excitable might be a better word."

"How did he react when you told him she had had an accident?"

"He was definitely anxious about it, and his reaction made me realize I'd made the right decision. People know accidents occur on a regular basis. Murder, on the other hand, is unexpected and has a tendency to shock the system."

As soon as the words came out of my mouth, I regretted them. However, I told myself a small city detective, with very little experience, probably wasn't going to notice my little slip.

"Have you had some experience to back up that statement, Titus?"

Maybe I'd underestimated her.

"I've watched a lot of crime dramas on television."

Once again, I regretted making a foolish statement. I doubted I could name even one television program devoted to crime and criminals. I hoped she wasn't about to ask me to elaborate on my answer.

I tried to analyze why a simple interrogation was tripping me up. I was a well-trained intelligence officer with years of experience, and I was used to being questioned under very stressful situations.

Perhaps that was the answer.

I was not in a stressful environment. I was in the heartland of America, sitting in a church with a worried young woman who was so beautiful she could have been on the cover of any fashion magazine.

"What made you so certain Farah Karimi had been murdered?"

I decided to add something extra to my scholarly legend and, along with that, throw in an attitude to get her attention.

"I was in the military before going to work for CIS. I've seen people with their throats cut before, Detective."

For a couple of seconds, Detective Saxon studied my face. Then, she lowered her head and wrote something in her notebook.

When she looked up again, she asked, "How well did you know Mrs. Karimi?"

"We spoke to each other several times in class. She was just learning English, so our conversations weren't very detailed or significant."

"Do you know . . ." she consulted her notebook again, "her husband, Bashir Karimi?"

"Yes, Bashir and I are actually good friends," I said, "and I have no idea how he's going to take this. He loved her very much."

"You're good friends with him?"

"Yes, Farah introduced us. When I shared my military experience in Iraq with him, we really hit it off."

"Do you know if they have any family in the area?"

"None that I'm aware of."

"That's unfortunate."

I asked, "Has he been contacted yet?"

"Officer Freeman called OU and discovered he was attending a class when his wife was killed, but, according to the professor, he left a few minutes before the class was over. When we're finished here, I'll be going over to his residence."

I slowly shook my head back and forth and tried to look very concerned. "As his best friend, I can tell you he'll take this very hard."

"Well, then," she said, closing her notebook, "would you mind following me over to his house while I break the news to him about his wife? This is a time he'll need his friends more than ever."

"I'd be happy to help you out, if that's what you want."

CHAPTER 22

As I followed the detective to a subdivision south of Norman called Eagle Cliff, I took the opportunity to call Danny Jarrar.

"Hi, Danny. It's Titus."

"What's up? Everything okay? "

"Everything's fine, but I need some information."

"Carlton told me about Simon Wassermann. I'm sorry, Titus. I know the two of you were good friends."

"I believe that bullet was intended for me."

"Carlton didn't sound as certain of that as you do."

"Well, you know how he operates—ever the cautious one."

"Anything new on the shooter?"

"Not yet. You haven't heard anything from your contacts, have you?"

"No. Is that why you called?"

"Not really. Tell me what you know about a detective named Nikki Saxon. She's with the Norman Police Department."

"Okaaaaay," he answered, stringing the word out to make it sound like I was asking about dating her. "Something going on I should know about?"

"I'm inquiring on a strictly professional basis."

"You're in trouble with the locals already?"

"Funny."

I told him about Farah Karimi's murder and the circumstances of my involvement.

Like me, Danny immediately considered the possibility Ahmed might be her killer. However, I also told him that Farah and her husband appeared to be keeping their Iranian nationality a secret. Then, I mentioned my suspicions about Bashir's military training and his denial of it.

"So, you think the husband killed her?"

"I did at first, but the police just told me he was in an OU classroom when it happened. However, I'm sure he'll be considered a person of interest, which is why I overstated my relationship with him to Detective Saxon. I'm following the detective over to his house right now so we can deliver the news of Farah's death to him in person. Do you know Detective Saxon?"

"Just barely. I met her at a seminar right after she made detective. We probably talked for about fifteen minutes then. Another time—maybe a year ago—she called me for some assistance with a drug-related case. That's it. I can't tell you very much about her, except that she's very attractive. You probably already noticed that, though."

"Hard to miss. How long do you think she's been a detective?"

"Probably three or four years."

"She seemed nervous when she arrived at the scene."

"Maybe it was her first time conducting an investigation without a partner. Most of their veteran officers are working a double homicide right now. The lady was pretty sharp when I talked to her. I'd be surprised if she wasn't extremely thorough."

"You're right. I slipped up, and she caught it immediately."

"Carlton won't think you're flying under the radar if the local police start probing into your background. Are you sure it's a good idea to get involved in this woman's murder?"

"I'm already involved, Danny, and, since her murder looks exactly like a combat kill, there's a possibility Ahmed is responsible. Naturally, if he killed her trying to get to me, I need to know that. In fact, if that's what happened, I'm going to feel responsible."

"While I agree the timing is suspicious because of Simon, I don't see why you would hold yourself responsible for her death."

I decided to tell him the truth. "Before her murder, I saw a car parked near the back entrance. It was out of place, and I'd never seen it before, but I didn't check it out. I would hate to think another person was murdered because of my negligence. "

"Did you give the police a description?"

"What could I tell them? I saw an unoccupied car when I arrived at the church, and it made me suspicious? That sounds crazy. And I can't tell them why I was surveying the cars in the parking lot without drawing attention to my real identity."

"The car was empty? Maybe whoever killed her was already there in the building."

"Yeah, maybe. She doesn't drive. Her husband always drops her off late. Somehow the killer must have known her schedule and waited for her inside the building."

"If you really want to help the police catch whoever did this, you may have to break your cover and tell them about the car. But I'm warning you, that won't play well with the Agency."

"Warning noted."

♦♦♦♦

Detective Saxon pulled her silver Toyota in the driveway of a mid-sized ranch house with a large oak tree in the front yard. As I pulled in directly behind her, I wondered how Bashir Karimi, an Iraqi engineering student, had the means to live in a neighborhood of redbrick homes and well-kept lawns. I'd pictured the couple living in a more modest house or an apartment closer to the campus.

The detective must have been thinking the same thing. As we walked up to the front door together, she said, "Your friend lives in a nice neighborhood."

"Yes, I've always loved their place."

The detective unclipped her badge from her waistband and held it in her hand as she rang the doorbell. As we waited, I noticed we were both looking around, observing the passing cars and other houses on the block. A minute went by with no answer, and she rang the bell again.

Another minute passed.

I suggested, "Maybe we should check the back."

"Wait here," she ordered and walked around the side of the house.

I gave her a few seconds and then followed her through the gate and into the back yard.

By the time I reached the rear of the house, she had already drawn her weapon and was entering the house through the back door.

I followed directly behind her.

She caught a glimpse of me out of the corner of her eye, but she didn't turn around. "I told you to remain at the front door," she said harshly.

Her body was taut, spring-loaded for whatever she might encounter in the house.

I drew my Sig, but kept it out of her sight. "Should you call for backup?"

She sounded impatient. "I just did, but I need to make sure Mr. Karimi isn't in here needing medical attention."

As she went from room to room, she called out, "Police. Mr. Karimi, are you here?"

When it was obvious no one was in the house, I holstered my weapon. Finally, she turned around and faced me, lowering her gun to her side.

"That wasn't very smart," she said sharply. "You should have stayed outside."

I ignored her reprimand. "Bashir seems to have left in a hurry."

We both surveyed the family room. There was a suitcase on the floor with several items of clothing spilling out of it, and a can of soda had been dropped on the carpet, but no one had bothered to clean it up.

The detective headed for the front door. "Let's go outside and wait for the other officers to arrive," she said. As she unlocked the front door, she said, "In fact, I believe you could leave now. I'll call you if I have any further questions."

While following her over to my Range Rover, I looked down the street and saw a black Nissan.

The car was exactly like the one I'd seen in the church parking lot earlier in the morning. It was slowly approaching Bashir's house from the west, about two blocks away.

"Detective Saxon, I'd like to show you a very important clue to Farah's murder," I said, opening the passenger's side door of my car and motioning her inside.

She hesitated.

The Nissan drew within a block of the house.

"What kind of clue? Could you wait for the other officers to—?"

"No, I couldn't."

I practically shoved her inside the Range Rover and ran around to the driver's side door, sliding in just as the Nissan cruised by.

I looked directly at her. "Don't show any interest in the car approaching Bashir's house. Just look at me as if I am the most interesting man on the planet."

She gave me her full attention. "Right now, you are definitely the most interesting man on the planet."

I started the car. "Okay, he's leaving the neighborhood. We're going to follow him."

"What? No."

"Put your seatbelt on."

"Mr. Ray. Titus, wait. You can't be serious." She sounded frantic. "I have two patrol cars on the way here. Why are you following that car?"

"Are you able to make out the license plate?"

Despite her agitation, she strained to see the plate. However, by that time, the Nissan was almost a mile ahead of us. It stopped briefly at a red light and turned right on State Highway 9.

"No, I can't see anything." There was a note of anger in her voice now. "Tell me what you're doing before I have you arrested."

As we came to the intersection, two patrol cars, with their lights flashing, turned in our direction.

When they passed us, she warned me. "My car's at Mr. Karimi's house. When those officers can't find me, they'll issue an alert."

As the Nissan cleared a set of railroad tracks just before the guardrail swung down, I shouted, “Oh, I can’t believe this.” A train whistle sounded in the distance. “Call your dispatcher,” I said. “Tell them you’re checking out the neighborhood or something.”

Since the guardrail prevented any oncoming traffic, I quickly made a U-turn and returned to the Eagle Cliff neighborhood. Detective Saxon didn’t say anything until I pulled in the driveway at Bashir’s house. Then she unsnapped her seat belt and turned to face me.

“Are you going to tell me what’s going on? What did that Nissan have to do with Farah Karimi’s death?”

To say she was angry would be an understatement.

I held her gaze for several seconds. Finally, I replied, “If you’d like to interview me about your case, you can come out to my house around seven tonight. I’ll give you the full story then.”

She looked away from me and stared out the window at Bashir’s house before replying. “I’m might take you up on that, Titus, because I definitely have a few more questions for you.”

After getting out of the car, she leaned back inside and said, “In fact, I’ll probably start with this one: Why are you carrying a concealed weapon?”

CHAPTER 23

At seven o'clock, Stormy and I were sitting in my living room waiting for the detective to arrive. The dog was looking up at me with his head cocked to one side.

His expression seemed to say, "What are you doing?"

"I have no idea what I'm doing," I told him. "But it doesn't matter, because I don't think she's coming."

Ten minutes passed, and then I heard a voice on the gate intercom.

"Mr. Ray, it's Detective Saxon."

After keying in the code, I told her, "Drive on in."

When the detective arrived in the driveway, Stormy and I were there to meet her.

She was still wearing the same clothes she'd had on earlier in the day, but for some reason, she looked different. I decided it was her hair. Several curly strands had come loose from her ponytail and were falling down around her face.

She smiled as she got out of her car. "And who is this?"

"I call him Stormy."

She bent down. "Hi, Stormy. You're a handsome dude." She turned to me. "I'm a dog person."

"We have something in common then."

She turned her attention from Stormy to the property. I saw her look at the road leading up to the barn and then glance back down to the lake and the forested area beyond the water. "When I took his class at OU, Dr. Ortega used to call himself a gentleman farmer. Now, I see why. This is a beautiful piece of property."

We climbed the steps to the porch and went inside. As soon as the detective entered the dining room, she gestured toward the bay windows facing the lake. "Oh, I love this view."

"The house also has a sunroom. The view of the lake from there is spectacular in the morning."

"That must be wonderful."

All of a sudden, I felt extremely awkward. Whether it was the banality of our conversation or the sheer normalcy of it, I wasn't sure, but for several seconds, I couldn't think of a single word to say. Then, as the silence deepened, I remembered the food.

"Have you eaten anything?"

"No, but I didn't come out here to eat, Mr. Ray. I'm supposed to get some answers. Remember?"

"I thought you'd agreed to call me Titus, Detective Saxon."

"Okay, Titus. If you'll give me some answers, you can call me Nikki."

"Nikki, then."

She smiled.

It was a beautiful smile.

"Are you sure you won't eat something?" I asked.

"Oh . . . maybe." She placed her hand across her stomach. "It's been awhile, and I'm starving."

"I've grilled us a couple of steaks."

"You've twisted my arm then."

♦♦♦♦

After the detective savored her first bite of steak, she pointed her knife toward me in a menacing fashion and said, "Talk."

At that moment, I was reminded of Carlton and his debriefing persona, and that made me question once again what I was about to do.

Despite my misgivings, I said, "As you may have already guessed,

Nikki, I'm not just in Norman to collaborate on a book with a professor."

She bobbed her head up and down. "You're right. After seeing a woman with her throat slashed, you appeared way too calm for a think tank pundit. I'm a good detective, but even a lousy one could have figured that out."

I didn't respond to her observation, and she took another bite of her steak and studied my face. After a few seconds, I said, "If I decide to tell you about my real job, I will need certain guarantees."

"Ummm . . ." she said, continuing to eat, "like what?"

"First, this conversation has to stay strictly between the two of us."

She looked off in the distance. Then she nodded her head. "Okay, unless you've come to Norman with plans to break the law, I can go along with that."

"Second, whatever evidence you and your officers turn up on the Farah Karimi case, you have to share it with me."

"Whoa," she said, putting her fork down and shaking her head. "I'm not sure I can do that."

"It's the only way I can help you catch Farah's killer."

"This isn't my first case, Titus. I've been solving homicides for four years now, and I can certainly manage this one without any outside help."

"Okay then, let me ask you a question. Who looks good for this murder?"

"I don't have a suspect right now, but, since Farah's husband has obviously disappeared, I have to assume he's somehow involved in her killing."

"I don't believe Bashir was responsible for his wife's death, but he certainly might know who killed her."

She immediately jumped on that statement. "Was Bashir driving the Nissan we were following today?"

I shook my head. "No, but I believe the person driving that car is connected with Farah's murder. He may even be her killer."

Nikki's eyes widened at my assertion, and I hurried on. "But I'm not telling you anything else unless you agree to my terms."

"Okay, I'll agree to share whatever evidence we find, primarily because what you've just said confirms my theory of who you really are and what you're doing here in Norman."

I was surprised at her statement.

"You looked surprised," she said, laughing.

"Well, you did say you were a good detective," I replied, "so I can't wait to hear what you've turned up on me."

"I'd be happy to do that." She pushed her plate away. "The steak was delicious, but I can't eat another bite."

"Would you like a cup of coffee before you tell me who I really am?"

"That sounds wonderful." She handed me her plate as I began to clear the table. "If you have some cream, add a splash to my cup."

"Done."

I told her to go make herself comfortable in the family room. Then I went out to the kitchen and brewed us each a mug of coffee. I had a small carton of heavy cream I'd purchased for making Alfredo sauce, so I opened it and poured some in her coffee.

When I entered the room with our cups, I saw that she had slipped off her shoes and was sitting on the couch with her feet curled up underneath her. I sat down opposite her in a leather recliner.

"Now I'm all ears," I said. "Who am I?"

As if suddenly embarrassed, she lowered her head for a brief moment.

Seconds later, she looked up and said, "I believe you're part of some kind of federal security detail that's been guarding Farah and Bashir Karimi. Maybe they were defectors or they were being threatened by the Iraqi government for helping the United States, something like that. I believe they were given a house and maybe even a salary while Bashir completed his studies at OU." She paused and gave me a quizzical look. "Am I right?"

She seemed very pleased with herself.

At that moment, I realized all I had to do was go along with her suppositions, and then not only could I protect my real identity, I could also stroke her ego at the same time. Before I decided how to reply, however, she rushed on with her theory.

"I'm guessing other members of your security detail have taken Bashir to a place of safety, because whoever killed Farah might go after him next."

She took a sip of her coffee and studied my reaction to this fantasy.

As she did so, I came up with two good reasons—or rationalizations—for telling her the truth and not going along with her suppositions. First, Nikki was a law enforcement officer, and, if I had to do so, I could probably justify my identity disclosure on that basis. Second, I desperately needed to find out if Ahmed had murdered Farah and, unless I told Nikki who I really was, I seriously doubted she would let me get anywhere near the murder investigation.

"I can understand why you've come to those conclusions, Nikki, but they're just wrong."

A moment of fear passed over her face. However, I couldn't tell if she was afraid of me or simply afraid of losing her job.

Maybe it was both.

I knew she had probably broken departmental rules by coming to see me on her own. She may have thought the rules didn't matter because, according to her conjecture, this was a federal case and the FBI was really in charge. Now that I'd denied her theory, however, she could be thinking she was in big trouble.

On the other hand, she might be afraid of me. If I wasn't a federal officer, then who was I? She knew I had a gun, and with my size advantage, I could easily overwhelm her small body in a physical struggle. To make matters worse, she was locked in an isolated house behind a security fence. Besides that, she might not have even told anyone she was coming to see me.

She shifted uncomfortably on the sofa, waiting for me to continue.

I thought she looked very vulnerable.

And extremely attractive.

Seeking to reassure her and return the smile to her face, I said, "However, there's one detail you do have correct. I *am* employed by the federal government."

Her dark brown eyes reflected confusion.

"But you're not with the FBI?"

"No, my agency primarily operates overseas."

She sat very still and thought about my answer.

I enjoyed watching her as she grappled with the possibilities.

Her eyes brightened. "You're with the CIA?"

I smiled at her. "Thank you for guessing correctly. Now I can always deny I ever told you."

"Really? CIA?"

When I nodded, she shook her head as if she didn't believe me.

"Well, forgive me, Titus, but I need more proof than just your word on that."

"You don't believe me?"

"Not really, no."

"Would a character witness help?

She hesitated. "Yeah, maybe. Who?"

"You know Danny Jarrar, the Deputy Director of OSBI?"

"Jarrar? Yes. Well, no, I don't really know him. I met him at a terrorist conference in Oklahoma City once. I've also talked with him on the phone a time or two."

"Danny can vouch for me. I'll give him a call."

Earlier in the day, after I'd left Bashir's house, I'd called Danny and updated him on the situation. I'd asked him to see what he could find out about the Nissan, and I'd told him I thought the last letter on the license plate was either K or H.

"Was the driver a foreigner?" he had asked.

"Yes. He had definite Arabic features."

"Why do you think he was cruising by the house?"

"I'm not sure. Maybe he was coming to meet Bashir, or maybe he was planning a hit on him too. If we can locate Bashir, we'll know a lot more."

"What's happening with the detective?"

"She's coming out to my house tonight for some answers."

"What?"

"I probably should have mentioned she saw I was carrying a gun."

"Are you crazy?"

"I'm considering telling her the truth."

"Sure, go ahead. Then I'll recommend you for one of our job openings here at OSBI."

"If she needs verification of my status, will you give it?"

"Think carefully before you do that."

"Believe me, I will."

"You know I'll vouch for you, Titus. I've always got your back."

♦♦♦♦

I left Nikki in the family room and went back to my bedroom for my Agency satphone. Danny answered on the first ring, and I briefed him on what I wanted from him. He agreed, and then I walked back to the family room and gave the phone to Nikki.

Her conversation with him was short.

When she hung up, she looked at me as if I'd grown a third eye.

"Okay, he confirmed you really do work for the CIA, but that's all he would say. So tell me, what's a CIA officer doing here in Norman?"

"Danny Jarrar and I have been good friends for a long time, so when I had to have surgery on my leg, Norman seemed as good a place as any for me to have some R & R."

She deliberated about my explanation for a few seconds, and, by the look on her face, I thought this story was going to satisfy her. Since I'd given her such minimal details, I also felt I could justify myself to Carlton later—if that became necessary.

"In your statement, you said you'd only known Farah Karimi for a few weeks. Was that true?"

I nodded. "That was true."

I explained about my decision to volunteer at the ESL class to keep myself from becoming bored during my medical leave.

"I first met Farah when I went to check out the ESL class. However, something I overheard that day might help you with this case. On the other hand, it could have no significance whatsoever."

Her voice held a note of reprimand. "Don't leave anything out. You know the smallest detail can make a big difference in a case."

After telling her about hearing Farah and Bashir speaking Farsi in the parking lot, I said, "When Farah introduced herself to me, she said she was an Iraqi who spoke Arabic."

"Farsi is spoken in Iran, correct?"

"Yes."

"Can I assume you speak Farsi?"

"Yes."

"And Arabic?"

"That too."

She rolled her eyes. "I'm happy to speak a little Spanish."

"Spanish is good."

She tucked a stray lock of hair behind her ear. "Why do I have a feeling you also *habla español*?"

I smiled but didn't respond.

"I'll take that as a yes."

She got up from the couch and retrieved her purse from the foyer table. "I want to make some notes while we go over this again."

When she sat back down, she pulled out the small black notebook she'd used when recording my statement earlier in the day and wrote something in it. "So you believe Farah and her husband were hiding their country of origin. Is that right?"

I nodded. "There's something else you need to know about Farah."

She pointed her pen at me and said, "You know, it's really nice to have some cooperation from the feds for a change."

I grinned at her. "You probably shouldn't get use to it."

"Don't worry. I'm smarter than that."

After I told her about Farah's use of the back stairs as a means of getting to class on time and her perpetual lateness, Nikki resumed her detective persona. "Since it appears there's only one car between them, perhaps her husband had an early morning class and didn't get back home in time to have her there at exactly nine o'clock. That might explain her tardiness."

"That could be it, but, as a whole, Iranians are not very punctual people. In fact, it's rare for them to be on time for any occasion. One time in Tehran, I was kept waiting for two hours by an Iranian businessman, and I never even received one word of apology for his behavior."

"Please don't tell me anymore or you might have to kill me."

Nikki's remark was so unexpected, I laughed at the old joke. Then, when she started laughing too, Stormy got excited and jumped up on the couch with her. I yelled at him to get off, but she kept petting him, insisting he be allowed to stay where he was. After he put his head on her lap, she picked up her notebook again.

"You promised to tell me about the Nissan."

Watching Nikki and Stormy together gave me such an unexpected surge of happiness, that, for a moment or two, I couldn't remember what she'd asked me.

"Yes," I finally answered, "I first saw the Nissan this morning after pulling into the parking lot. As I'm sure you understand, it's an operational habit to keep tabs on anything out of the ordinary, and the Nissan drew my attention because I'd never seen it before, and it was parked close to the back entrance."

"Was it occupied?"

"No. There was no one inside."

"So you think the driver was already in the building when you arrived?"

"I believe that's the most likely scenario. He could have hidden underneath the stairwell or just inside the kitchen and waited for her there."

She looked thoughtful. "You're assuming the assailant was a man."

"Aren't you?"

"Purely from a statistical standpoint, this type of murder is usually committed by a male, but there's no direct evidence of that so far. Unless . . ." she paused and gave me a suspicious look, "you know something about the murderer that I don't."

"I assure you I don't know who murdered Farah," I said, "but since my area of operations is centered around the Middle East, I'd like to make sure my arrival here in Norman and Farah's murder are purely coincidental events."

She nodded. "I get that."

"I guess now would be a good time to confess I didn't tell you everything this morning."

"Why am I not surprised?"

I tried to look contrite, but she didn't look like she was buying it. "So, tell me what you left out."

"After checking Farah for a pulse, I went down the stairs and out to the parking lot to see if I could spot anyone fleeing the scene. That's the moment I noticed the Nissan was gone."

"I'm guessing you didn't tell me this earlier because as an unassuming writer you couldn't easily explain your actions or why you had noticed the Nissan in the first place?"

I started to quibble with her description of me, but then I said, "That's right."

"Anything else?"

"No, that's the extent of what I know. Now, it's your turn."

She didn't respond immediately. Instead, she flipped through several pages in her notebook, pausing every now and then to read what she'd written there. Her delaying actions made me wonder whether she was having second thoughts about our agreement.

However, after a few seconds of consulting her notes, she began describing what she'd found at the scene. "The evidence is pretty sketchy right now, but I can tell you one odd thing. I went through the contents of Farah's handbag, and, while it contained the usual items a woman might carry, there was no cell phone. When one of our officers asked Susan Steward about a number for Farah's husband, though, she said it should be on Farah's phone. So, we're certain she owned a cell phone."

I nodded in agreement. "She definitely had a cell phone. I saw it the first day when she showed me how to play a word game on it."

"I was at her house all afternoon, and it didn't turn up there. We'll get her phone records tomorrow. Maybe they'll tell us something."

"What did you find at the house?"

"Well, it appeared Bashir emptied out a small safe in the bedroom before he left. So wherever he is, he probably has cash and his passport."

"What about a computer?"

"According to one of our techs, there were two laptops in the house on a wireless network. However, when we arrived, we found only one of them."

"Could you tell whether the one left behind belonged to Farah or to Bashir?"

"We're assuming it belonged to Farah, but we'll know for certain tomorrow."

"Finding that Nissan should be a top priority. I told Danny I thought the last letter of the license plate was either K or H, and he's going to pull in his state resources to help us locate it."

"I already have notices out on both the mysterious Nissan and Bashir's Honda."

"I'm afraid Bashir has had enough time to leave the state by now."

"Yeah, that's a big possibility," she said. "Do you think one of the ESL students notified him of his wife's death, and that why he left his OU class so abruptly?"

"If that's what happened, he may have left out of fear for his own life. Yet, I don't think he's the kind of man who would run, especially if someone had just killed his wife."

"You really know Bashir? I thought you were lying about that."

"I don't know him as well as my scholarly persona implied," I admitted, "but when I met Bashir, even though our encounter was brief, he struck me as a man who would fight instead of run."

"Maybe he went to a safer place until he figured out how to do that—the fighting part, that is."

"You could be right. A well-trained officer recognizes retreat is sometimes the best option."

"Was Bashir in the military?"

"I believe so, but that's just speculation on my part."

"Speculation is a big part of this job."

"Were there any photos at the house showing Bashir in a uniform?"

As she started running through the pages of her notepad again, Stormy jumped down from her lap and trotted over to the door. After letting him outside, I asked Nikki if she'd like another cup of coffee.

"No thanks," she replied. "I really should be going." Closing her notebook, she said, "I don't remember seeing any photographs at the house, and I didn't make any notes about them, but I'll check when I go back to Bashir's house tomorrow."

"Would it be a problem if I joined you there?"

She considered my question. "No, I don't think so. The captain has all the other detectives working a double homicide. Did you hear about that?"

I nodded. "One of your officers told me about it. Is that why you were so nervous when you were taking my statement this morning? Was Farah's homicide your first case to work without a partner?"

As she got up from the couch, I saw fire in her eyes.

"I wasn't nervous when I was questioning you this morning," she stated emphatically, "and I've worked homicides alone for two years now."

In one quick fluid movement, she slipped her shoes on, grabbed her purse, and headed for the front door.

Meanwhile, I followed her, trying to make amends for my blunt question and struggling to explain what I'd observed.

"I didn't mean to sound like you weren't doing a thorough job," I said, "and maybe nervous wasn't the right word. I probably should have said you seemed uncomfortable in those surroundings."

As she turned to face me, I watched her anger slowly disappear.

"No, you're right," she said quietly. "I did feel uncomfortable, but it wasn't related to the murder. The truth is . . ."

She paused for a couple of seconds and then started over again. "The truth is I hadn't been inside Bethel Church for many years, and I found it painful to be there. When I went there as a child . . ." She shook her head. "Well, let's just say it was a difficult time for me."

"I'm sorry if I offended you."

"I wasn't offended."

She gave me a weak smile and offered me her hand. "Thanks again for the dinner, Titus, and for letting me meet the real you."

I didn't dissuade her from that notion.

CHAPTER 24

I was barely awake when Carlton called the next morning.

"You sound as if you're just getting up," he said.

"That's because I am."

"I thought you always got up every morning at six o'clock."

"It *is* six o'clock."

"Oh, that's right. You're on Central Time there."

I knew Carlton was fully aware of the time difference between Oklahoma and Virginia. However, just like his love of being a detailed person, he also took great pride in arriving at work every morning earlier than anyone else. The track of our conversation was simply a ploy for me to acknowledge he'd already been at work for several hours.

Instead of feeding his ego, I asked, "Has Ahmed been found?"

He gave an exaggerated sigh. "The FBI is coming up empty-handed so far. The Venezuelan student who owned the van has completely disappeared, and his friends keep insisting he decided to quit school and return to Caracas."

"Well, maybe he did. Did they check the airlines, bus stations, rental cars?"

"The FBI knows how to conduct a manhunt, Titus."

He sounded exasperated, but I didn't think his feelings were directed at me. He simply hated being dependent on other organizations to move along an investigation.

He continued, "They're certain he didn't fly back to Caracas. Buses are another matter because they present numerous possibilities. He could have taken a bus into Mexico and caught a plane from there. He could have rented a car, then taken a bus, then taken a plane."

"You don't sound very encouraging."

"That's because I'm giving you the FBI report. On the other hand, I told Katherine to pull the records for car sales in the Austin area, because we know if Ahmed was the shooter, he had plenty of cash for the operation. He could have purchased his own car after dumping the van, thus avoiding all public forms of transportation."

"You're running your own investigation and not coordinating with the FBI?" I made a *tsk, tsk, tsk* sound. "Frankly, Douglas, I'm shocked."

Carlton hated being teased about his occasional rule breaking, and he quickly replied, "I'll share things in a timely manner when it's appropriate."

"So you found something?"

"Possibly. In San Marcos, just south of Austin, we located a car dealer who said he had sold a new car to a Hispanic male for cash. It got my attention because it was a cash deal and the dealer said the buyer was in a hurry. That was on Saturday, just one day after Wassermann's killing. I have someone in San Marcos checking on this report, even as we speak."

"Let's hope the buyer was the Venezuelan. Did the car dealer say he was alone or was he with someone?"

"I'll let you know as soon as I know something."

Carlton's evasiveness made me wonder if Ahmed had already been spotted with the Venezuelan in San Marcos. If so, then Ahmed al-Amin was connected to the Venezuelan's van and was definitely Wassermann's killer. There was no other explanation, because both Carlton and I knew a Venezuelan kid hadn't taken out Wassermann.

Trying to pull more information out of him, I said, "Since I haven't heard from you, I'm assuming Katherine hasn't picked up any chatter about the hit yet. She said if Wassermann's killer was Ahmed, she expected to have some type of communication into Tehran about his success in killing me. Hasn't there been anything yet? It's been almost a week now."

"No, but the operations center at NSA is reporting a slowdown in communications across the board. We'll be discussing this issue with several of our division chiefs later today."

"Who doesn't know the NSA has the ability to intercept every kind of communication out there? Perhaps the terrorists are relying on human couriers now, or they're coding their messages differently."

"We're looking into it," he replied. "Anything new with you?"

Here was an opportunity to tell him about Farah's murder and to mention a certain female detective, who was now aware of the true identity of his covert operative.

I reported, "Stormy has learned how to catch a ball."

♦♦♦♦

The moment I ended my call with Carlton, my iPhone rang. The screen indicated the call was from the Norman Police Department.

"Hi, Titus. It's Nikki."

"It's good to hear from you."

Strangely enough, I wasn't just mouthing a cliché.

Last night, after Nikki had left the house, I couldn't stop thinking about her. Although she appeared to be a tough detective and a smart interrogator, she also struck me as an emotionally fragile and vulnerable woman.

That dichotomy intrigued me.

She said, "I've got a few new details to share, but, if you don't mind, I'd prefer to discuss them with you later."

The background noise coming from her phone indicated she was in a room full of people.

"I don't mind at all. I'm getting ready to leave for a physical therapy session, but after that, I'll be free the rest of the day."

"Can you meet me at Bashir's house around one-thirty? We can talk then."

"I'm looking forward to it."

For once, I was telling the truth.

♦♦♦♦

I drove to Bashir's house around one-twenty and was pleased to see Nikki's silver Toyota was the only car in the driveway.

When Nikki met me at the door, she had her cell phone up to her ear, but she waved me inside. Using hand gestures, I indicated I wanted to look through the house, and she nodded her head and motioned for me to go ahead.

The Karimi's house was furnished in a style common to most wealthy Iranians. The furniture was large and ornate, and the colors used in the draperies and upholstery fabrics were bold and vibrant. However, missing from the decor were any family heirlooms—Persian rugs and tapestries, family paintings—which were typically passed down from generation to generation and extremely prevalent in most Iranian households.

I understood why Nikki had not recorded anything in her notes about framed photographs on display. There were no wedding photos or family pictures in evidence anywhere.

After scrutinizing the rooms and finding nothing of interest, I sat down at the kitchen counter and leafed through a telephone directory, looking for any items or locations the couple may have underlined or marked in some way that would give us a clue as to where Bashir could have gone.

However, this proved to be an exercise in futility. Most likely—like all young people today—they had just used the internet whenever they wanted information.

Nikki was still on her telephone when she wandered into the kitchen. Apparently, she was listening to someone dictate a list of items to her. She kept repeating "okay" after writing down a line or two.

Today, she was wearing a patterned red and black jacket over a knee-length solid black dress. Some of her long brown hair was pinned on top of her head, while the rest of it fell loosely around her face. She kept brushing strands of it away as she talked.

For some inexplicable reason, she looked even more beautiful today than she did yesterday.

She snapped her phone shut and sat down beside me at the counter. Looking down at the telephone directory I was holding, she asked, "Find anything?"

"Nothing." I replied, pushing the book aside and pointing to her notebook, "but you look as if you've had a productive morning."

"Puzzling might be a better word. Tomorrow I should have a printout of both Bashir and Farah's phone records, but, to get us started, I asked the phone company to give me the last five numbers the couple had called or received."

"And what was puzzling?"

"According to their records, the last phone call Farah ever made was to her husband's cell phone at nine fifty-two yesterday morning. The call lasted about two minutes. However, you said you found her body on the stairs at around nine-twenty. That's puzzling unless the—"

I finished the sentence for her. "—the person who murdered her made that call. Maybe that's how Bashir found out so quickly his wife had been killed."

"That could be it," Nikki agreed. "If the killer called Bashir immediately after the murder, perhaps Bashir was in on it. Maybe that's why he left his OU class early."

"Or after murdering Farah, the killer called Bashir to taunt him, tell him he was next, and he rushed back home to get out of town quickly."

"Either scenario is possible," she said.

She looked around the room, trying to analyze the scene. "So, let's see . . . He comes back here and . . ."

"He gets out this suitcase," I said, pointing to the partially filled suitcase we'd seen the day before, "and starts throwing clothes in it."

"Yeah, that's pretty obvious."

"But, tell me detective, why did he stop packing? No matter where he was headed, he was going to need clothes when he got there. "

Nikki answered slowly, "He could have packed two suitcases and decided at the last minute to take only one of them."

"That's a possibility."

Warming to this scenario, she quickly added, "He stopped here in the family room, opened this one up, took out some of the clothes he wanted, and then left this suitcase behind."

"That makes sense. He decided to travel light. That could mean he wasn't going very far."

She sounded excited. "He could still be in Norman."

"What about friends in the area? Where did he eat, buy gas, do his banking?"

"We're still working on the friends' angle. We didn't find any credit card statements in the house, but we did discover he has a substantial checking and savings account. I've subpoenaed those records already."

"I can see why you didn't have any notes about photographs in the house," I said, pointing around the room. "They must not like pictures of themselves."

Nikki corrected me immediately. "Oh, they liked photographing themselves all right, or at least Farah did. It turns out the computer we took from here yesterday belonged to her. Her photographs were about the only interesting items on it."

"What about the sites she visited on the internet?"

"They weren't much help. She wasn't a prolific web surfer. Her most recent pages were several days ago when she looked up some English vocabulary words. She didn't use email or the social networks either."

"What kind of photographs did she take?"

"Campus scenes, statues, flowers, sporting events, those kinds of things. There were the usual photos you might expect of her and her husband."

"Such as?"

"Oh, there were shots of the two of them in this house or by the oak tree out front. They had photographed each other riding bicycles, cheering at a football game, walking around the campus—nothing out of the ordinary."

"What about pictures of their vacations? What places did they frequent?"

"I don't recall anything like that. Every photo I saw looked as if it had been taken here in Norman."

"What about—"

"Except," she said, interrupting me, "I saw a few photographs taken at a hotel in the City."

"In Oklahoma City? What hotel?"

"The Skirvin Hilton. It's a luxury hotel built back in 1911. It's right in the middle of the downtown area."

"Did it look as if they were staying there or just taking pictures because of its historic significance?"

"Oh, they were definitely staying in a room at the hotel. I recognized the distinctive décor immediately. There were several pictures of them in one of the hotel's restaurants too."

"Okay, detective. What do you think? Is it possible that's where he's gone? It's not a logical choice for a hideout, but maybe that's why it's the perfect choice. If he's familiar with the surroundings, he would also feel safe there."

"I don't know, Titus." She chewed on her lower lip for a second. "I guess it's possible, but—"

"You've put a bulletin out on his car, and nothing's turned up yet." I said. "What kind of parking does the hotel have?"

She looked thoughtful. "I believe there's an on-site parking garage."

"So, if he's staying there, his car would be off the streets and out of sight." I grabbed my car keys out of my pocket. "Let's go check it out."

She got off the barstool. However, she made no move toward the door. "I can't do that, Titus," she said. "Oklahoma City isn't my jurisdiction. If something went down while you and I were snooping around, it would jeopardize my case. The proper procedure is for me to call the OKC police department and let them take a look at the hotel."

That was the last thing I wanted to happen.

If Bashir was at the hotel, and they took him in for questioning, I'd never get a chance to interrogate him by myself. I couldn't let that happen. I needed to be absolutely certain his wife's death had nothing to do with Ahmed or with me.

"No, you're right, Nikki," I said. "What if we do it this way? I'll call Danny Jarrar at OSBI and have him meet me at the Skirvin. He's got all the credentials you need to take a look at this possibility before involving anyone else."

As she considered my suggestion, she took her time unsnapping her purse and placing her cell phone and notebook back inside. When she slung her bag over her shoulder, she looked up at me and nodded her consent. However, I could tell she was disturbed that I was going to be looking into Bashir's whereabouts without her.

"Okay, that would work," she replied. "I'm supposed to be over at the Medical Examiner's office anyway. Farah's autopsy is scheduled in about an hour."

"When you get back to the station, would you mind emailing me a photo of Bashir from Farah's computer?"

"Sure. Give me an email address." She took out her phone and entered my CIS email address into her contacts.

I headed out the door. "I'll call you the minute I know anything."

"Call me even if you don't know anything."

That was an easy promise to make.

CHAPTER 25

Since I needed to gas up the Range Rover before getting on I-35, I decided to wait until I was at a gas station before calling Danny. I never got the chance, though, because even before I made it to the gas station, he called me.

He sounded excited.

"I think I may have found your guy."

"You found Bashir?"

"No. Sorry. I meant the guy driving the Nissan. Don't get your hopes up, though. I may be way off base on this. Are you available to meet me?"

"Sure. I was just about to call and ask you for a favor anyway."

"Does that favor have anything to do with a rocket launcher?"

"Let's hope not. Besides, I would never ask you for the same favor twice."

"Trust me. That's a favor I would never grant twice."

Since Danny said he was finishing up a seminar at Tinker Air Force Base in southeast Oklahoma City, he told me to meet him at Twigs' Diner at the junction of I-35 and I-240 near an old movie theater.

As I headed north on I-35 toward our rendezvous, I had the distinct impression something big was about to happen. During a mission, I often had this feeling—Carlton called it my "gut premonition"—that an operation was about to be split wide open.

Unfortunately, my gut premonition never foretold if the outcome was going to be very good or very bad.

♦♦♦♦

Twigs' Diner desperately needed a paint job on the outside. However, the inside looked clean and well kept—though a bit outdated.

The floor was covered in large black and white tiles, and all the booths were upholstered in red vinyl, matching the padded chairs at the tables in the center of the room.

When I entered the diner, I passed by a scruffy teenage boy eating a hamburger at the counter. Then, I took the last booth in a row of four booths at the back of the restaurant.

Except for the boy at the counter and an older couple seated at a table, the place had no other customers. The restaurant was a good choice for a quiet conversation, and I suspected Danny frequented the place for just such conversations.

I ordered lemonade, and the moment the waitress brought it, Danny also arrived.

He started harassing me as soon as he slid in the booth.

"You look well. Did Detective Saxon put that smile on your face?"

I gave him a drop-dead look, and he chuckled.

The waitress, who had greeted Danny personally, immediately reappeared with a white mug full of steaming black coffee for him.

He pointed at my lemonade and asked, "Why are you drinking that stuff? They make the best coffee in the world here."

"I need my Vitamin C."

"They have this drink called orange juice for that. You drink it in the morning with your toast."

He took a sip of his coffee, and then started swiping through some screens on his iPad. The whole time he was doing this, he was telling me why he loved Apple products so much.

Finally, he got to a screen with some photographs on it, but he didn't show them to me until he'd placed his order for a Supreme Omelet.

"You should order some eggs here," he advised me. "They're the greatest. That's how the diner got its name."

"What does the name Twigs have to do with someone knowing how to fix a couple of eggs?"

"Willie, the owner, used to work at another place where a guy used to come in every day and order two eggs with cheese and sausage. It wasn't long before the customer would simply hold up two fingers and say, 'Twigs,' and Frankie knew he meant his two-egg order. Some of the other customers started doing the same thing, so Willie decided to open up his own place and name it Twigs. Eggs are the house specialty."

As with most of Danny's stories, there was no need for me to comment, because, before I could even get a word in, he was on to another subject. However, this time his next subject was the Nissan.

He told me how he'd cross-referenced my description of the late model black Nissan with my recollection of the driver and the last letter of the license plate. At this point, he swiveled his iPad around and showed me some photographs. They were obviously taken by a long-distance lens.

"First, I want you to look at these six photographs and see if any of them look like the guy at the wheel of the Nissan."

"Give me a minute to study them."

I was glad his food arrived so I could concentrate. Otherwise, I would have been tempted to tell him to shut up while I tried to compare my memory to the snapshots.

There's something to be said for silence.

The six photos were all of Arabic-looking men in their twenties or thirties. I filtered out the restaurant's background music, the fried food smell of the diner, and Danny salting down his omelet. Then, I floated back to the brief glimpse I'd had of the driver at Bashir's house just moments before I'd opened the door to the Range Rover and started the engine.

I pointed to a picture of a light-skinned Arab man with thick, dark hair and a trimmed moustache. He was sitting at an outdoor table. "This was the guy."

The camera had caught him about to take a drink, his open mouth revealing crooked teeth and a pair of thin lips. His nose had been broken at least once, maybe twice.

The excitement in Danny's voice was apparent. "This one?"

"Yeah, that's him. That's the guy I saw driving the Nissan past Bashir's house."

"Okay, then we've hit the jackpot. This guy drives a black Nissan and his plates are 407JEK."

"Who is he?" I asked impatiently.

"He's a Palestinian. His name is Shahid al-Nawar. He's one of about a dozen Arabic men we've had under surveillance for a few months."

"Is he affiliated with Hezbollah?"

"Definitely. He came here on a student visa two years ago. He went back to Jordan last summer, and that's when the Israelis alerted the FBI about him. Before he returned to the States last fall, he had travelled not only to Pakistan, but also to Iran. The Israelis were even able to pinpoint him at a training camp outside of Tehran a few years ago."

"What's he doing here in the States?"

"That's just it. We don't know. He mostly hangs out with the other Arab students and goes to class occasionally. Of course, we can't keep him under constant surveillance; there's not enough manpower for that. This photo was taken of him after the Israelis notified us of his travels. Now we treat him like the rest of these guys and run a forty-eight hour stakeout on him every two weeks or so."

"Where does he live?"

"He rents a house off Peters Avenue in Norman. Two of these guys," he pointed to photos of two other men, "live with him."

I studied the faces of his roommates again. They looked slightly familiar, but I wasn't sure why.

Danny pointed to Shahid's photo and asked, "Do you think your detective has any evidence tying him to Farah Karimi's murder?"

I ignored the reference to Nikki being *my* detective and said, "They're still processing the forensics, but I know they didn't find the weapon that killed her. Right now, other than the fact I saw his car in the parking lot before she was killed, there's nothing to link him to her murder."

"Could Ahmed Al-Amin have hooked up with Shahid?"

"Since Wassermann said Ahmed entered the States with another Hezbollah group, that's certainly a possibility."

We stopped talking as the waitress refilled Danny's coffee.

When she left, Danny took out his cell phone. "I'm going to set up some surveillance on Shahid."

After he'd called his office, I brought up the subject of Bashir. I told him I had a hunch Bashir might not have left town but had simply gone to ground somewhere in the area. When I mentioned the Skirvin Hotel, and why I thought he might have gone there, Danny was eager to go with me to see if we could find him.

We decided to take his car and leave my Range Rover parked at Twigs' Diner. Danny assured me Willie would take good care of it.

I wanted to believe him, but I had to wonder about a man who thought Twigs was a good name for an eating establishment.

♦♦♦♦

On the way over to the hotel, I pulled up the two photos of Bashir, which Nikki had sent to my email. When Danny parked the car, I handed him my iPhone and asked him if recognized Bashir Karimi.

He studied the photos for a minute. "No, I've never seen him before; but you're right, he definitely looks Persian."

Since Danny could legitimately flash his badge and question anyone inside the hotel, we agreed I'd be his silent partner unless we found Bashir inside the hotel. In that case, our roles would be reversed, and Danny would be an observer while I questioned Bashir.

Danny had already given me a history lesson on the Skirvin Hotel in the car, but I wasn't prepared for the luxurious and elegant feel of the place. It looked as if it belonged to a bygone era of oil barons and wealthy cattlemen.

When we walked up to the reception desk, Danny used the straightforward approach.

He flashed his creds at the young female desk clerk, showed her the photos of Bashir, and asked if he was registered. The clerk called the hotel manager, who looked as if he too belonged to a bygone era.

However, he proved to be exceptionally cooperative, and, within a few minutes, he was able to tell us no one was registered at the hotel under Bashir's name. That didn't surprise us.

Still trying to be helpful, the manager invited us to wait in his office while he took the photographs of Bashir and went to make further inquiries from his hotel staff.

As soon as we were alone, I said, "Look, Danny, if we find Bashir is hunkered down here, we have no way of telling how he's going to react to a confrontation. I mean, if he's innocent of her murder, he's going to be grieving over his wife's death. On the other hand, if he killed his wife, he could be violent. You don't really need to be involved in this. Let me go and—"

"Titus, stop," Danny said sharply. "Don't keep blaming yourself for the hit on Wassermann. There was absolutely nothing you could have done about that."

He jabbed his finger in my chest, emphasizing each word. "We're doing this together. End of story."

I stared down at him for a few seconds. "Okay. End of story."

The manager returned and announced they had a guest named Motaz Asadi, who appeared to be Bashir Karimi. He was staying in one of their mini-suites, Room 426.

"Call Mr. Asadi," Danny said to the manager, "tell him he failed to sign the registration form when he checked in. Say you're bringing it up now. Give us a few minutes to get up to the fourth floor before you make that call."

A few minutes later, Danny and I were positioned along the wall outside Room 426. On the floor to our left was a room service tray with the remains of what appeared to be a chicken sandwich.

Less than a minute went by, and then we heard the telephone ring inside the room.

It rang twice before someone picked it up.

Both Danny and I had our guns out, ready to stop Bashir if he got spooked by the phone call and decided to flee the room.

The door remained closed.

Approximately three minutes after the manager made the call, Danny knocked on the door.

"Mr. Asadi, it's Stephen Coleman, the hotel manager."

When Danny faced the peephole, I saw him trying to hide his facial features by scratching his forehead, just in case the occupant of the room was expecting an older man to match the voice he'd heard over the telephone.

The locks on the door were disengaged within a couple of seconds, and, when the door swung open, we both rushed in.

A startled Bashir brandished a knife from behind his back when he saw us.

Danny shouted, "Drop it. We're not here to hurt you."

Bashir calmly pointed the weapon at Danny, and then, for the first time, focused his attention on me.

He looked confused when he recognized me.

"Bashir," I said, "my friend is with law enforcement. We're here to help you."

"Drop your knife," Danny ordered, "and we'll lower our weapons."

Bashir considered this while continuing to stare at me. I nodded my head at him, encouraging him to comply.

He maintained his position, so I slowly walked over and placed my handgun on the dresser.

Bashir's eyes remained defiant for a few seconds, and then he lowered his arm.

He didn't resist when Danny took the knife from him.

"Who are you?" he asked, slumping down on the bed. "How did you find me?"

While Danny did a walkthrough of the room, I pulled a chair closer to the bed and sat down in front of Bashir.

In less than a minute, Danny gave me the all clear sign, and then he sat down on a sofa across the room from me.

He didn't holster his gun, though.

I touched Bashir on the shoulder. "I'm so sorry for your wife's death," I said softly.

He shrugged me off, his facial expression reflecting both anger and grief. "Who are you?" he asked me again.

Although his clothes were wrinkled and disheveled, and he looked as if he hadn't slept in awhile, he still maintained the same air of self-assurance I'd noticed at the ESL dinner.

"I'm exactly who I said I was the other night at the dinner when we first met," I said calmly. "I'm writing a book on the Middle East with a professor at OU, but I'm also a volunteer in the ESL class."

Bashir gave me a look of incredulity.

I could tell he didn't believe a word I'd said.

Bashir turned and addressed Danny, "And you?"

"I'm Danny Jarrar. I'm an investigator with the Oklahoma State Bureau of Investigation. Titus and I are good friends. When you turned up missing yesterday, he asked me to help him find you."

Danny took out his badge and held it up for Bashir to see, but he showed no interest in it.

Bashir turned back to me. "And now that you've found me, what happens?"

"I want you to help us find your wife's killer."

Bashir took a deep breath and bowed his head, pressing his hands against his temples as if his head were pounding.

I said to him in Farsi, "You don't have to know who I am to believe I want to help you."

He looked up quickly, his eyes narrowing as he stared at me.

Finally, with desperation in his voice, he said to me in Farsi. "He killed her. Now I want to kill him."

CHAPTER 26

After a few seconds of silence, Bashir asked me in English, "Where did you learn Farsi?"

When I simply looked at him and didn't respond, he nodded his head as if he understood my reticence. Then he asked, "You knew Farah and I weren't from Iraq, didn't you?"

"Yes," I answered. "I suspected you and Farah were Iranians."

After I told him about overhearing their Farsi conversation in the church's parking lot, he pointed out, "Yet, you never ask us about this deception."

"It was really none of my business, and I thought you might have a good reason for deceiving people."

"Yes," he agreed with a decisive tone in his voice, "we did."

Bashir lowered his head for a moment. Seconds later, he looked up with a pained expression on his face. "Were you there at the church yesterday when she was killed?"

Although it was difficult to meet his gaze, I answered truthfully. "I was the person who discovered Farah's body."

Upon hearing this, his composure completely collapsed, and he started weeping.

Danny holstered his weapon, went over to the bathroom, and brought Bashir back a glass of water.

As he handed it to him, Danny said, "We're both very sorry for your loss, Bashir."

"Thank you," Bashir said, taking a sip of water. "Do you really want to help me find the man who killed her?"

We both gave him our assurances that we did, but then I told him he would have to tell us everything—what he was doing living in the States under a false identity, who would want to kill his wife, and why he ran from his house in Norman.

He promised, "I will tell you all this and more."

♦♦♦♦

Bashir moved from the king-sized bed to an overstuffed chair in the living area where Danny was seated on a sofa. I retrieved my gun from the dresser and sat down next to Danny.

"I will begin with my real name," Bashir said. "It is Behnam Kashani, but my passport is in the name of Bashir Karimi."

"Did you get—?"

Bashir interrupted me. "No, do not ask me any questions. It will be easier if I tell you my story first. Afterward, I will be glad to answer whatever questions you may have for me."

Sensing his need of control, I relented. "Sure, that's fine."

He nodded his approval and began his story.

"I was born in Iran in 1980, the year after the Iranian Revolution and after the Shah was overthrown. My father often told me he believed the day the Shah had to leave Iran was the saddest day of my grandfather's life. My grandfather was very close to Shah Pahlavi and his family, and, due to that relationship, when the Shah was in power, my grandfather became a very wealthy man. First, he invested in steel. Then he ventured into banking, and later into automobiles. These were industries the Shah assured him would not be nationalized.

"However, once the Shah was deposed, my grandfather urged my father to step down from all their business ventures and join the Iranian Revolutionary Guard Corps, which was in its initial formation right after the revolution. My grandfather predicted the IRGC, whose responsibility is internal security, would become the only means to riches and success in Iran's future. Within a few years, my father became one of the IRGC's senior commanders."

Bashir sighed heavily and continued, "I'm relating this history because I want you to know I was raised in a very wealthy and prestigious household in Iran, and it encompassed two worlds, one of the military and one of business. Naturally, when I became of age, I yielded to my father's wishes and joined the IRGC. However, because of my family's wealth and connections, I was also able to pursue a degree at the University of Tehran at the same time, and that's where

I met Farah."

Despite his request, I interrupted his story. "Could you clarify one point, Bashir? Is your father an ardent Islamist like most members of the IRGC?"

Bashir nodded his affirmation. "According to my grandfather, my father maintained a very secular lifestyle when he was growing up in the Westernized society the Shah had built; however, once he joined the IRGC, he adopted the militant's strict adherence to the tenets and practices of Islamic law."

"I'm sure that affected your upbringing," I said.

Bashir cleared his throat. "Yes it did. I was also an Islamist until I met Farah. As you Americans describe it, I fell in love with her at first sight. However, after I got to know her, I discovered she had rejected the Muslim faith. She had become a Christian, a follower of Jesus Christ."

This time it was Danny who interrupted him. "Oh, wow! I'm sure that didn't sit well with Daddy."

Subtlety was never Danny's strong suit, and I was afraid his comment might be offensive to Bashir, but instead he agreed with Danny's observation and went on with his story.

"You're right, of course. My father and I had many painful arguments, and I finally agreed to stop seeing her. However, during our time apart, I started reading a Bible she had given me, and then I understood why she had become a believer. I too became a believer. A few days later, I sought her out and we were reunited. However, she agreed with me to keep our relationship and my new belief a secret until I could decide how to break the news to my father. A few—"

Suddenly, a soft melody from a cell phone started playing, and Bashir immediately let out a cry of anguish and rushed across the room to a nightstand. He whipped open the drawer, withdrew the phone, and silenced the ring.

As he continued staring down at the phone, I walked over and took it from his hand. The screen name was displaying "Farah."

"Who's using Farah's phone?" I asked.

His words were barely perceptible. "The man who killed my wife."

"Why is he calling you?"

"When I finish my story, you'll understand," he replied, walking back over to the living area.

After he sat down, his chin dropped to his chest, and he vigorously rubbed his eyes. At that moment, I wasn't sure he was capable of continuing. But, moments later, he raised his head, and, with a determined look on his face, resumed his story.

"One of my responsibilities in the Guard was to investigate document forging. A few weeks after I started seeing Farah again, I received some information on a known forger, a man who operated near Azad University on the outskirts of Tehran. After reading the evidence against him, I decided there was enough information to make an arrest. However, after talking it over with Farah, instead of arresting the man, I offered him a huge sum of money to prepare passports, travel documentation, and other papers we would need in order to leave Tehran and start a new life in America."

"Were you afraid of your family?" Danny asked." Is that why you wanted to leave?"

"No. While I knew my family would disown me, I never thought they would harm either of us. What we both wanted more than anything else was to live a normal life as believers of Christ. I knew that was never going to happen in Iran, and the only place I knew it could happen was here in America.

"Six months before I met Farah, my grandfather had passed away. Before he died, he had deposited a substantial amount of his wealth in Swiss bank accounts, and, when he died, some of that fortune became mine. So, once we had made our escape from Iran, Farah and I flew to Geneva, Switzerland, where I made arrangements for the funds from my inheritance to be transferred to accounts here in the United States. We did all of this without telling anyone we were leaving Iran and coming to America. Once we arrived, though, I contacted my father."

At this point, Bashir's voice cracked. "He told me I was no longer his son. I was dead to him."

He stared out the window with a faraway look in his eyes for a few moments. Watching him deal with the pain of losing his family was difficult.

I changed the subject. "Why did you choose to come to Norman?"

He gave me a weak smile. "We considered several places, but, in the end, Farah was the one who decided we should live in Norman.

"I wanted us to live near a university so I could pursue a degree, and I also felt we would be safer in a community where there was a large international population. When I was looking at OU as a possibility, Farah got excited about coming to Oklahoma. Later, I realized this excitement was due to her poor English. When I told her we could live in Norman, Oklahoma, she thought I was saying normal, and that's what we both wanted, just a normal life. Even when I explained it to her, she still insisted Norman was where she wanted to live."

Bashir gestured toward the window, and said. "We were married at a church not far from here, and, while we were looking for a residence in Norman, this hotel was our first home."

"That's how we found you," I told him. "Farah's computer had photographs of the two of you here at the hotel."

"That was careless of me to leave her computer behind," Bashir replied, shaking his head, "and it was my carelessness that got her killed in the first place."

"I know you want to blame yourself for her death," Danny told Bashir, "but instead you should focus your energy on helping us find her killer."

"You're right," Bashir agreed. "That's what I must do."

"So tell us what you know about the man who murdered your wife," I prompted.

"To do that, I need to tell you what happened two months ago."

I saw Danny remove a pen and notepad from his coat pocket. So much for technology—he had left his iPad in the car.

"Our passports identified us as Iraqis, and, for that reason, we were very careful about making Arabic friends because I didn't want our accents to betray us as Iranians. However, after living in Norman for over a year, I could tell Farah was getting homesick. So, two months ago, after she met a Jordanian woman at a grocery store, I gave my consent for us to attend a meal at the woman's home. I thought a family meal would do Farah a lot of good, because she hadn't joined the ESL class yet, and I knew she needed to make some friends in Norman.

"The dinner seemed harmless at the time, and it was wonderful to see Farah enjoying herself. She especially liked playing with the children in the family. However, when the meal was almost over, the Jordanian woman's nephew and his two roommates arrived. I immediately recognized one of the roommates, although he gave no indication he knew me."

"Was he an Iranian?" I asked.

"No, he was a Palestinian I had met about a year before I left Iran. He was attending a training camp for Hezbollah recruits being conducted by the IRGC. My commander and I had spent a couple of days at the camp observing their training methods, so I knew I wasn't mistaken about his identity." Bashir took a long, slow breath.

"He's the man who killed my wife. His name is Shahid al-Nawar."

At this disclosure, Danny looked over at me with a look of triumph. Getting up from the sofa, he said, "Excuse me. I need to call my office."

After Danny stepped out in the hallway, Bashir said, "I need to take a break." Then, he headed for the bathroom.

While Bashir and Danny were out of the room, I raided the room's mini-fridge and grabbed a soda. A few minutes later, Danny walked back in the room. When he saw Bashir was in the bathroom, he said, "The surveillance team can't locate Shahid. I've ordered an additional unit to Norman, so we should get some results soon. If that—"

Danny cut himself off when he heard the bathroom door open.

Bashir looked emotionally depleted, and I held up the soda can. "Would you like one?"

"No, thanks."

Danny got himself something to drink, and when we sat back down, I asked Bashir, "What makes you so certain this man killed Farah? You said he gave no indication he knew you."

Bashir replied with disgust. "He knew who I was, or rather, who I had been, as soon as he saw me, but I didn't know that until a week after the dinner. That's when he approached me in a parking garage on the OU campus and held a knife to my throat. Then, he made me get inside his car where we could talk. Once inside, he told me he had recognized me at the dinner and had been curious as to why I was living here under a false identity.

"His curiosity led him to get in touch with his contacts inside the IRGC, and they told him I had supposedly drowned while on holiday at a Caspian resort—I'm sure this story was fabricated by my father to guard his reputation. Shahid said his contacts told him I was from a very wealthy family, and that my father was a high-ranking official in the IRGC. He said he knew my father wouldn't want the authorities to know I was a Muslim traitor living among the infidels in America.

"However, he assured me if I met his demands, he would keep my betrayal a secret. He went on to explain how he was responsible for building a network of Hezbollah cells in the area, and that I could buy his silence by giving him one million dollars. This money would be used to provide housing, transportation, and financing for his network, enabling him to fulfill his responsibilities.

"I suspected he simply wanted these funds for his own personal use, because I knew, if his mission was sponsored by Hezbollah, he had plenty of money for his operational needs. He refused to say what his objectives were in building these networks, but I believed his mission had to be coming straight from the IRGC high command and, more than likely, was a plan for some kind of attack inside the United States."

I looked over at Danny, and, by the expression on his face, he appeared just as surprised as I was by this astonishing revelation. I had assumed Bashir's story was going to conclude with his father sending someone after him to bring him home or to kill him because of his rejection of Islam. Bashir's involvement with a Hezbollah cell leader was an unexpected twist, and I was sure Danny was thinking the same thing.

"When I absolutely refused to do what Shahid was asking of me, he threatened Farah and my family back in Iran. He said if I didn't help him, he would kill my wife, and then he would arrange to have all my relatives murdered. At that point, I asked him to give me ten days to get the money together.

"I didn't tell Farah about Shahid's blackmail because, since she had started making new friends in the ESL class, I'd never seen her so happy, and I didn't want her to worry. Instead, I decided to appease Shahid by giving him half of the money and pretending to go along with the rest of what he wanted—at least until I could figure something out. Then, the night before we were to meet, he unexpectedly showed up at my house.

"Farah remembered Shahid from the dinner party, and she immediately assumed we had developed a friendship from that time. Shahid tried to be charming, showing a great deal of interest in her, but she was completely unaware he was simply baiting me, demonstrating that he could get at my family anytime he desired to do so.

"He became especially interested in a word game Farah had discovered for her iPhone called Words with Friends. It was helping her learn lots of English vocabulary. When she showed him she was able to send text messages to other players by using the chat feature on it, he immediately downloaded the app and insisted I do the same. After he left our house that evening, he used the word game to text me where he wanted to meet me the following day."

When Bashir paused, I asked, "Shahid sent you a message through the word game last Friday night when we were at the ESL dinner, didn't he?"

"Yes, I told you I'd received a phone call, but—"

Danny cut him off. "Why didn't he just text you? Why was he so interested in chatting with you on the word game?"

Bashir explained, "We know your government has sophisticated monitoring technology that analyzes all electronic communications according to languages. However, Shahid said the chat from an English game app would not be targeted. You don't even have to play the game to use the chat feature, so he was going to make sure the members of his cell only communicated with each other through this word game from now on."

"Let's hope he's wrong about that app," I said, but I still made a mental note to talk to Carlton about it as soon as I could get free.

Danny asked, "So what happened last Thursday when you gave him half of the money?"

"He seemed to take it as a good sign I was going to cooperate with him. However, when I was at the ESL dinner with Farah on Friday evening, he sent me a message to meet him on Monday morning. At that time, he informed me I needed to help him lease an apartment and purchase a van for four cell members arriving in Norman in a couple of weeks. He was very agitated about it.

"I tried to persuade him not to get me involved with his activities. However, when he continued to insist on my participation, I realized he knew the task he'd been given was more than he could handle. Shahid is a fighter, but he knows nothing about administration and logistics; plus, he's barely proficient in English. In the end, I agreed to help him set everything up; however, I only did so in order to give myself time to come up with a different plan." Bashir grimaced and shook his head. "Now, I believe he knew I was deceiving him all along."

He stopped talking and rubbed the back of his neck for several seconds. He seemed reluctant to finish his story, and, knowing how it was going to end, I fully understood his hesitancy.

"Once I left Shahid," he continued, "I knew I could never meet with him again. That's when I started formulating a plan for us to leave Norman. When Shahid tried to contact me on Monday afternoon through the chat feature, I resigned from the word game site and removed the app from my phone. Thinking back on it now, I realize I acted foolishly. Perhaps if I hadn't done so, Farah would still be alive."

Bashir bowed his head, grasping the back of it with both hands and shaking it back and forth.. It took him several seconds to get control of himself before he could continue.

"Yesterday morning, after I dropped Farah off at the church for her ESL class, I went on to my class at the University. About halfway through the lecture, I received a text from Farah asking me to call her. I left the classroom immediately and placed the call. When Shahid answered Farah's phone, all he said was, 'I warned you.' Seconds after he hung up, there was a text sent from her phone with a photograph attached."

Bashir couldn't control his emotions anymore. As he spoke, he started weeping. "It was a picture of my wife . . . she was covered in blood . . . he had killed her."

Danny and I remained quiet. After a few seconds, Bashir got up, walked over to the nightstand, and drained the glass of water Danny had offered him earlier.

When he sat back down, I asked, "Why did you come here to the hotel, Bashir? What were you planning to do?"

"I needed a place to think," he answered, staring at me for a moment before he continued, "and I know you are not going to understand this, but I also needed a place to pray about what I needed to do next."

I met his gaze.

"I'm sure you wanted to hunt Shahid down and kill him, but, as a believer, you couldn't do that, so you weren't certain what to do next. I know such restraint goes against all your training."

He seemed surprised by my description of his feelings.

"That's exactly what I felt. I've been in this room praying since I got here because I couldn't decide who to call or where to go. I was hoping God would answer my prayers and then—"

"—and then we showed up," I said, finishing his sentence.

He nodded. "Yes, you showed up."

"It would appear God did answer your prayers, Bashir."

CHAPTER 27

I could tell Bashir was worried when Danny told him he was about to be put in protective custody and moved to a more secure location. However, he didn't say anything until Danny went down to the manager's office to make arrangements for us to leave the hotel.

When Danny stepped out of the room, Bashir asked me, "Will I be arrested for entering your country under a false passport?"

I assured him, "Not if you help us capture Shahid and bring down the networks he's established here."

He nodded.

"After that," I continued, "you should think about helping our government understand what's going on in Iran these days. I'm sure you have some very valuable information about your country's military, perhaps even their nuclear program."

He reacted with surprise and a note of anger in his voice. "You mean become a defector?"

"That's exactly what I mean."

He stared down at the carpet and didn't reply.

Finally, he looked up at me and said, "Farah and I came to America in order to live a normal life together, to practice our faith without fear. Betraying my country was not on my mind. I never imagined doing such a thing. "

"Sometimes life takes some surprising turns. It happens to all of us." I shook my head and added, "It's certainly happened to me."

I mulled over the irony between Bashir's story and my own recent stay in Iran. He was an IRGC officer, who, having been converted to Christianity in Iran, escaped to America. I was a CIA officer, who, having been converted to Christianity in Iran, escaped to America. Yet, despite our common ties, I would never be able to disclose this information to him.

There was a note of fear in his voice when he asked, "How will I be treated if I do this?"

As I was reassuring him the Agency would extend him every professional courtesy, up to and including honoring his military rank, Danny came back in the room and announced we were leaving immediately. Within minutes, four OSBI agents arrived to drive Bashir and his car to a secure location at Tinker Air Force Base in Midwest City, where an FBI counterterrorism team was standing by.

As soon as Bashir left, Danny said, "If we can identify the Hezbollah cell Shahid has been running, we might be able to shut down their entire network. This could really be big, Titus. The Agency will be mining information from Bashir for years."

"At least now I know Ahmed didn't murder Farah."

Danny nodded. "At this moment, I can't see how Farah's murder is connected to Ahmed Al-Amin."

"I need to let Carlton know that Shahid has been communicating through that word game. Carlton mentioned NSA chatter was off this week. Perhaps Shahid told his jihadist friends about that chat feature and now they're all using it."

"I already took care of that," Danny said. "While I was downstairs, I made a call to Carlton."

I started to protest, but he held up his hand.

"Don't worry. I kept you completely out of it. I simply told him I had a source who had informed OSBI that some of the terrorist networks operating inside the United States might be communicating with each other through a word game. Naturally, he said he'd never heard of Words with Friends, but you can bet it's under the microscope right now."

"Thanks for keeping me out of it."

"I also called Detective Saxon. She's meeting us at your place in an hour."

"At my place?"

"You don't mind do you—?"

"I guess it's fine, but—"

"—because I want you there with me when we tell her about Bashir's situation. We can't very well meet at the police station because then I'd be put in the awkward position of having to explain your presence."

"No, you're right. My place is perfect."

Or at least it would be perfect if Stormy had obeyed my strict instructions about his bathroom habits.

♦♦♦♦

When I got to my house, Nikki was parked outside the gate, and, within a few minutes, she was standing in the driveway bombarding me with questions.

"What happened? When Director Jarrar called, he said Bashir was at the Skirvin and they were putting him in protective custody. What's he doing in protective custody?"

I punched in the security code while she was questioning me. Then I turned around and made a capital "T" with my hands.

"Time out, Detective."

She laughed. "Okay. Sorry. I'm not a very patient person."

"I can't tell you anything until Danny arrives."

"Right."

Stormy scampered across the room to greet us, and while Nikki was making cooing noises at him, I went through the house turning on lights and checking things out. When I unlocked the patio doors, Stormy rushed outside.

Thankfully, he had been a very conscientious dog during the long day he had spent inside the house.

When I went to get us some sodas out of the refrigerator, Danny arrived with a couple of pizzas, and he and Nikki spent a few minutes exchanging greetings. As we sat down to eat, I noticed everyone was on a first name basis.

"So, Danny," Nikki asked, "what happened with Bashir today?"

Danny took a big gulp of soda before replying. "Before I tell you about Bashir, why don't you to tell us about Farah Karimi's autopsy. I want to see if those results corroborate the story he told us about her death."

Nikki put her pizza down and quickly wiped her mouth with a napkin. "The written results won't be ready until tomorrow, but here's the important stuff. The ME confirmed she died instantly from a knife wound across her throat. Her assailant was behind her when she was struck, and she showed no defensive abrasions on her body. She obviously had no time to defend herself before she was killed. The ME believes the weapon the killer used was some type of curved blade. She called it a dagger but also some strange word I don't remember. It's in my notes."

I asked, "Was it a *Pesh-kabz*?"

Nikki nodded. "That sounds about right. Are you familiar with that weapon?"

"It's the militants' weapon of choice in the Middle East," I answered.

"Used almost exclusively in Pakistan and Afghanistan." Danny added.

Nikki nodded her head thoughtfully as she digested that bit of information. Then, out of the corner of my eye, I noticed her studying me for a couple of seconds before glancing over at Danny. While I knew it had to be disconcerting to be dealing with two veteran intelligence officers, she seemed determined to hold her own and not be surprised by anything we had to say.

She continued, "The only other interesting part of the autopsy was that Farah had a small tattoo on the inside of her right wrist. It was a cross."

"Those types of tattoos are the way Christian women in Muslim countries show their solidarity with each other," I explained. "It's an extremely courageous act on their part to get one."

"I've read how difficult it is to be a Christian in a Muslim country," Nikki said. "Is that why you think she was killed?"

"No," I replied, "according to Bashir's testimony, she was killed because he refused to help a Palestinian named Shahid al-Nawar set up a Hezbollah terrorist network in this area."

Nikki's eyes widened. "You believed him?"

"Yes," I answered. "Of course, everything he said is being checked out," I pointed toward Danny, "but both of us felt he was telling the truth."

"What is the truth? Why was Farah killed?"

"Danny is much better at recapping a story than I am, so he's going to give you the highlights of what Bashir told us."

Danny grinned at me because when we'd worked together at the Agency, I'd always let him give our debriefers the operational narrative. He was a good storyteller, plus he loved the limelight.

"First of all, Bashir and Farah Karimi aren't Iraqis." Danny told Nikki. "They're both from Iran, and he comes from a very wealthy and well-connected family. His father commands a unit of their internal security militia, the IRGC. Basically, they're radical Islamists. Bashir himself was a member of this militia.

"Then, Bashir met Farah, who, as you already know, was a devoted Christian. This caused conflict between Bashir and his father, and while Bashir broke up with her for a short while, they got back together after he also converted to the Christian faith. He was able to convince Farah the only avenue to happiness for them was to leave Iran for good, so he obtained false identity papers for both of them, and they fled the country.

"They arrived in the States posing as very wealthy Iraqi immigrants because of a fortune he had inherited from his grandfather. They chose to come to Norman so he could pursue a degree, but also because Farah thought the city's name sounded like normal. She saw this as a sign they could live a normal life here."

At this point Nikki broke in. "How sad for her in light of what happened here."

Danny nodded in agreement. "For almost a year, they lived in Norman without a problem, but a few weeks ago, Shahid al-Nawar, a Palestinian, who was already under surveillance by my office, recognized Bashir as a former IRGC officer. Shahid discovered, through his contacts back in Iran, the IRGC had been told Bashir had drowned while on vacation. Armed with this information, Shahid confronted Bashir and, along with demanding money, insisted Bashir help him set up a Hezbollah network here.

"Behind Shahid's demands was the threat of violence against Farah and Bashir's family back in Iran. Bashir gave him half the money and decided to pretend a measure of cooperation until he could come up with a plan. However, last Sunday evening, when Shahid insisted Bashir help him find housing and transportation for a four-member team arriving in this area in a few weeks, Bashir broke off all contact with Shahid. Bashir is convinced that was the moment Shahid decided to kill his wife. He even sent Bashir photos of his dead wife over her cell phone after he killed her. So, Bashir went into hiding until he could figure out what to do."

Nikki stared at Danny, and then shook her head in disbelief. "That's an incredible story. I presume you've alerted the FBI and Homeland Security?"

"About two hours ago," Danny replied, grabbing the last piece of pizza.

"So, I'm about to be bumped from this case?"

Danny nodded. "You might have twenty-four hours, but then it belongs to the FBI. You'll be getting a call from Homeland Security and our Counterterrorism unit soon. I've had photos and all the information we have on Shahid faxed over to your office already, including the license plate number of his Nissan."

Nikki bobbed her head up and down. "Okay, so I've got twenty-four hours to find Shahid."

"That may be harder than you think. I've had a couple of teams out trying to track him down, and they haven't had any luck so far. They weren't able to locate him either at his house or on campus."

With a sense of urgency, Nikki replied, "I need to make some phone calls." She excused herself and walked into the living room with her cell phone.

"I think I'll head over to Midwest City and check on Bashir," Danny told me. "I want him well coached on what to say if Shahid calls him again, and, if I'm not there when the FBI arrives, they'll try to shut me out of this operation."

"If you need me, I'd love to help," I said, hoping it didn't sound like I was begging.

"I know you're dying to get in on this action," Danny replied, "but I believe you have enough on your plate trying to stay one step ahead of Ahmed. Besides, I can't stand how pathetic you sound when you're begging for something."

I glanced in the living room to make sure Nikki hadn't overheard Danny's remark about Ahmed. She was still talking on the phone.

Danny noticed my reaction and slapped me on the back as he was leaving. "Maybe the detective will let you help her find Shahid. I think she really likes you."

♦♦♦♦

While Nikki was on the phone with her office, I opened my laptop and checked my Agency emails. There was only one, and it had arrived earlier in the day after I'd left the house. It was from Carlton. As promised, he had instructed Katherine to do a data run on Paul Franklin. I skimmed over the information, paying particular attention to anything within the last five years.

Paul Franklin lived on the west side of Norman in an area called Brookhaven. The house was valued at over half of a million dollars, but he also owned several rent houses near the University. During the summer months, he usually traveled around the Middle East. Last year he'd been to Gaza, Jordan, and the West Bank. In the last five years, he'd given a substantial amount of money to organizations calling for a Palestinian state. He was on the board of several liberal think tanks, and he was also a State Department consultant.

Nothing on the data sheet surprised me, yet something about Katherine's information began to gnaw away at me. It was sitting right there on the outer edges of my brain nibbling away at my neurons. I was quite familiar with the feeling; it usually meant I was overlooking some important detail in a mission.

Nikki came back in the kitchen. "Did Danny leave?"

"He went to check on Bashir. Was there anything new at your office?"

"No, I have every available patrol out looking for Shahid and the Nissan. I'm supposed to meet with my captain first thing in the morning to go over the case, so I probably ought to get back to the station and finish up my paperwork."

"Do you have time for a cup of coffee before you go?"

She glanced at her watch. "If we make it quick."

"It's a nice evening. Would you like to sit out on the patio?"

She smiled. "And have you serve me coffee? Sure."

When I brought the mugs out to the patio, Nikki was sitting in an Adirondack chair and Stormy was lying beside her. There was a full moon overhead, and I decided to leave the overhead patio lights off, because the soft glow from the perimeter's automatic security lights made it easy for us to see each other. It would have been the perfect romantic setting, if only Nikki and I weren't together for the sole purpose of discussing a young woman's murder.

"Thanks," she said, as she took her mug. "You remembered my cream, I see."

"That's the only personal thing I know about you. You like cream with your coffee."

"Okay, what personal thing would you like to know?"

"I don't want to interrogate you. Just tell me about yourself."

"Hmmm. Let's see. I'm not a very good housekeeper. Your house is much neater than mine is."

"That's probably because you're not an obsessive compulsive person like I am. Be thankful for that."

"Does that mean you go around making sure all the pictures are hung straight and your cabinet doors are completely shut?"

"Yes," I answered a bit embarrassed. "But we're not talking about me."

She laughed. "You're right. Okay, something else. Let's see. Well, like most women, I enjoy shopping for clothes. Now that I'm a detective, that's where I spend all my money. In fact, not having to wear a uniform was my motivation for trying to make detective in the first place."

"I don't believe that. The part about the clothes shopping, sure, but I'll bet you've always wanted to be a super sleuth. Were either of your parents on the police force?"

"No."

A moment of awkward silence followed her emphatic reply. Finally, after several seconds, it became obvious she wasn't going to elaborate on her answer.

"See, I started asking questions," I said. "It's a trade hazard. You of all people should understand that. Please forgive me."

I noticed her nervously tapping her finger against her coffee mug, a gesture I'd seen her making the day before when she was interviewing me after the murder.

"No, it's okay," she replied. "It's hard for me to talk about my childhood, mainly because people usually end up feeling sorry for me, and I hate that."

"You don't have to tell me anything. Believe me when I say I'm big on privacy."

"You took a chance with me yesterday, so I'm going to do the same with you today."

I reached over and touched her hand.

"I'm a very hard-hearted guy. I promise not to feel sorry for you."

She gave me a less than enthusiastic smile. "Okay."

However, she waited a few seconds before starting to talk. When she did begin to speak, her voice was so low I had to strain to hear her.

"I never knew the identity of my father. I'm sure my mother never knew his name either."

She looked over at me. Perhaps she expected some sort of response, but when I didn't give one, she continued. "When I was three years old, my mother was sent to prison for being involved in an armed robbery. After I was older, I learned she was high on meth at the time. Since the courts weren't able to locate any of my relatives, they placed me in an institution called The Children's Home. It's run by a group of churches and resembles something between a boarding school and a foster home."

"Is it located here in Norman?"

"No, it's in Moore, a few miles north of Norman. It looks like a college campus, but instead of dorms, there are eight large houses. I lived in one of them with ten other children of various ages. A married couple—we called them Mom and Dad—took care of us, and they did everything normal parents do for their children. On Sundays, we all attended church together. I admit that was one of the most enjoyable times of the week for me, because, as we sat together in the service, it felt like I belonged to a real family."

"Why did you tell me yesterday you weren't happy when you were attending Bethel Church?"

"My house parents changed churches and joined Bethel when I was thirteen. The church itself was wonderful, and, without the guidance of some of the youth workers there, I wouldn't have made it. However, when I was thirteen, my life turned upside down because I was suddenly forced to become reacquainted with my mother. She was paroled after being in prison for ten years, and it's the policy of The Children's Home to try and reunite families."

"Did you visit her when she was in prison?"

"No. She could have had regular visits from me, but she wanted nothing to do with me. Once she was out of prison, though, she insisted she wanted to take care of me again."

"I can't imagine how hard that was on you."

"I was in turmoil for almost a year while she was allowed to visit me under the supervision of my house parents. Later, she was permitted to take me out to eat by herself, and, finally, I had an overnight stay at her apartment."

"How did you feel about her?"

"I went through a lot of different emotions. I was angry and embarrassed that my mother was an ex-con, but I was also upset that I had to leave my foster family. Whenever my mother and I were alone, she hardly spoke to me at all. Truthfully, I never felt as if she cared about me at all. However, my overwhelming emotion was guilt. I didn't want to live with her, be around her, or get to know her. Yet, I knew I shouldn't feel that way because she was, after all, my mother."

As if sensing Nikki's painful recollections, Stormy raised his head and moaned softly. Nikki bent down and touched him lightly on the head. He whimpered once, and then lowered his head once again.

"Did your mom have a job? Could she support you?"

"No, not at first. When she got out of prison, she worked as a waitress at several different restaurants, but she hardly made enough money to pay her rent. For over a year, I only saw her occasionally, while I continued to live with my house parents. Then, out of the blue, she had money. She claimed it was because she'd become an apartment manager. She even bought a car. When she got permission for me to spend a weekend with her, the administrators at The Children's Home were about to begin the process of having me released into her care permanently.

"After dinner, on Friday night of that weekend, she told me she had invited some friends over. I wasn't happy about that because the only friends she had ever mentioned were ex-cons, so I decided to stay upstairs in my room. Around midnight, my mother came upstairs and told me they were going out. I went to bed after they left, but I was awakened about four o'clock the next morning by two police officers banging on the front door. My mother and her friends had been arrested for trying to rob a convenience store."

"So that was how she was getting her money?"

She nodded. "The police charged the three of them with two other robberies, and they found evidence my mother was also dealing drugs out of the apartment manager's office." She shook her head. "I can only imagine why she wanted me around the place."

"Is she still in prison?"

"No, she died of breast cancer while serving another fifteen-year prison term."

"Did the authorities get you some help to deal with this? The psychological trauma must have been tremendously hard for a teenage girl."

She nodded. "I was in counseling until I graduated from high school; however, I believe it was my faith that sustained me during those years. I prayed a lot during that time."

"You're obviously a very well-adjusted woman with a tremendous future ahead of you now."

Nikki smiled at my compliment.

"I was so determined not to be anything like my mother, that even before I graduated from high school, I decided to go into law enforcement. I went to OU, majored in criminal justice, and, when I graduated, I was immediately accepted into the police academy. I think the best revenge against my childhood is becoming a success at this job."

Nikki scooted forward in her chair and said, "Now, I think it's time for me to go. I've still got a lot of work to do tonight."

"Thanks for telling me this, Nikki. At least now I can say I know a few more things about you than just how you like your coffee."

She laid her hand on my sleeve. "Next time, it's your turn."

"Could I ask you one more question?"

She smiled and said, "Oh, sure, what's one more question."

"What's the most important thing in the world to you?"

She looked at me as though I might be teasing her.

"Are you joking?"

"No, I'm quite serious."

"Well, I thought it was fairly obvious. For me, the most important thing in the world is becoming a success at my job."

CHAPTER 28

After finishing breakfast the next morning, I called Nikki to get the latest update on Shahid. However, she was just going into a meeting with her captain and said she'd have to call me back.

When I got off the phone, I asked myself, "If I were Shahid, where would I be right now?"

Although there were no witnesses to Farah's murder, Shahid still would have had to consider the possibility someone had spotted him in the church's parking lot. Thus, leaving town would have been his first option.

However, since he was responsible for running a network here, with more cell members arriving soon, he would have been forced to go with his second option—remaining in town and finding a place to hole up, preferably a place with a garage so he could hide the Nissan.

Danny had told me Shahid had been living in a rent house in one of the poorer neighborhoods of the city. However, when Danny's agents had arrived at the location, it looked as if Shahid and his roommates had moved out in a hurry.

So, where did Shahid and his roommates go?

Suddenly, that gnawing feeling I'd been dealing with since reading the data on Paul Franklin resurfaced, and I remembered the photos Danny had shown me of Shahid's roommates. They had seemed familiar to me then, and now I remembered why.

On the day I'd gone to see Paul Franklin, there had been two Arab students in the hallway outside Franklin's office. They'd been arguing about a rent payment. I suddenly realized the men Danny had identified as Shahid's roommates were the students I'd noticed outside of Franklin's office.

I pulled up the email Carlton had sent me yesterday about Franklin and reread it. Besides his expensive home on the west side, Franklin also owned rental property near the University.

I called Katherine's number at Langley.

"Hi, Katherine. It's Titus Ray."

"Titus, how nice to hear from you. How are you?"

"Great. Listen, I need a favor."

"Okay, so much for small talk."

"Sorry, I'm in a hurry." I replied with a half-hearted apology. "I got the data you pulled up on Paul Franklin. I'm interested in the addresses of those rent houses he owns here in Norman."

"I'll look them up and send them over to Carlton."

"There's no need for that. Email them directly to me as soon as possible."

"It sounds suspiciously like you're trying to keep Carlton in the dark about something."

"It's strictly a time thing. I'm in a big hurry."

She was quiet for a few seconds. "I don't believe you're shooting straight with me, but I'm going to do this because I like your dog."

"Stormy sends his love."

♦♦♦♦

Within an hour, Katherine had sent me the addresses of the four rental properties owned by Franklin. I immediately recognized one of the locations. It was the address on Peters Street where Danny had told me Shahid had been living with his two roommates. I crossed that one off the list, since Danny's agents from OSBI had already discovered Shahid and his friends had cleared out.

I wondered if all four of Franklin's properties were being rented by Arab students. Reviewing the conversation the professor and I had had several weeks ago, the most likely answer was yes. In fact, if

Franklin enjoyed expressing his sympathy for Arab causes—especially Palestinians without a homeland—there was no better way to do that than to provide housing for them.

Whether Franklin knew one of his renters was a militant extremist, sent here by Hezbollah to establish a network of terrorists on American soil, was a matter for the FBI to deal with. However, I certainly hoped he hadn't committed such a treasonous act.

As I prepared to leave my house in search of Shahid, I knew the odds of locating him before Nikki had to turn her case over to the FBI were not good, but I was still going to try. I owed Farah and Bashir that much.

In some strange way, I felt a responsibility toward them. They had come to America seeking a place of refuge, a place where they could worship God as they pleased, and my country had failed them. Javad and Darya had protected me in Iran, but no one had protected Bashir and Farah in America.

Stormy was out by the lake chasing birds, so I put some food and water on the patio for him, threw a few items in the backseat of the Range Rover, and set my car's GPS for the first address on my list.

It felt good to be on the hunt once again.

♦♦♦♦

All of Franklin's rental properties were located in a ten-block area north of the University and south of the downtown area of Norman.

As I entered the vicinity, I recognized many of the homes—from the early 1900's—had probably been upper-to-middle-class residences back then. However, as I drove by them now, I noticed they were presently occupied by poor college students, families struggling to survive, and senior citizens waiting to die. The yards were overrun with weeds and cluttered with trash and kids' toys. Most houses seemed to be in need of extensive repairs to make them look even halfway decent again.

Surveillance was not going to be difficult, though, because each side of the street was lined with vehicles. I took a parking spot two houses down from my target and settled in.

No one appeared for over an hour.

Finally, an Arab woman, with her hair discreetly covered and her long skirt almost touching the ground, came out the front door. She was pushing a baby stroller and she passed by me without a second glance.

I moved on to my next address because I couldn't imagine Shahid, plus his roommates, being able to stay in such a small house with a crying baby.

When I arrived at the second location, I realized there was a better possibility of finding Shahid and his friends because the homes were much larger. Most were two-story residences with detached garages. A couple of them were so large they had been converted into duplexes. Once again, the narrow street was crowded with parked cars, and this time I was forced to park almost directly in the sight line of the house I was observing.

After a few minutes, I began to feel uneasy. Whether it was my sense of exposure at being parked so near the house or my instincts telling me I'd found Shahid's base, I wasn't sure. However, before leaving my house, I'd thrown a couple of props in the car just in case I needed to get out and walk around the neighborhoods, so, as I got out of my car, I grabbed a clipboard from the backseat and headed in the opposite direction from the target house.

Then I called Nikki.

"Can you talk now?" I asked her.

"Your timing is perfect. I'm about to go over to Midwest City to interview Bashir. Did I hear a horn honking? Where are you?"

"Right now, I'm playing a hunch and watching a house at 707 Surrey Avenue. Are you familiar with that part of town?"

"I know it's a pretty rundown neighborhood. What are you doing there?"

I briefly explained how I'd connected Danny's photos of Shahid's roommates to the two Arabs I'd seen outside of Franklin's office. Then I told her about the information I'd received from the Agency about Franklin's rent houses.

"Let me get this straight," she said. "You think since Shahid was living in a rent house owned by Paul Franklin, he might be hiding in another one of his properties?"

"You sound skeptical."

"That's only because I am."

"The house I'm watching also has a detached garage. You haven't found Shahid's car anywhere, and it's been two days. Maybe that's where he stashed it."

"Okay," she replied, reluctantly. "I'll swing by there and take a look."

I gave her the address, but we agreed to meet two blocks south at a convenience store. I arrived by foot just as she was parking her car.

As soon as I slid in the passenger seat, she said, "You look like a magazine salesman with that clipboard."

"I was going for the census-taker look."

"This isn't the year a census is taken."

"You think people around here know that?"

She smiled. "No, I guess not."

As I described the two-story house on Surrey, I could tell she was reluctant to pursue a search warrant without something substantial to go on. My gut feeling wasn't going to impress a judge.

"When I was walking over here," I told her, "I saw an alley at the back of the property. What if I go take a peek in the garage and see if there's a black Nissan parked inside?"

She thought about my suggestion, but I saw the same look on her face I'd seen the day before when I'd asked her to go to the Skirvin Hotel with me.

"That could go wrong on so many levels, Titus. I don't even want to think about it."

"You're right. Bad idea. I'll go back to my car and see if anyone turns up at the house."

She looked relieved.

"I'm driving over to Midwest City now," she said. "I need to have a statement from Bashir before I turn my files over to the FBI. I'll call you when I get back."

"Right. We'll talk later."

I got out of her car and retraced my steps back up the block.

When I reached the alleyway leading to the back of the houses on

Surrey Avenue, I turned in and cautiously made my way to the rear of Franklin's property where I hoped I was going to find a black Nissan.

As soon as I reached the back of the house next door to Franklin's property, I threw my clipboard in a big green trashcan. Then, I unholstered my gun. As I held it at my side, I carefully surveyed Franklin's property from the cover of the neighbor's privacy fence.

Large trees dominated the backyard of Franklin's rent house, and I was certain their foliage would obscure the view of the garage from anyone in the house who happened to be looking outside. As I looked at the decrepit wooden structure from my vantage point, I was happy to see there was a window on the west side of the garage. However, it was so dirty, I wasn't sure I'd be able to see anything inside.

Suddenly, my attention was drawn to the opposite end of the alley where I spotted Nikki making her way toward me. Her gun was drawn, but she was holding it at her side. When she saw me, she tilted her head in the direction of the garage, lifting her gun slightly to indicate she would cover me while I went to look in the window.

As she stood facing the garage, she positioned herself against the neighbor's fence. It wasn't the ideal location because her back was to the alleyway, but there weren't any other good spots where she could keep her eye on both the house and garage at the same time. This bothered me, but since I'd planned to do the whole thing without her anyway, I didn't really think it mattered.

As it turned out, it mattered a lot.

I hurriedly covered the distance from the fence to the garage and slipped along the west wall until I came to the window. Using my free hand, I brushed aside the accumulated dirt and grime and looked inside. It was dark, and it took my eyes about a minute to adjust so I could see the vehicle parked inside.

It wasn't the Nissan.

It was a Chevy Malibu.

I couldn't tell what model it was, but I didn't stay long enough to find out. At that moment, all I wanted to do was to leave the area as quickly as possible.

I hadn't been out of sight for more than a couple of minutes. As I rounded the corner of the garage, I was expecting to see Nikki exactly where I'd left her.

However, she wasn't there.

Instead, she was on the east side of the garage, where Shahid was holding a dagger to her throat.

I aimed my gun directly at his head. He was no more than ten feet away, and it was going to be an easy shot.

"Drop your gun," he said in heavily accented English, "or I'll cut her throat."

Now that we were face to face, I could see his nose had been broken at least twice. And, because of the way Farah had been murdered, I also knew he had a lot of skill with the dagger. While I was certain he would die if I shot him, Nikki might never recover from the damage he could do to her in the seconds before I sent him off to his hellish fate.

I raised both my hands—my pistol in the right one—and, while never taking my eyes off him, I slowly bent my knees and placed my gun on the ground just a few feet from where Nikki had dropped her own handgun.

As Shahid pressed the knife further into Nikki's flesh, he demanded, "Open up the garage door."

The dilapidated wooden door was an old-fashioned manual type. I grasped the metal handle and pulled it up on its rollers. It made a loud, grinding noise as I did so.

Shahid ordered, "Step back."

I did as I was told and stepped away from the door.

I didn't fully understand his actions until I saw him maneuvering Nikki toward the car.

Then I clearly saw he intended to take her as his hostage.

That was never going to happen.

I spoke rapidly to him in Arabic, "You're making a big mistake by taking her. I'm much more valuable to you."

He stopped in his tracks and studied me for a moment.

"Who are you?" he finally asked me in Arabic.

"I'm a federal government investigator," I replied, "and I know you killed Farah Karimi." I gestured toward Nikki. "She's only a civil servant. I'm worth more to you than she is."

I wasn't sure he was going to buy this lie. It would depend on how much he knew about the way our government worked. The scenario I had drawn for him was plausible only in the Middle East where wealthy government officials were regularly kidnapped and later used as bargaining chips.

Nikki was handling herself well during my brief dialogue with Shahid—she wasn't struggling—but her eyes were clouded over with fear. I had no doubt she must have been frustrated at not being able to understand my conversation with the terrorist.

Shahid sneered at me. "Why would you offer to take her place?"

"In this country, we value women."

He made an ugly guttural sound.

"Open the trunk," he demanded.

For a moment I thought he hadn't accepted my offer and was about to shove Nikki inside. Instead, he ordered me to take everything out of the trunk.

I removed a couple of smelly rags, a red gasoline container, some white cord, and two heavy duffel bags. I placed them all on the garage floor.

He motioned toward the duffel bags. "Throw those in the back seat."

I opened the door behind the passenger seat and threw the duffel bags inside. For a brief moment, I wondered if they contained the money Bashir had given him.

"Turn around."

The second I had my back turned, he shoved Nikki against me. He did it so forcefully the impact momentarily stunned me.

However, I quickly regained my balance and pivoted back toward him. By that time, though, he had already retrieved my gun from the ground and was pointing it at both of us.

"Get the rope," he told Nikki. "Tie it around his wrists."

Nikki's breathing sounded labored, and she had difficulty getting the twisted cord undone. When she finally did so, Shahid forced me to place my hands behind my back, while she wound the cord around my wrists and tied the ends together.

Holding my gun right up to her temple, Shahid stepped closer and inspected the knots. After testing them, he made her tie them tighter.

When she finished, he motioned toward me. "Now get in the trunk."

I maneuvered myself inside, experiencing a brief flashback to being transported across Iran in a similar fashion. Now, however, I was more worried about Nikki's safety than my own.

When Shahid grabbed the truck lid, I quickly lowered my head. However, in the seconds before he slammed it shut, I saw Nikki throw herself on the ground and dive for her gun.

At that moment, the trunk banged shut, and I was engulfed in total darkness.

CHAPTER 29

Inside the trunk, I could hear several shots being fired in rapid succession. A couple of seconds later, I heard the driver's side door open and the engine roar to life. Then, the Chevy was put in reverse and backed out of the garage.

I had to assume Shahid was at the wheel, and as he maneuvered the car through the residential neighborhood streets, I felt certain Nikki was dead.

However, after a few agonizing moments thinking about her, I tamped down my emotions and looked at the situation objectively.

Shahid had been very close to Nikki when he'd fired at her, but her action of grabbing the gun had startled him, so there was a possibility—albeit a small one—that he'd missed her.

Even though I knew her chances of being alive were very slim, I prayed for her in a way I had never prayed for anyone before. At the same time, I worked at loosening the cords binding my wrists.

Getting my hands free was my only chance of survival because Shahid had made a huge mistake—he'd failed to pat me down before ordering me inside the trunk. While I no longer had a weapon, my iPhone was still in my pants pocket, and if Nikki were still alive, she could put a GPS tracker on it.

However, I knew I couldn't count on that happening. To have any chance of survival, I needed to get to my phone and contact Danny Jarrar before Shahid decided my usefulness to him was over.

Because Shahid's role in Farah's murder had been discovered, it didn't surprise me a few minutes later when I realized we were on the expressway and headed out of Norman. I assumed he was making his way south to Texas and from there straight to Mexico. I had no doubt his friends in the drug cartels would manage to get him on a plane and home to Syria from there.

However, after he'd driven for approximately thirty minutes, I felt the car decelerating, and we left the freeway. In another five minutes, after a couple of right turns, Shahid stopped the car, and, within a few seconds, I heard the car door slam.

Was this it? Was he about to open the trunk and shoot me with my own gun?

Although I'd rubbed my wrists raw, I hadn't been able to free my hands from the cords.

As I strained to hear what he might be doing, I positioned my legs so I could at least knock him down as soon as he opened the trunk.

Then, I waited.

And waited.

And waited some more.

It was probably another twenty minutes before I heard him approach the car. Instead of opening the trunk, however, he began tinkering with the rear fender. After a few seconds, I realized he was changing the license plate on the Chevy. Evidently, he'd stopped somewhere and stolen some plates.

Suddenly, I had hope.

Shahid had to believe Nikki was alive, and she had alerted the authorities. Otherwise, why would he be concerned about the car's license plate?

As he struggled to attach the plates, I heard him cursing in Arabic.

Finally, after several minutes, he pounded on the trunk a couple of times. "The woman is dead," he said. Then, as if to emphasize his point, he hit the trunk again. "You hear me? She is dead."

Yeah, I heard him.

♦♦♦♦

His words made me more determined than ever to get my hands

free, and as he returned to the freeway, I redoubled my efforts.

I didn't make much progress.

Perhaps an hour after he'd switched the license plate, he called someone on his cell phone. He spoke to them in Farsi. His tone was deferential.

"Reporting in."

Several minutes of silence ensued.

Was he on hold? Was he listening to someone?

"I had to leave," he finally said.

After a few more seconds of silence, I heard him say, "Remaining there would have put the others in jeopardy."

Silence again.

"Yes, I have followed the correct procedure. I have a hostage, and I am in a different car."

"On the I-35 highway," he said, as if answering a question. "The next town is Gainesville, Texas. I will be at the camp in forty minutes."

There was a long pause before his next response, and, for several moments, I thought he might have disconnected the call, but then I heard him say, "Yes, I understand. It must be done. I will make the sacrifice."

The conversation ended.

♦♦♦♦

About five minutes later, after concentrating my efforts on just my right wrist, I felt the knots loosen.

At last, I was able to free my right hand and then the left. Both wrists were bloody and raw, but I hardly noticed. All I could think about was getting to my phone.

Once I'd maneuvered myself into a position where I could remove it from my pocket, I hit the mute button and texted Danny a terse message.

"Text me ASAP."

I heard from him immediately.

"With FBI. Tracking u."

"Why?"

"Nikki called."

Nikki was alive!

Danny texted: *"Status report."*

"Locked in trunk. Stopping 40 minutes."

"Destination?"

"Unknown."

"Hostiles at destination?"

"Unknown."

"U hurt?"

"No."

"Ten minutes out."

"Nikki?"

"In surgery. Hang in there."

As if I had any other choice.

♦♦♦♦

While I was glad to hear Nikki was alive, my emotions were tempered by the fact she was in surgery. However, I reminded myself surgery probably meant she had a good chance of surviving her wounds.

Nikki had already proved herself to be a fighter, and I took comfort in that. I also prayed.

Determined to have my own fighting chance, I felt around the perimeter of the trunk, searching for anything I could use for a weapon. I tried to be as quiet as possible. The last thing I wanted was for Shahid to realize my hands were no longer restrained.

As I felt into the crevasses at the edges of the trunk, I hesitated to use my iPhone as a light source because I didn't want to run the battery down. But when I came across a short piece of plastic, I switched it on and took a quick peek to see what I'd discovered.

It turned out to be a piece of green plastic in the shape of a cylinder. It was about twelve inches long and a quarter-inch thick. One end looked as if it had been broken off from something, and that was the part that interested me.

It was sharp and pointy.

The car slowed slightly and traffic noise picked up. I knew we must have arrived in Gainesville. Within seven or eight minutes, Shahid had passed through the town, and we quickly picked up speed again.

Since I no longer had to concentrate on getting my hands free, and I had a weapon—or the semblance of one—I started thinking about Shahid's phone conversation.

From Shahid's responses, it sounded as if the person on the other end of the line had some type of authority over him. Not only had Shahid sounded intimidated by the person, he had also used a unique Farsi word for reporting, a word used when a soldier was giving operational details to his commanding officer.

I also considered the implications of Shahid referring to the place where we were going as a "camp." As brazen as it sounded, it was entirely plausible Hezbollah had set up some type of training camp in the middle of this Texas ranch country and was using the facility to prepare recruits for operations inside the United States.

Locating the camp outside of Gainesville made a lot of sense. The larger neighboring town, Denton, was home to two big universities. Large ethnic groups being seen together wouldn't have seemed unusual, and, as in Norman, Arabic students living together wouldn't have drawn any undue alarm.

The most troubling aspect of Shahid's conversation, though, was what he'd said about being a sacrifice.

Islamic jihadists making sacrifices tended to create gruesome headlines.

♦♦♦♦

Once again, the car slowed. However, this time, traffic noise decreased so I realized we were exiting the freeway.

After stopping for a moment, Shahid turned the car west. The ride wasn't as smooth as the freeway; it was more like a secondary road than a highway. I estimated the car's speed at around fifty.

We drove for almost thirty minutes.

I got another text from Danny.

"More intel?"

"Nothing."

"FBI needs to assess. Stall at destination."

"Will do."

"Clothes?"

For a few seconds, I was puzzled by his question. Then I understood he was afraid I might be mistaken for a hostile if the environment went hot, especially if the Feds didn't know how I looked or what I was wearing.

Was "census taker" a good enough description for me?

"Jeans. Blue shirt."

"Five minutes out."

I found myself hoping the FBI were quick assessors because I wasn't waiting for them if an opportunity presented itself for me to take Shahid down.

We had travelled on the secondary road for about ten minutes when Shahid suddenly made a sharp left turn. The car skidded a bit as we hit what sounded like a gravel road. About a mile later, he slowed, took a right turn, and stopped the car.

I waited with my plastic weapon in hand and reminded myself to breathe.

CHAPTER 30

Shahid didn't get out of the car immediately. His behavior worried me, and I listened intently for any voices nearby. I heard nothing. Several minutes went by.

Then I heard Shahid mumbling something in Arabic. It sounded like a prayer to Allah.

Finally, he opened the car door.

I knew his key fob had an automatic trunk release, so I was prepared to move as soon as I heard the click of the latch. I just prayed my injured leg would cooperate.

Suddenly, the trunk lid flew open.

I sprang forward, jabbing the pointed piece of molded plastic straight through Shahid's left eye.

It hit him square, blood spurting everywhere, and he doubled over in agony, while I tumbled out of the trunk after him. I wrestled him to the ground and tried to grab the gun from his hand.

He was in a lot of pain and cursing at me in Arabic, but he still held on to the gun. When he tried to get to his feet, I delivered a blow to his head that sent him reeling. He finally dropped the gun. It landed next to a Ford pickup.

As I lunged for it, shots rang out.

I grabbed the gun and scooted around behind the pickup.

Bullets were whizzing by my head. They were coming from an old barn located about one hundred yards away. I returned fire, but I knew immediately I was outgunned.

A white two-story house was off to my left, and I saw Shahid head over there, while I continued to be pinned down by the gunfire.

Seconds later, I heard a noise behind me.

I quickly turned and leveled my weapon.

It was Danny.

"About time," I said, lowering my Sig.

"Is this what you call waiting?" he shouted, aiming his weapon toward the barn.

"Best I could do."

I saw several FBI agents dodging bullets while fanning out across the property.

"Shahid went inside the house," I told Danny. "I'm going after him."

As he protested, I ran toward the porch, taking the steps in one leap and barreling through the front door of the farmhouse.

I swept the front room with my weapon and took cover behind the wall separating the living room from the dining room.

I could still hear shots being fired outside, but the house itself seemed quiet. I crept forward slowly, going from room to room until I knew the first floor was clear.

Then, I heard someone coming down the stairs.

I positioned myself just inside the foyer, close to the front door, which gave me a clear view of the bottom half of the staircase. I knew it had to be Shahid, and I was betting he'd found a gun inside the house and was intent on joining the fight outside.

I wasn't going to let that happen.

It was indeed Shahid.

His left eye was completely swollen shut and his face was contorted in either rage or pain. It was hard to tell the difference. However, he had no weapon in his hand. He wore his weapon around his waist.

It was a suicide belt packed with explosives.

The moment he saw me, he raised the detonator in his hand and shouted, "*Allah Akbar*."

I immediately turned and sprinted out the front door, throwing myself down the porch just seconds before the bomb went off.

♦♦♦♦

I was disoriented and confused for what seemed like a long time. Finally, the fog lifted, and I saw Danny and an FBI agent hovering over my face.

I assured them I was okay.

As reality set in, I realized the whole area was swarming with FBI agents. Some were in blue windbreakers. Others were decked out in SWAT gear. I also heard the distinctive thump, thump, thump of a helicopter overhead. Ambulances arrived and medical personnel started setting up a triage area near the old barn.

When I refused medical attention, Danny took a set of car keys from one of the agents and motioned me inside a maroon Crown Vic sedan.

"Are you sure you're okay?" he asked, looking me over.

"Positive."

"Good. We're getting out of here."

He made a tight U-turn across the front lawn of the farmhouse and drove a quarter mile down a driveway to a gravel road where he turned left.

Just like Shahid, he skidded as he hit the loose rock.

"What's the hurry?" I asked.

"Trust me. We needed to leave."

"I trust you, but why the hurry?"

"After Nikki told me Shahid had kidnapped you, I called—"

"Whoa," I said, interrupting him. "I've changed my mind. Tell me what happened to Nikki."

"All I know is Shahid shot her a couple of times," he said, "but she was able to contact the dispatcher and make it back to her car. That's when she called me on her cell phone. She said the two of you had found Shahid, and that he'd taken you hostage. Her speech was pretty garbled, but I got the gist of it. She was giving me the Chevy's license plate number when she stopped talking. I think she must have passed out."

"The plates wouldn't have mattered because Shahid switched them almost immediately."

He nodded. "A couple of federal agents were debriefing Bashir when I got Nikki's phone call. The story I gave them was that Shahid had been located, and had taken a hostage. The hostage was my . . ." he paused and made quotation marks with his hands, "undercover agent."

"So now I'm an undercover agent?"

"Makes a good story, don't you think? Anyway, as you saw, the FBI called in a lot of firepower to go after Shahid, but that's also the reason I had to get you out of there as quickly as possible. I didn't want them questioning you too closely."

He quickly glanced over at me and added, "I'm sure you'd agree an FBI interrogation would *not* have been good for your career."

"You're right about that." I punched him on the shoulder. "Thanks for everything, Danny."

With a big grin on his face, he replied, "Just watching your back as always."

"Yeah, right."

He turned serious. "Immediately after Nikki called me, we started tracking you on your cell phone."

"Did Nikki give you my iPhone number? I've always called you on my Agency phone."

"I got it off your business card," he said. Then he started laughing. "Remember? The one you shoved in my face trying to impress me with your promotion to Senior Fellow?"

I ignored his loud cackling and said, "When Shahid was on the phone, his responses made it sound as if a superior was ordering him to that ranch. Shahid even called it a camp. I'm betting that location is some type of staging area for recruits before they're deployed elsewhere. Shahid might have even trained there himself."

"With the stockpile of weapons we found in that barn, I'm sure you're right. We also found more suicide vests. Speaking of which, why do you think Shahid blew himself up like that?"

I thought about his question for a moment.

"At the end of the conversation I overheard, he mentioned

something about making a sacrifice. He said it had to be done. Maybe it had to do with his failure in Norman. At any rate, I believe what I heard was his agreeing to take on a suicide mission, probably wearing the belt to a crowded stadium or mall. But when he got to the ranch and knew the place had been discovered, he just decided to take out as many law enforcement personnel as possible."

"How were you able to find Shahid in the first place?"

I told him about Katherine's research on Paul Franklin. Then I explained how I'd made the connection between the photographs of Shahid's roommates that he had shown me at Twigs' Diner and the Arab students outside of Franklin's office.

Danny shook his head. "With his diplomatic background, do you really believe Paul Franklin is involved with bringing terrorists into the country?"

"I couldn't say for sure, but the death of his wife had a tremendous effect on him. If he hates America like he hates Israel, I'm sure he's more than willing to help Hezbollah get a foothold here."

"So what went wrong at the house on Surrey? How was Shahid able to take you hostage?"

I decided not to tell him about Nikki showing up in the alley unexpectedly, because I was afraid he might think her late arrival played a role in what went down there. I certainly had no intention of letting him blame her for my mistakes.

"I believe Shahid had lookouts in the neighborhood or had seen me at the front of his house earlier, or maybe he'd just driven into the garage before Nikki and I arrived. In any event, he must have been hiding on the other side of the fence, and, when I went around the side of the garage to look through the window, he slipped around behind Nikki and disarmed her. He was going to take her with him, but I convinced him to take me instead."

"That must have been a hard sell."

"I told him I held a high position in the government, and he could hold me for ransom."

"And he believed you?"

"I can be a convincing guy."

"Or he was just gullible."

"At least we're speaking of him in the past tense."

"So how did Nikki get shot?"

The moment I started explaining how Shahid turned his back on her, Danny got a call on his cell phone. He listened a moment and then hung up.

"That was the hospital," he said. "I asked them to call me as soon as they had any word on your detective."

My stomach churned. "And?"

"She's out of surgery and in recovery."

♦♦♦♦

Danny took me back to the address on Surrey so I could pick up my Range Rover. The police had cordoned off the entire block, but he took my car keys and went to retrieve my car, while I waited in the Crown Vic.

While Danny was showing his credentials to the officer stationed outside the house, my attention was drawn to two men standing on the front porch. They were talking with Paul Franklin. Even from across the street, I could tell Franklin was distraught.

A few minutes later, Danny pulled up in my car.

After I took the keys from him, I pointed over toward the house. "See the white-haired guy with the Feds? That's Paul Franklin."

Danny observed him for a moment. "He seems pretty upset."

"That may be, but—"

"I haven't gone soft, Titus," he said with a note of irritation in his voice. "His ties to Shahid and Hezbollah will be thoroughly investigated."

I pressed him. "Don't let his appearance fool you. His thoughts are lethal."

"Leave Paul Franklin to me." He shoved me in the direction of my Range Rover. "Go see Nikki. She's in room 5601."

♦♦♦♦

I drove over to Norman Regional Hospital on Porter Avenue. However, before taking the elevator up to the fifth floor, I stopped in a restroom and scrubbed off the grime leftover from throwing my body in the dirt at the farmhouse. Although my shirt still looked filthy and my face had several cuts on it, I felt a little more civilized.

When I arrived on the fifth floor, I was surprised to see there was no security guard stationed outside Nikki's door. Before that changed and I was put in the position of having to explain my presence, I quickly pushed opened the door and walked in.

The sight of Nikki, though, brought me to a complete stop.

She was hooked up to two machines. Both of them were putting out a steady rhythm of irritating beeps.

Her right shoulder was swathed in a white gauze wrapping, and her dark brown hair was covered in a blue hospital cap. The sound of her breathing seemed to indicate she was in a deep sleep.

However, as I took a seat beside her bed, her eyes fluttered a couple of times.

Seconds later, she opened them.

Giving me a weak smile, she said, "You're . . . here."

"In the flesh."

She licked her lips in slow motion.

I held a paper cup with a straw in it up to her mouth and gave her a sip of water.

She stared at me with a glazed look.

"What . . . happened . . . to you?" she asked. There was a noticeable slur to her words.

"I don't think you'd remember tomorrow if I told you everything right now, but it's all good. Shahid is dead."

She nodded her head slightly and closed her eyes again.

Suddenly, a large, African-American nurse appeared in the doorway. She looked surprised to see me.

"Sir, are you family?"

"Yes ma'am, I'm her uncle, Titus Ray."

She nodded her head and gave me a big smile as she walked on in the room. "This young lady just came down from the recovery room, so the anesthesia hasn't worn off yet. You can sit with her, Mr. Ray, but she may not be able to talk to you for awhile."

"I was told she had been shot."

She nodded her head. "They had to remove two bullets, both of them from her right shoulder, but the surgery went well, and she's going to be just fine."

"She looks so pale."

"Well, she lost a lot of blood before the ambulance brought her in. They transfused her in the operating room, so I'm sure you'll see her color improving soon."

The nurse walked over to Nikki's bedside. "I'm about to take her vitals, but you're welcome to stay if you like. The doctor just spoke to her police captain, and he's going to station some officers outside her door very shortly."

I got out of the chair, brushed Nikki's cheek with my hand, and said, "I'd better go. I'll see her tomorrow when she's awake."

As I turned to leave, Nikki opened her eyes slightly and whispered, "Bye, Uncle Titus."

CHAPTER 31

When I called Nikki's room the next morning, she sounded coherent and cheerful. However, when I mentioned I was coming up to the hospital to see her later in the day, she persuaded me to stay away until she was released.

"I have twenty-four hour protection right now," she explained. "Danny wanted to keep you out of this investigation, so he gave my department some fairytale about Shahid discovering one of his Arab recruits was actually an OSBI undercover agent. He also told my captain I was shot while trying to stop Shahid from taking the agent hostage. When my captain heard this, he put a security detail around me in case one of the cell members decided to come after me."

"He's right to be cautious."

"Danny told me what happened at the farmhouse. I can't believe you weren't killed."

"If the FBI hadn't showed up, I wouldn't be here right now. Your phone call to Danny saved my life."

She was quiet for several seconds.

Finally, she said, "I'm sorry I messed up yesterday."

"How did you mess up?"

"I shouldn't have been so wishy-washy about going with you to check out the garage. If we had coordinated our plans, it might have turned out differently."

"I completely understood your reluctance to get involved. You felt a responsibility to follow departmental rules."

"Yes, but I was already breaking the rules by allowing you to help me with the investigation. I think if I had been willing to follow your instincts in the first place, we could have done a better job of making a plan before I simply charged in there."

"I don't agree with your assessment at all. You did what you had to do."

I tried making her feel better by changing the subject. "Are you able to remember what happened?"

"I'm still a little hazy about events after I was shot, but I remember everything before that happened," she replied. "When you were looking inside the garage, I was standing with my back to the privacy fence, covering you in case anyone came out of the house. Then, all of a sudden, Shahid came up behind me and put a knife to my throat. He told me to drop my gun, and that's when you came around the corner of the garage."

"He must have seen me when I was parked across the street from the house. He probably slipped outside to watch the house from the neighbor's yard. I had a strong sense something was going on inside the house when I parked there, and I shouldn't have just ignored my feelings. I should have waited."

"Those duffel bags inside his trunk made it look as if he were getting ready to leave. If you hadn't acted when you did, he could have gone to Denton, strapped on that suicide belt, and killed hundreds of people. If that had happened, think how you'd feel today."

"I'm just sorry I put you in a situation where you got shot."

"We got the person who murdered Farah Karimi. That's the important thing."

I thought of Bashir Karimi and wondered if Shahid's death had brought him any measure of comfort.

I said, "I saw you go for you gun when I was getting inside the trunk. What happened after Shahid shut the trunk lid on me?"

"He fired two shots at me before I could get a shot off at him, and then he took cover inside the garage. When he pulled the car out, I tried hitting his tires, but I was a lousy shot, and, in my own defense,

I was feeling pretty weak by then anyway."

"Danny said you made it back to your car."

"My car was parked on the street at the end of the alleyway. I remember telling myself I had to get to my car so I could follow you, but how I made it back there is still a little unclear. I don't remember talking to Danny at all. I've tried to bring up the details, but they just won't materialize."

"Yesterday, your nurse told me you're going to be fine."

"That's what the doctor said this morning. He may even release me tomorrow."

"That soon?"

She laughed. "It surprised me too."

"I guess I shouldn't be surprised. I've been praying for you."

"You have? That's not something I'm used to hearing."

"Well, it's not something I'm used to saying either."

"Once I get out of here, you'll have to make good on that promise to tell me more about yourself."

"When you get home, I'll bring you over a pot of my famous chili and let you interrogate me."

It was good to hear her laugh again.

♦♦♦♦

The moment I got off the phone with Nikki, I called Paul Franklin's office to reschedule my meeting with him. His secretary said she would have to call me back later because Professor Franklin was taking some time off to deal with some personal issues.

I suspected those issues included having a chat with Homeland Security.

It had been forty-eight hours since I'd heard anything from Carlton about the search for Ahmed, so I sat down at my computer to send him an email.

I worded my message very carefully.

I didn't want it to sound as if I thought he wasn't doing his job—any operative making that mistake would never get another choice assignment. However, just as I was about to push the send button, my satphone rang.

It was Carlton.

His voice was loud and agitated. "What were you thinking?"

For one insane moment I thought he knew I was about to send him a nagging email.

"Sir?"

"I just viewed the satellite feed from a raid yesterday at a ranch near Denton, Texas where the FBI captured about a dozen Muslim extremists. Guess whose face I saw on that screen?"

"Yes, sir. I can explain that."

"Did Danny Jarrar get you to go undercover for him?"

"Ah . . . no . . . not really. I didn't—"

"If that's a denial, then why did the OSBI undercover agent look exactly like you? Do you want to get fired? Is that what this is all about?"

"No, sir, not at all."

"Good," he said, pausing for several long seconds, "because we've confirmed it was definitely Ahmed Al-Amin who shot Simon Wassermann."

Confirmed—I liked the sound of that.

However, I refrained from any I-told-you-so remark.

Carlton continued, "I managed to convince Deputy Ira to let you go after him."

I was stunned by this news.

In fact, as my mind absorbed his statement, the part of my brain responsible for forming words and coherent thoughts simply stopped functioning altogether.

"Did you hear me?"

"Yes, I heard you," I said, finding my voice at last, "and I definitely want the assignment. Does this mean I've been taken off medical leave?"

"In a manner of speaking. You need to wrap things up there, and check in here at Langley on Monday morning."

"What made the Deputy change his mind about me?"

"He owed me a favor, and I cashed it in. Let's leave it at that."

"And Ahmed? Where is he?"

"I'll brief you when you get here on Monday morning."

I thanked him for the opportunity to bring Wassermann's killer to justice, and he acted as if my gratitude wasn't necessary. However, I knew he expected me to acknowledge what he'd done for me.

When I tried to explain how I'd been involved in the Denton raid, he just brushed it off and told me my actions were proof I needed to get back to work.

After I hung up the phone, Stormy walked over and dropped his ball at my feet.

I picked it up and held it in front of him. "So tell me what I'm supposed to do now?"

He didn't have a clue.

However, after thinking about it all afternoon, I did.

CHAPTER 32

The next morning, after making my chili and putting it in a crock-pot to simmer all day, I telephoned Nikki. She told me she was being released from the hospital within a few hours, and then she gave me directions to her house.

Around noon, I went by my bank and took care of several business transactions.

An hour after I returned home, I had two visitors.

They produced dozens of documents for me to sign.

Then, I was off to see Nikki.

♦♦♦♦

Nikki lived in a residential area on the east side of Norman off Alameda Avenue.

Her small, ranch-style home was a combination of gray and charcoal-colored bricks with windows bordered by black wooden shutters. Along the sidewalk leading up to the front door were rows of pink and red begonias. Two large geranium plants in black wooden buckets anchored each side of her small front porch.

I approached her door with a mixture of joy and sadness.

Nikki appeared at the threshold the moment I stepped on the porch.

She looked a lot different from the last time I'd seen her in the hospital. Now, her color was back to normal, and she had on a pair of jeans and a sleeveless white blouse. Her hair was falling about halfway down her shoulders, and she was wearing a blue arm sling around her neck.

As I walked in the door with my pot of chili, she said, "That smells delicious."

"Where shall I put it?"

"Follow me."

As I walked through her living room, I remembered what she'd said about being a messy housekeeper. However, I could see no evidence of this claim. The room was decorated in different shades of blue and had big yellow throw pillows everywhere, and it looked very inviting.

When we arrived in the kitchen, she had me put the crock-pot on an island in the center of the room. "I made us some cornbread to go with the chili," she said, "but it's going to be a few minutes before it's ready. Would you like a glass of tea while we wait?"

I nodded. "Sounds good."

While she was getting the tea out of the refrigerator, I had one last argument with myself. Then I said, "I need to go back out to my car. I'll just be a minute."

Nikki had already filled two large tumblers with ice and was just in the act of pouring tea into them when I returned to the kitchen. When she saw me, she put the tea pitcher down.

Coming around from behind the kitchen island, she said. "Well, this is a surprise."

Stormy obediently sat down beside me while she stroked his head. As a precaution, I held onto his leash to keep him from jumping up on her.

"I didn't think you'd mind if I brought him with me."

"No, of course not."

After I took his leash off, Stormy followed us into the living room. Nikki sat down on the couch, and I sat down opposite her in a blue leather chair, while Stormy wandered around the room sniffing the carpet.

"Let's not talk about Farah's murder or the Shahid investigation tonight," Nikki said. "My captain has scheduled me for two interviews tomorrow, and I know that's just the beginning. When the Feds release my name to the press, the reporters will probably be camped out on my street for days."

"You're right. You're about to be grilled by all kinds of government agencies. You should ask Danny to keep the press off your front porch, though."

Stormy came over to the couch and sat down at Nikki's feet. She winced as she leaned over to pet him, and I immediately asked her if she were okay. However, she brushed me off.

"I'm not talking about myself tonight. It's your turn."

"I've led a very boring life."

"I seriously doubt that."

"I can assure you the parts I'm able to talk about are really very boring."

"Okay, tell me about your childhood then."

I gave her a short version of growing up in Flint, trying to make it as dull as possible. But then, Nikki turned into Detective Saxon and refused to accept my superficial descriptions of my family relationships. Instead, she began firing questions at me. As a result, I ended up being honest with her about my dad's alcoholism, and the toll it had taken on the family.

I even told her about my failed marriage to Laura.

Just as I finished, the oven timer went off, and we went back to the kitchen where I ladled out two big bowls of chili, while Nikki removed the cornbread from the oven.

As she was cutting it into squares, I sampled a piece. "This is terrific. I'm lousy when it comes to making cornbread, although I do have one fan." I pointed down at Stormy.

"Really? I've never heard of a dog who eats cornbread."

As I related the time Stormy ate my cornbread in the storm shelter during the tornado, Nikki laughed so hard it made her shoulder hurt.

In the days that followed, it was hard to get that sound out of my head.

♦♦♦♦

After we sat down to eat, Nikki said a blessing over our food, and that was when I decided to tell her about my recent conversion to Christianity.

"This may not take very long, because, as much as I'd like to do so, I can't give you a very detailed account of my circumstances at that moment."

"That's fine. Just tell me what you can."

"I was on assignment in an Islamic country," I told her, "and to say things hadn't gone as planned would definitely be an understatement. To make matters even more difficult, in the midst of a very hostile environment, I had broken my leg and couldn't leave the country. However, with the help of one of our allies, I was taken in by a Christian couple. During the months I lived with them, they so modeled a life of faith in front of me, I knew I wanted that same kind of life for myself.

"While that decision was momentous for me, what has been even more earth-shattering is the realization it was only the first step in a lifelong journey. Sometimes I feel like a child learning to walk. I keep stumbling all over the place. The first time I didn't lose my temper, I was very proud of myself, but then I turned right around and exploded at someone. I haven't figured out if my desire to serve the Lord can possibly be compatible with my career as an intelligence officer. But right now, I know for certain that's what I'm supposed to be doing."

"If you're looking for affirmation," Nikki said, "I wholeheartedly agree. I'm sure you're very good at what you do."

"My boss at the Agency seems to agree with you." I hesitated for a brief moment. Then I added, "I'm leaving for Langley tomorrow."

Nikki looked shocked. "You're leaving tomorrow?"

I found the disappointment in her voice oddly comforting.

"Yes, I have an assignment waiting for me at Langley on Monday morning."

"Didn't you tell me you were supposed to be on medical leave for a year?"

"I was, and I have to admit I'm surprised they're going to waive my leave, but there are some special circumstances involved in this assignment."

She remained quiet for a few seconds. Then, she started to speak, but, after opening and closing her mouth a couple of times, she just shook her head and turned silent once again.

I tried to help her out. "I know this isn't easy when you have a dozen questions you'd like to ask me." She attempted a smile. "I'm really sorry I can't be more forthcoming with you."

Finally, she asked, "What will you do with Stormy?"

At the mention of his name, Stormy trotted over to her.

"That's the reason I brought him with me tonight. I wanted to ask you if Stormy could stay with you while I'm out of the country."

She pushed her empty chili bowl away and started scratching Stormy behind his ears. As he stood there with his teeth showing, panting, and smiling from ear to ear, I was shocked to realize I was going to miss him—I was going to miss having a dog in my life.

"Oh, my," she said to him, "you're so handsome. How could I ever refuse you anything?" She turned to me. "Of course, I'd be glad to keep him for you. But does that mean you'll be coming back to Norman?"

I nodded. "Yesterday I got in touch with Eric Hawley. He's the realtor handling Phillip Ortega's property. I had him make Ortega an offer on his property, and he accepted it. Now the place is mine."

She shook her head back and forth. "I can't believe he sold it to you just like that. Professor Ortega loved that place."

"I gave him a substantial amount of cash, so he wasn't all that reluctant to sell. I also believe Hawley really encouraged him to accept my offer, because not only is Hawley going to get a big commission out of this sale, I've also asked him to manage the property while I'm away."

She got up from the table and took our bowls over to the sink. She didn't say anything while she poured coffee into two mugs. When she finally spoke, there was a tearful catch in her voice. "How long will you be gone?"

"That's hard to say. It could be a week or it could be a year. There's no way of telling."

"Can you tell me how dangerous this assignment is?"

I answered her honestly. "Most of my assignments are dangerous in one way or the other. But consider what the two of us went through this week in Norman, and I wasn't even on an assignment here."

"Of course, you're right," she said, returning to the table with a cup of coffee for each of us.

I added, "However, I have to believe the job I'm doing overseas limits the danger from spreading over here."

"I certainly saw the implications of that with Farah's murder."

Even though we said we weren't going to talk about it, we ended up discussing Bashir and the investigation of the Hezbollah cells for the remainder of the evening. For my part, I welcomed the conversation because it delayed my inevitable goodbye. However, after retrieving Stormy's toys from my car, I knew the time had come for me to leave.

"I've never had this problem before," I told her. "I usually don't have to say goodbye to anyone."

Forcing a smile, she said, "I'm not saying goodbye, Titus."

I walked toward the front door.

However, before opening it, I turned around and gave her a hug.

It proved to be very awkward because of her arm sling, and, as we pulled away, we both laughed a little nervously.

"Before you go," she said, "would you answer a question for me?"

"Sure."

"You asked me the other day what I considered to be the most important thing in the world to me. How would you answer that question?"

I took a second before replying.

"I don't know for sure, Nikki, but I believe I'm closer to an answer right now than I've ever been before."

The next morning, I left for Langley and the hunt for Ahmed.

THE END

Or just

THE BEGINNING

ABOUT THE AUTHOR

Luana Ehrlich is a freelance writer, minister's wife, and former missionary with a passion for spy thrillers and mystery novels. She began her series of Titus Ray novels when her husband retired from the pastorate. Now, she writes from an undisclosed location, trying to avoid the torture of mundane housework, grocery shopping, and golf stories. However, she occasionally comes out of hiding to see her two grandsons or to enjoy a Starbucks caramel macchiato. She resides in Norman, Oklahoma.

A NOTE TO MY READERS

Dear Reader, Thank you for reading *One Night in Tehran*. If you enjoyed it, you might also enjoy reading **Book 2 in the series, *Two Days in Caracas***, which is also available on Amazon.

I'd love for you to do a review of *One Night in Tehran* on Amazon or on the Goodreads website. Since word-of-mouth testimonies and written reviews are usually the deciding factor in helping readers pick out a book, they are an author's best friend and much appreciated.

Would you also consider signing up for my newsletter? When you do, I'll send you a copy of Titus Ray's famous chili recipe, and you'll receive insider information, plus all my updates, about the series. You can sign up at the contact page on www.LuanaEhrlich.com. In addition, you'll be able to find out more about the Titus Ray Thriller Series at www.TitusRayThrillers.com.

One of my greatest blessings comes from receiving email from my readers. My email address is author@luanaehrlich.com. I'd love to hear from you!

Read the first scenes from ***Two Days in Caracas*** on the following pages.

Excerpt TWO DAYS IN CARACAS

PART ONE

Chapter 1

Monday, June 4

I needed to move. I needed to do it soon. I was standing inside the doorway of an apartment building on *Calle Alturas*, just a few blocks from downtown San José, Costa Rica. It was an ideal location, but I knew my presence was going to start drawing attention any minute.

Right now, the torrential downpour made it appear as if I were simply seeking shelter from the rain. However, such tropical afternoon showers usually gave way to sunny skies very rapidly in this part of the world.

Once that happened, I would need to move quickly.

I studied the house on the corner. Then, I scanned my surroundings for a building public enough for me to monitor the residence from a distance.

The overall construction of the house, with its concrete-block walls and iron bars across the windows, appeared typical for the neighborhood.

I could see nothing unusual about it.

However, its innocuous look didn't mean anything. In fact, the normality of the place made it easy for me to believe it might be Ahmed Al-Amin's safe house in San José.

On the other hand, I wasn't totally convinced Ahmed was even in Costa Rica in the first place.

When I'd arrived at the CIA's Operations Center in Langley, Virginia, Douglas Carlton, my operations officer, had briefed me on the status of Ahmed Al-Amin, the Hezbollah assassin I was tracking. Afterward, I'd questioned one of the Agency's logistics analysts on the authenticity of the San José address he'd given me.

"How can you be certain Ahmed is at this location?" I'd asked him.

"Because we're getting pings from all the texting."

I shook my head. "I can't believe Ahmed is using an unencrypted cell phone. He's one of Hezbollah's top operatives, and if he's using his cell phone, he certainly knows our satellites can track him."

"Oh, it's not Ahmed who's doing the texting. It's the Venezuelan kid who's with him. Every night he sends a text message back to his girlfriend in Austin. Ahmed might not even know the guy is using his cell phone."

Would Ahmed really be that oblivious to what his traveling companion was doing? Somehow, I doubted it, but I didn't argue with the impossibly young analyst.

Instead, I turned my attention to Josh Kellerman, a briefer from Support Services, who spent the next thirty minutes going over my legend, explaining the myriad of details involved in the cover identity I would be using in Costa Rica.

My business card indicated I was Rafael Arroyo, Vice President of Sales for Global Resources. Kellerman gave me a brief overview of the industrial refrigeration units I was supposed to be selling, along with several boring, but very colorful brochures.

The Rafael Arroyo legend was one I'd used on previous trips to the Middle East, although then I'd been given an Arabic name. Strangely enough, I felt very comfortable in the skin of a refrigeration salesman.

Following my briefing with Kellerman, I went over to meet with Sandy Afton. She was in the southwest wing of the Agency's New Headquarters Building where Support Services had an area the size of a department store, which was solely devoted to men and women's clothing. Although the women's section was twice as large as the men's section, I'd never questioned the need for this.

As soon as I arrived, Sandy showed me the clothing choices she'd made for me. I approved most of them, and, after that, while my suitcase was being packed by one of Sandy's assistants, I changed into a *guayabera* and a pair of dark slacks for my flight to Costa Rica.

When I'd come out of the dressing room—looking like a refrigeration salesman—Sandy had deposited the clothes and shoes I'd just removed—along with my wallet and any other items identifying me as Titus Ray—inside a metal box about the size of a small footlocker.

The last thing I did was hand over the keys to my Range Rover. I did so reluctantly, because, although I'd just purchased the car two months before, I'd already fallen in love with it—or, maybe I'd simply fallen in love with the idea of owning my own vehicle.

I said, "My car is parked over by the west gate in the parking lot used by Security."

"Why is it parked over there?"

"Because there's a handgun underneath the front seat, plus a spare in the glove compartment, and I have extra ammo clips in the side pocket of the duffel bag in the back."

She smiled. "I can see why they wouldn't let you drive inside the complex. Speaking of weapons, I know you don't want me to issue you a firearm before you leave, so I've instructed the embassy in San José to provide you with whatever you need when you get there."

I seldom requested the necessary credentials permitting me to get on a plane with a gun. Doing so was too much of a hassle and only served to draw attention to me.

I never wanted to draw attention to myself.

Never.

Sandy said, "I've already spoken with Ben Mitchell about the type of weapon you'll need."

Carlton had set me up with Ben Mitchell, the "Economics Officer" assigned to the American Embassy in Costa Rica. He was my contact while I was in country. In reality, like me, he was a covert intelligence officer.

Carlton had told me Mitchell had been with the Agency for five years and was classified as a Level 2 officer. While I was a Level 1 officer, I didn't think Mitchell's lower status would be a problem for me on this particular mission.

I wasn't acquainted with Ben Mitchell, but that didn't surprise me. I'd been in Iran and Afghanistan for the past seven years, and I hadn't traveled south of the border during that time.

Mitchell was scheduled to meet my flight from Miami. Meeting a refrigeration salesman from Global Resources was a natural thing for him to do in his role as the American Embassy's Economics Officer.

I was sure he would think Rafael Arroyo was a great guy.

However, as it turned out, Mitchell didn't come to the airport in San José to meet Rafael Arroyo, because, after leaving Agency's headquarters in Langley, Virginia, I had decided to change my plane ticket and take an earlier flight.

After landing in San José, I'd rented a car and arrived at my present location without having had any contact with Ben Mitchell.

That's the way I preferred to work.

Completely alone. Solo.

Now though, as I observed the boxy concrete house from the shelter of the apartment building, I was beginning to regret my decision to ditch Mitchell.

Having another set of eyes at the rear of the house might prove beneficial, and, since I'd come to the address directly from the airport, I didn't have a weapon on me.

Knowing what I knew about Ahmed, I had no intention of confronting him without some kind of firepower.

When I'd entered the *Calle Alturas* neighborhood earlier, I'd spotted a man and a woman inside a Toyota Highlander parked about a block away from the safe house. I knew they had to be members of the surveillance team Mitchell had brought in to keep an eye on the house until I arrived. They were clearly amateurs, and if Ahmed were in the house, it wouldn't be long before he would notice them as well.

If he hadn't already spotted them.

The rain finally let up, and I stepped out of the doorway and walked over to a small pastry shop located next door to a video store. Three small café tables had been placed on the patio in front of the pastry shop, and when a waiter had finished drying off one of the wrought-iron chairs, I sat down and ordered *un café sin leche*.

Once the waiter had gone inside to get my coffee, I felt inside my pants pocket for my satellite phone and punched in the numbers I'd memorized before leaving Langley.

When Ben Mitchell came on the line, I told him my location and asked him to meet me. He said he would be driving a late model Jeep, and then he hung up on me.

He sounded ticked off.

♦♦♦♦

I was savoring the last drops of my second cup of Costa Rica's finest beverage when I spotted Mitchell driving down *Calle Alturas*.

He followed my instructions and parked one block south of my location. As he made his way up the busy street carrying a hard-shelled briefcase at his side, I had plenty of time to observe him.

The first thing I noticed was that he was about my height—six feet—but, unlike me, he appeared very young. He had a round, boyish face, and his thick, dark hair was disheveled, as if he'd recently been caught up in a windstorm. However, since there was no wind to speak of, I suspected this was simply the type of modern hairstyle adopted by guys under forty these days.

Although he wasn't obvious about it, I saw him carefully assessing his surroundings, including me. However, he barely gave the faded green house on the corner a cursory glance.

When he reached the pastry shop, he extended his hand, put a smile on his face, and said, "Mr. Arroyo, I'm Ben Mitchell."

We shook hands, and, as he seated himself, he signaled the waiter he wanted what I was drinking. While the waiter was getting his coffee, we chatted about Global Resources.

For any interested observers, I took out one of the company's brochures and made a big show of unfolding it and pointing out the features of an expensive refrigeration unit.

Once the waiter had placed his coffee on the table and left,

Mitchell leaned in toward me and asked, "What exactly do you think you're doing?"

His smile had disappeared.

"I'm tracking a terrorist who killed one of our covert operatives in Dallas last month. Weren't you briefed in on this?"

"Of course, I was briefed in."

Mitchell picked up a spoon and studied it.

He appeared to scrutinize it so intently, someone might have thought he collected spoons for a hobby. After a few seconds, he laid it back down on the table and looked up at me.

I noticed his eyes were slightly dilated, and I saw a muscle on the left side of his face begin to twitch. I immediately recognized these as signs Ben Mitchell was having trouble controlling his temper.

I recognized the symptoms because I had often exhibited them myself.

He said, "I was told to meet you at the airport later today. Mind telling me what you're doing here now?"

I was amused by his anger, and, until a few months ago, I would have enjoyed seeing just how much I could have harassed him before he finally exploded. Now, though, I resisted that temptation and explained myself—sort of.

"I took an earlier flight."

He nodded his head but kept looking at me, as if he expected me to continue giving him an explanation.

I thought about the nonchalant way he'd done the recon on the cement house while appearing not to do so, and I decided to give him what he wanted.

"Look, I came in earlier than expected, because I've been doing this long enough to know my chances of staying alive are always better if I do the unexpected. Being predictable gets you killed."

He shifted his eyes over to a couple of kids riding their bikes down the sidewalk and gave them his full attention for a few seconds.

I sensed his anger was dissipating, and it made me wonder if Ben Mitchell was a short fuse but quick recovery kind of guy.

He turned and looked at me once again. "How long have you been with the Agency?"

I knew that old trick—gain control of your emotions by changing the subject—and he had just executed it perfectly.

"I was recruited back in the late '80s."

"An old-timer, huh?"

"I prefer the word seasoned."

He gave a short laugh. "Okay, how do you want to play this?"

I suggested he move his surveillance team in the Toyota Highlander further down the street and then have them point the vehicle in the opposite direction. I also told him I wanted a specific description of anyone they saw entering or leaving the house.

He called and gave Josué, the driver of the Toyota, my instructions. Then, I explained about the exfiltration procedure Carlton and I had worked out at Langley. The plan's endpoint culminated when we had Ahmed safely tucked away in a luxury cell at the Jihadi Prison Camp at Gitmo. Before that happened, though, Mitchell and I still needed to give the details some fine-tuning.

He glanced down at his watch. "I'm due back at the embassy in fifteen minutes. Will you be sticking around here?"

"Looks like Josué and his partner have this covered for now. I'll go check into my hotel and meet you back here in a couple of hours. Let's meet at the restaurant on the corner."

He agreed, and then he headed back to his Jeep. Once I saw him drive off, I picked up the black briefcase he'd left behind and made my way over to my rental car.

Just to make sure I wasn't under surveillance, though, I made several stops along the way—once to select a CD from a sidewalk display, once to purchase some fresh pineapple from a fruit vendor, and once to buy a lottery ticket from a kid with a dirty face.

As far as I could tell, no one appeared to be the least bit interested in me, and, when I drove away from the neighborhood, I felt certain my prospects for capturing Ahmed were excellent.

Later though, I wondered if I'd stayed around the neighborhood a little longer, if I could have prevented what happened next.

Made in the USA
Lexington, KY
10 October 2017